She didn't n
didn't need

She had lived by those decisions, had dedicated herself to her career, and for seventeen years she hadn't—except in the rare weak moment—regretted it. Nothing had changed.

So why did she now feel like such a liar?

Because something *had* changed. Smith. Somehow, in the last twenty-four hours, she had begun seeing him in a totally different light. He was no longer just a casual friend with whom she had little in common, but a man. A potentially special man. A man who could make reality of dreams she hadn't yet dared to dream.

But a man like Smith certainly didn't need her.

Dear Reader,

Many of you love the miniseries that we do in Intimate Moments, and this month we've got three of them for you. First up is *Duncan's Lady*, by Emilie Richards. Duncan is the first of "The Men of Midnight," and his story will leave you hungering to meet the other two. Another first is *A Man Without Love*, one of the "Wounded Warriors" created by Beverly Bird. Beverly was one of the line's debut authors, and we're thrilled to have her back. Then there's a goodbye, because in *A Man Like Smith*, bestselling author Marilyn Pappano has come to the end of her "Southern Knights" trilogy. But what a fantastic farewell—and, of course, Marilyn herself will be back soon!

You won't want to miss the month's other offerings, either. In *His Best Friend's Wife*, Catherine Palmer has created a level of emotion and tension that will have you turning pages as fast as you can. In *Dillon's Reckoning*, award-winner Dee Holmes sends her hero and heroine on the trail of a missing baby, while Cathryn Clare's *Gunslinger's Child* features one of romance's most popular storylines, the "secret baby" plot.

Enjoy them all—and come back next month for more top-notch romantic reading...only from Silhouette Intimate Moments.

Yours,
Leslie Wainger
Senior Editor and Editorial Coordinator

Please address questions and book requests to:
Silhouette Reader Service
U.S.: 3010 Walden Ave., P.O. Box 1325, Buffalo, NY 14269
Canadian: P.O. Box 609, Fort Erie, Ont. L2A 5X3

A MAN
LIKE SMITH

MARILYN
PAPPANO

Published by Silhouette Books
America's Publisher of Contemporary Romance

SILHOUETTE BOOKS

ISBN 0-373-07626-6

A MAN LIKE SMITH

Copyright © 1995 by Marilyn Pappano

Printed in U.S.A.

Books by Marilyn Pappano

MARILYN PAPPANO

has been writing as long as she can remember, just for the fun of it, but a few years ago she decided to take her lifelong hobby seriously. She was encouraging a friend to write a romance novel and ended up writing one herself. It was accepted, and she plans to continue as an author for a long time. When she's not involved in writing, she enjoys camping, quilting, sewing and, most of all, reading. Not surprisingly, her favorite books are romance novels.

Her husband is in the navy, and in the course of her marriage she has lived all over the U.S. Currently, she lives in North Carolina with her husband and son.

For Sandy Olson—
loyal Texan, fellow writer, saddle tramp
and good friend.
May all the trails you go down be happy ones.

Chapter 1

In her thirteen years as a reporter for the *New Orleans Times-Picayune*, Jolie Wade had covered more murders than any one person should ever have to know about. She had interviewed crooks as petty and insignificant as pickpockets and as important and powerful as organized crime boss Jimmy Falcone. She had dealt with men—and women—who earned their living killing other men and women, had traded insults with some of the toughest people in town, had turned her back on people who could kill her without feeling even the slightest remorse.

And in those thirteen years, nothing had ever unnerved her like the appointment she was about to keep.

She drove to the end of Serenity Street, heart of a tiny, painfully familiar neighborhood, the shabbiest section of the French Quarter. She had grown up on Serenity in a crowded apartment on the third floor of one of those old houses two blocks back. As a child, she had skipped along its sidewalks and had played in the park here at the end of the street. As a teenager, she had lost her heart and, later, her virginity, in the same park. Later still, she had lost many of her hopes and dreams and all of her illusions here.

And all to the same man she had come to meet tonight.

Tucking her purse under the seat, she got out of the car and locked the doors. The park looked deserted, but then, it always had that look at night. There were lots of shrubs to hide young lovers ... or young thugs, out looking for an easy mark. At five foot four and not even a hundred and ten pounds, she probably looked like the easiest mark of all, but she was tough, she reminded herself. Life and hard work—and Nicky Carlucci—had made her tough.

The sound of her car door closing seemed to echo in the quiet night. She must be out of her mind to show up here. Just because Jamey O'Shea, one of the few people from the old neighborhood that she remained in occasional contact with, had called and asked her to come was no reason to risk her safety like this. So what if Nicky had decided after eighteen long years that he wanted to talk to her? There were better ways to reach her than through Jamey, better places to meet than with old memories.

The park was nothing more than an empty lot, bordered on two sides by the neighboring houses, across the back by a tall brick wall that provided privacy to the house on the other side and enclosed across the front with a rusted wrought iron fence. The house that had once stood there had burned down before she was born, and the owners, uninsured and as hard-luck poor as everyone else on Serenity, had simply walked away from the land. A few dedicated parents, her own included, had taken it on themselves to clear away the rubble, to haul off the trash and plant grass and shrubs and turn it into a safe place for their kids to play. It had been a tiny pocket of loveliness and security on a street that knew too little of either.

Now it was overgrown, uncared-for. Graffiti was scrawled on the walls, and the stepping stones that created winding paths were broken, unsteady beneath her weight. Twenty years ago she had felt safer here in the middle of the night than at home in the bed she had shared with her younger sister. Tonight, tough or not, she was uneasy.

She walked only as far as the light from the nearest streetlamp that hadn't been broken could reach—not far.

Stopping there, she looked around, her gaze searching the shadows, then quietly called, "Nicky?"

There was a moment of silence. The tree frogs hushed, the crickets stopped, and the whippoorwill in one of the few trees ceased its song. After a time, everything returned to normal, then went askew again as Nicky Carlucci stepped out of the shadows and approached her.

How many times had they met here over the course of their three-year relationship? she wondered. A hundred? Her first guess brought a cynical smile. Easily ten times that, probably closer to twenty times. Wherever they had gone, whatever they had done, they had always met here first. Nicky had always taken her home when their evenings were finished, but he had never picked her up there. Her parents hadn't approved of him. They had wanted better for their daughter than a Serenity Street punk, and that was all they'd seen in Nicky. Even when he had begged, borrowed and scraped together enough money to go to college, they hadn't believed he would ever make anything of himself. Even when he'd started law school—long after he had cut Jolie out of his life—her folks had still thought he was nothing more than a low-life punk.

And, in the end, they had been right. After all his hard work, Nicky had accomplished only one thing: he had become one of the better educated and more talented crooks in the city.

He stood in the lamp light for a moment without speaking, and she used the time to study him. Physically, the past eighteen years hadn't changed him much. He was lean and looked tough, as always. Growing up as he had, living only his earliest years with his mother and dividing the next twelve years between abandoned buildings around the neighborhood and the sanctuary of St. Jude's four blocks down and one street over, he couldn't have survived if he hadn't been tough.

He carried his age well, she thought. He was only a few years from forty, but there were no lines, no telltale wrinkles. Of course, he didn't seem to have a conscience to cause him any worry. He apparently felt no guilt for the laws he'd broken, no remorse for the things he'd done. Even now, under federal indictment for a number of crimes and facing the near-certain probability of years in prison, he showed no regret.

He certainly showed no regret for what he'd done to her so long ago.

He lit a cigarette, a habit she'd found nasty twenty years before and disliked even more now, held the match until the flame was licking a breath away from his fingertips, then dropped it to the ground, where a bit of yellowed grass smoldered before the flame died. "You won a bet for me. Jamey bet ten bucks you wouldn't 'come. I knew you would."

He had always been so sure of her when they were teenagers, too. He had never asked; he had told, demanded or simply taken. She'd been too easy for him, her best friends had insisted when he had dropped her. She'd given and given until he'd had everything, until there had been no reason for him to come back. She could bet, they had been certain, that the new girl he was seeing up in Baton Rouge wasn't so easy.

Maybe she hadn't been . . . or maybe she had. All Jolie knew was that when he'd come back from Baton Rouge after law school, it had been without the woman he'd been so determined to marry that he had broken Jolie's heart without a second thought.

"Aren't we a little old for clandestine meetings?" she asked, forcing her voice into its usual, even keel.

He blew out a stream of smoke that curled upward between them, then gave a hoarse laugh. "Honey, most of my life has been conducted in clandestine meetings."

"I guess in your business, it's in everyone's best interests."

"Censure, Jolie?" He laughed again. "I thought a journalist was supposed to be unbiased. Besides, from what I understand, you spend plenty of your time in the shadows, too."

That was true enough. Sometimes the people she met with couldn't afford to be seen talking to her. Some of her best sources of information could suffer a serious reversal of fortune if just how friendly they were with her ever became public knowledge.

Was that the case with Nicky? Had he chosen this park for their meeting because it was shadowed, dark and far from where anyone might expect to find either of them these days and not because—as she had thought—of old memories and the thousand and one nights they had slipped in and out of here together? Did he even remember any of those nights?

With an involuntary shiver, she took a step back. "It's late, Nicky. I've got to be at work in another eight hours, and I'd like to get some sleep first. What do you want?"

"I'd rather be called Nick. I'm a little old for Nicky."

She knew that. She knew, in fact, that he actually preferred his given name, Nicholas, but that was a gesture of respect given him only by people who didn't know him or who were afraid of him. *She* knew him, and she wasn't afraid of him.

He studied her a moment before going on. "I understand you're damned good at what you do."

She acknowledged him with nothing more than a shrug.

"So was I."

"A damned good crook wouldn't get caught."

Now it was his turn to shrug. "Maybe. Maybe not. I've read just about everything you ever wrote about Falcone."

Jimmy Falcone. She had known the most powerful organized crime boss in southern Louisiana—currently under indictment, along with Nick, for every crime the FBI could nail him with—would eventually enter into the conversation. That was why Nick had won his bet with Jamey. She was something of a local expert on Jimmy Falcone. She'd made a name for herself tracking him and his activities, both legal and illegal, for the past thirteen years. She knew his organization probably as well as the FBI did...but Nick knew it better. For about ten years now, he had been one of Jimmy's most loyal and most trusted advisors.

"Get to the point, Nick," she said impatiently. She wanted to go home, have a drink and then pamper herself

with a long, luxurious bubble bath. She wanted to wash
away the memories, the disappointment and the distaste that
was rapidly growing inside her.

He took one last pull from the cigarette, then flicked it
away and spun on his heel, disappearing into the shadows.
Jolie watched the butt arc through the air, a thin glowing
point in the darkness, then land nearby. Though only bare
earth surrounded it, she took the few steps necessary to
grind it out beneath her running shoe before returning to the
stepping-stone path.

Nick returned, carrying a thick green folder, the kind that
was accordion-pleated and closed on three sides. She automatically reached for it, but he held on to the open side with
both hands. "You can use this however you want—keep it,
turn it over to the feds, toss it. There's just one condition,
Jolie."

"What?"

"Keep me out of it. If any of Jimmy's people connects me
to this, I'm dead. I know that probably doesn't matter much
to you, but I'd kind of like to hang around a while longer."

If it had been any man besides Nick talking about any
man besides Jimmy, Jolie likely would have thought he was
exaggerating, but not Nick. Not about Jimmy. Jimmy Falcone was cold. The only life that meant anything to him was
his own. Only he and God knew exactly how many deaths
could be laid at his feet, but the number was frighteningly
high. Even though Nick had done more to keep Jimmy out
of jail and his business prospering in the past ten years than
anyone else, if Jimmy thought for a moment that Nick was
betraying him, he would give the order for his death in the
blink of an eye.

So why was Nick apparently doing just that?

She pulled on the folder, freeing it from his grip, and began thumbing through the contents. It was difficult to see in
the dim lamp light, but there were pages of computer-
generated notes, some photographs and a number of tape
cases, each holding four microcassettes. Evidence against
Falcone. Documentation of his illegal activity. Wouldn't her
law-and-order colleagues—Michael Bennett, a New Or-

leans cop, Remy Sinclair, the FBI agent that Falcone had recently tried to kill, and Smith Kendricks, the prosecutor who was taking Falcone to trial in the near future—love to get their hands on this? She would bet Kendricks hadn't even dreamed of being lucky enough to come up with a co-operative Nick Carlucci.

She looked up at Nick again. "If this stuff is of any value—"

"It is."

"Then why aren't you taking it to the feds? Why aren't you using it to make a deal for yourself?"

"I'm not interested in making deals."

"What *are* you interested in?"

He was looking at her, but he wasn't seeing her. His gaze pierced straight through her and veered off somewhere in the distance. When he answered, it was a flat monotone that was all the more effective for its lack of emotion. "Justice."

Five minutes ago, she would have laughed at such an answer. She would have replied that justice was a noble concept with which Nick Carlucci had not even a passing familiarity. That look, though... that look proved her wrong. Which of Jimmy Falcone's wrongs was Nick putting right? she wondered.

Taking a few steps toward the iron fence, toward the light, she flipped through the top few pages again. "Since you've become a defender of justice," she said, deliberately injecting a note of cynicism into her voice, "why don't you give this stuff to the government? Kendricks can make better use of it than I can. I can only write newspaper articles that make Falcone look bad. Smith can use it in court to—"

Hearing a rustle behind her, she spun around. She saw nothing, but from the back of the lot came the soft sound of a gate closing. That gate was the only other exit from the park; it led into the narrow strip of yard of the rear house and onto the next street. Remaining utterly still, after a moment she heard the closing of a car door and the sound of an engine that soon faded.

With a shiver, she clutched the folder tightly and walked quickly toward her own car. The Nicky she knew never would have walked off and left her that way. He would have waited until she'd made it safely to her car before pulling his disappearing act. Then, as she unlocked the car door, she muttered a curse aloud. The Nicky she knew had done a hell of a lot worse than leave her standing alone in the middle of a park. He'd pulled another disappearing act back then, this one at a time when she'd needed him desperately, and he'd done it without a moment's concern for her.

Safely locked inside the car, she dropped the folder in the passenger seat. Making a U-turn, she drove back down Serenity Street to Decatur, then headed home. Thoughts of a drink, a soothing bath and bed had disappeared from her mind.

Thanks to Nick, she had work to do.

Assistant U.S. Attorney Smith Kendricks sat at his desk, the newspaper spread open in front of him. Seated across from him were two of the best cops he'd ever worked with—Michael Bennett and Remy Sinclair. In one way or another, each of them had some involvement with the investigation into Jimmy Falcone's activities. Michael's wife—and Remy's cousin—Valery had been a witness to one of the murders Jimmy had ordered, and Remy had been the agent in charge of the FBI's investigation until Falcone's people tried to kill him. He had survived the shooting and a subsequent attempt and was now, along with his bride, Susannah, one of the government's prime witnesses against Falcone.

Michael and Remy were both also the best friends Smith had.

And they were both familiar with the problem facing him now.

"How does she do it?" he asked, tapping his fingertip on the column where Jolie Wade's latest story ended.

"She's a resourceful woman," Michael replied, while Remy simply made an annoyed sound but didn't say anything.

Smith knew well how each of his friends felt about the reporter. Michael had known her for years; he liked her and had a mutually satisfying, strictly off-the-record working relationship with her. Remy, however, like most FBI agents, saw all reporters as thorns in the bureau's side. He didn't willingly cooperate with her on anything, even though it had been *her* sources who had provided the information necessary to nail Remy's dirty partner a few months back. His respect for her abilities was given only grudgingly—but at least it *was* given.

What Smith wasn't so sure about were his own feelings for Jolie. Personally, he liked her. She was intelligent, direct and tenacious as hell. She had an uncanny way of knowing who could be trusted and who couldn't. She was passionate about her work, about truth and honesty and the people's right to know. She was a damn good writer, willing to work and work hard for every story she got. She had spent thirteen years on the local paper and had developed an extensive network of sources and informants, better than any local cop had. She didn't always approve of the way the local law enforcement did their jobs—the NOPD, the FBI and the U.S. Attorney's office had all come in for their share of front-page finger pointing—but she was always fair. Whenever she criticized them, it was because they *had* done something wrong.

Professionally... With the government's case against Jimmy Falcone set to go to trial in four weeks and with Smith prosecuting, the last problem he needed right now was Jolie in her investigative mode. She was doing more than simply covering the news today; she was *uncovering* new news.

And it dealt with *his* case.

In very accurate, very intimate detail.

In more accurate and more intimate details than even he and the FBI had.

Smith closed the newspaper and leaned back. It was Friday evening, past quitting time, and he was supposed to have dinner tonight with Michael and Remy and their wives. Instead, he imagined he was going to still be here long after the blackened fish Michael had promised was a mere memory, dealing with his boss and likely with Shawna Warren, the case agent who had replaced Remy after his shooting.

Despite their dedication to preserving and upholding the laws of the land, he suspected neither Alexander Marshall nor Shawna would object if freedom of the press was somehow expunged from the Bill of Rights.

Hell, Jolie, he thought with a scowl; then a grin took over. "You have to admire her timing. She'll go home and spend a pleasant, relaxing weekend, while the rest of us—both the government and Falcone's people—scurry around frantically trying to find out how she knows what she knows."

Now it was Remy who was scowling. "You don't have to admire anything about her. You just have to haul her in here and demand that she give up her source."

"Right," Michael agreed sarcastically. "And after that, you can turn the tides, balance the budget and end world hunger. Jolie's got so damn many sources because she takes care of them. People tell her things because they know she *won't* give them up. Not ever. Not for anything."

Leaving his desk, Smith went to the window and gazed out. The sun was edging farther west, but it was still muggy and hot outside—typical weather for New Orleans in July. He liked Louisiana summers. Of course, he spent his days here in the office or in court and his evenings in one air-conditioned place or another, but he liked the heat—the intensity of it. The lethargy it brought on. The slower pace it required.

He liked the flavor of summer in the South.

Forcing his mind back to the matter at hand, he sighed. Remy was right. He could have Jolie brought into his office, could demand that she reveal her source, and when she refused—because Michael was also right; she would never give up an informant—he could have her arrested. He could go before a judge and get search warrants for her home, her office, her car. He could give the FBI free rein to scrutinize every last minute detail of her life. By the time they finished with her, she wouldn't know what privacy was. She wouldn't have a single, solitary secret left.

He hated to do that to her.

But he would, if there wasn't any other option.

"I've got to get going. I'm already late," Michael said, rising from his chair. "If you finish up here in time, come on over. We'll keep dinner warm for you."

"Thanks, but don't count on seeing me." By the time he finished with Alexander and Shawna, he wouldn't have the stomach for anything as spicy and highly flavored as Michael's Cajun dinner. He would probably go home to a dinner of aspirin and antacid.

He'd known from the time he was a boy, Smith thought as Remy and Michael left, that he would become a lawyer and would go into some sort of government service. That was what Kendricks men did, for at least the first fifteen to twenty years of their careers; his father, grandfather, uncles and cousins had been prosecutors, attorneys general, congressmen and ambassadors. He had never doubted that he would follow in their footsteps, had never considered that he might even have a choice. He had gone to Harvard Law, as everyone before him had, and then he had gone to work for the Justice Department.

That was twelve years ago, and he'd never regretted it.

But the thought about aspirin and antacid hadn't been a joke. Lately he *was* finding himself taking more than just work home with him from the office. In the past few months it was headaches and tense muscles, and his stomach felt as if it were doing its damnedest to supply him with an ulcer. He needed to relax. He needed a personal life. He needed one day when he wasn't working on or planning for or worrying over the Falcone case.

He needed to see that bastard, and all the bastards who worked for him, in prison.

This case had become personal. The moment Falcone had decided to get Remy off his back by framing him for murder, Smith's professional judgment had been skewed, and he had never gotten it on track again. He never prosecuted cases without merit. He always wanted to see the bad guys punished and justice prevail.

But he wanted more this time. He wanted Falcone and Carlucci and all the others to suffer. He wanted them to pay for everyone they had hurt, for every crime they had ever committed or even thought about committing. He wanted not just justice, but revenge.

Maybe Jolie Wade could help him get it.

Or maybe she would stand in the way of it.

He didn't know the reporter as well as he would like to. Unlike Michael, who considered her a friend, Smith could only claim her as a professional acquaintance. He'd done a few interviews with her and had spoken with her a number of times in the past—always with other media representatives present—about one case or another. He had even run into her a time or two socially—pleasant, cordial, forgettable encounters.

Except he hadn't forgotten them.

The simple fact—one he hadn't admitted to Michael or Remy or even himself—was that he was attracted to her.

And she intimidated the hell out of him.

Thanks to his education and his upbringing, there wasn't a social situation he couldn't handle. Thanks to his job and, again, his upbringing, there wasn't a class of people out there he wasn't comfortable with—servants or socialites, rich or poor, white collar or blue, good guys or bad, victims or criminals.

Except Jolie Wade. She was in a class by herself.

He knew little personal information about her. She was about his age, possibly a few years younger. She was single. Her ambition was legendary, and so was her talent. He knew that her competitive spirit carried over from work into other areas of her life; she regularly competed in and often won local 10-K runs, and she was rumored to hold her own in tennis and to be one hell of a poker player.

He also knew that she was brash, aggressive and blunt spoken. As a prosecutor, he appreciated the direct air about her, the way she met his gaze *and* his questions head-on; as a man, it sometimes unnerved him.

He knew she had a soft, rounded Southern drawl and a strong sense—as Southern women seemed to have—of who she was. She had a fierce pride, a stubborn streak the proverbial mile wide and personal ethics stronger than any society could have pushed on her.

And she had the prettiest green eyes he had ever seen.

From the desk behind him, the intercom interrupted the silence. It was his boss, summoning Smith to his office. He scowled at his reflection in the window glass before turning away. He had been expecting the call from Alexander, but that didn't make this meeting any more pleasing a prospect. Still, he slipped into his suit coat, straightened his tie and collected his briefcase from the credenza, then shut off the lights as he left his office.

It had been a long day. He had already put in nearly twelve hours at his desk, including lunch. Now he had to be the outlet for Alexander's—and probably Shawna's—frustration before he could even think about going home.

It was a sure bet that Jolie Wade was already home, kicked back and taking it easy or getting ready to go out for an evening of pleasure.

It was an even surer bet that no one in the Falcone camp would kick back and take it easy—and not just this weekend. Jimmy would make sure that no one found a moment's peace until Jolie's source was identified or his trial started, whichever came first.

Missing out on Michael's dinner didn't seem such a bad price to pay for that.

As he had expected, Shawna was waiting with Alexander. Like Remy, like Smith himself, she was a lawyer by education; six years ago she had given up a promising career with the most respected law firm in Washington, D.C., to join the FBI. The same traits that made her damn near impossible to work with in her own office—she was tough, methodical, precise and very detail-oriented—made her very popular indeed in the U.S. Attorney's office. When Shawna delivered a case, it was neatly wrapped and tied with a bow. She was so thorough that convictions—or guilty pleas— were practically a given on her cases.

But, again like Remy, she had little tolerance for reporters, which she was making clear to Alexander when he motioned Smith into the office.

Without interrupting her, Smith sat down in the empty chair opposite her and settled back to listen. He'd heard it all before from Remy, from Alexander, from Shawna. He'd even let off some of the same anger himself a time or two. It was tough when you were doing the best damn job you could while adhering to the limits and restrictions of the law, and along came someone like Jolie, operating under few limits and restrictions and finding out all sorts of things that had eluded your best efforts.

When Shawna ran out of steam, Alexander asked, "What do you propose we do?"

"Bring her in. Question her. Arrest her."

Smith shook his head. "That won't accomplish anything."

"She has a reputation for protecting her sources. I know," Shawna said snidely. "But that reputation has never been tested. Take her before a judge, get her slapped with a contempt citation and put her in jail for a while. Maybe then she'll decide that the reality of protecting her sources isn't as easy or as noble as the theory."

Again Smith shook his head. "If we charge Jolie and she goes to jail, we'll be making a martyr of her. She already has tremendous respect in this city, both among the law-abiding citizens and the not-so-upstanding. That will only boost her status, to say nothing of bringing media across the country down on us. They always pick up on it when a reporter goes to jail for shielding a source."

"So what do you suggest, Smith?" Alexander asked.

He shrugged. "I think we should talk to her—*talk*, Shawna, not threaten. It can't hurt to ask where she got her information, even if she's not likely to tell. Other than that, about the only logical thing to do right now is take her story and see if you can develop anything from it. Maybe there's enough there to point you in the right direction."

There was a moment's silence while his boss considered his suggestion. Neither Alexander nor Shawna was happy with it; he could see that in their expressions. He could also see that they knew he was right. Maybe this article was a one-shot thing with Jolie. Maybe she'd come across some information and that had been it. Maybe she would be willing now to share it with them.

And if it wasn't a one-shot story? If she had more information, enough maybe for a series of articles? If she wasn't willing to share it?

They would find out soon enough.

Then they could take whatever action might be necessary.

"All right," Alexander agreed. "Shawna, you see what you can do with the story, and, Smith—" Pausing, he smiled. His boss so rarely smiled that Smith rightly took it as a warning. "You see what you can do with Jolie. Deal with her. This weekend. Come in to see me with good news Monday morning."

Deal with her, Smith thought resignedly. People didn't deal with Jolie Wade; they got dealt with by her. He wasn't a man who accepted failure easily—that was part of what made him such a good prosecutor—but he was likely to come out of any dealings with Jolie on the losing end.

But he also wasn't a man who turned away from doing his job. Deal with her, Alexander had said, and that was what he would do.

At least, he would try.

Jolie stood at the counter in her small kitchen, barefoot and dressed in shorts and a T-shirt, surveying the salads she had just finished making. Hers was a chef's salad, filling a decent-size serving dish and swimming in blue cheese dressing. It was heavy with turkey and ham, three kinds of cheese, and enough tomatoes, onions, olives and croutons to hide the fact that there was very little lettuce in the bowl. The salad she had made for Cassie was in a regular-size bowl, consisted primarily of spinach and sprouts and would be eaten perhaps with a drizzle of fresh lemon juice but most likely dressing-free.

Such differences in the eldest and youngest of the Wade kids, she thought, fishing a plump black olive from her bowl and licking the blue cheese off before biting into it. She loved real food and was willing to pay for her indulgences with daily runs, while seventeen-year-old Cassie was a vegetarian who hadn't eaten sugar or fat in other than negligible amounts in more years than she could remember.

The differences didn't stop there. Jolie loved rock and roll, while Cassie's musical tastes ran to the more esoteric; the haunting, lyrical strains of some group who seemed to speak little, if any, English drifted down from upstairs. Jolie dressed for comfort in well-worn jeans and trousers, T-shirts and sweaters and shorts, while Cassie wore dresses, usually long, shapeless and black. Jolie loved bad movies, while, for Cassie, if it didn't have subtitles or was shown at anything other than the artsy little theater over near the school, it wasn't worth seeing. Although Jolie loved her dearly, it was hard to believe that the same blood pumped through their veins.

But it did.

"Cassie," she called, carrying the bowls and silverware through the house to the living room. "Dinner's ready."

"I'll be right down." Though she shouted to be heard, Cassie's voice sounded serene, unruffled. She was an elegant young woman, possessing more grace, more class and style than all the other Wades put together. Occasionally Jolie wondered where it came from and why she hadn't gotten at least a small portion of it herself.

She set the bowls on the coffee table and was returning to the kitchen for their drinks—soda and steaming herbal tea—when the doorbell sounded. Detouring to the door, she tiptoed to see out the peephole. She expected to see long-haired, leather-jacketed Trevor, the latest in a long line of young men who had fallen head over heels for Cassie.

Instead, she saw Smith Kendricks.

Sinking back onto her heels, she reached out to unfasten the dead bolt, then rose onto her toes and checked again. It was still Smith standing in the porch light's yellowish glow.

Still the last person in the world she would expect to find at her door on a sultry hot July night.

As the bell pealed again, she undid the locks and opened the door halfway, leaning against it to study him through the screen door. He was over six feet tall and lean without being lanky. His bearing was elegant, his clothing expensively casual, his style understated. A pretty boy—that was what they would have called him, somewhat derisively, twenty years ago on Serenity Street.

In the past twenty years, she had come to appreciate pretty boys.

Given half a chance, she could come to appreciate Smith Kendricks very, very much.

But half a chance was more than she would ever get. She knew Smith's type, and she was about as far away from it as a woman could be.

Ah, but she could dream, couldn't she? Dreaming had brought her this far, to a successful career and a neat little house half a city and an entire world away from Serenity Street.

Crossing her arms over her chest, she gave him a smug smile. "Slumming, Kendricks?"

"I thought I'd see how the little people live," he replied, clearly amused by her greeting. He always looked so serious, so superior, so—hell, so *rich*—that she forgot, from the last time she'd seen him to the next, that he had a sense of humor.

"'The little people'?" she echoed. "Is that a reference to my social status or my physical stature?"

"Which would offend you more? Being considered common? Or being called short?"

"Being called short." She *was* common, as ordinary and working-class as a person could be, and she wasn't ashamed of it. She wasn't ashamed of being short, either, but, oh, how she would love just once to have legs a mile long.

"How about vertically challenged?"

"Maybe I'm not short. Maybe you're just tall."

He acknowledged the possibility with a nod, then asked, "Is this a bad time?"

That was her cue to back up, open the door and invite him inside. She didn't. "For what?"

"To talk."

"Business?"

Again he nodded, and again she thoughtfully considered him through the mesh door. No doubt he was here about her story; she had expected some sort of contact from the government, although she had figured it would come from the FBI—maybe from Remy, because he knew her, or Shawna Warren, because she was in charge of the case. What did it mean that the assistant U.S. Attorney himself had come? And what did it mean that he had come to her house on a Friday night, when he surely had better things to do, instead of showing up at the newspaper or summoning her to his office on Monday?

"I can save you the trouble," she said at last. "The answer's no."

"So what's the question?"

"'Will you tell us who your source is?' That's what you're here to ask, isn't it?"

Instead of answering, he looked toward the well-lit room behind her. "Can I come in?"

After a moment's hesitation, she unlatched the screen door and stepped back. When he stopped in the broad doorway leading to the living room and looked around, she made a sweeping gesture. "Welcome to my humble home."

He made no secret of his interest in the room. After a thorough inspection, he turned and gazed down at her. He seemed to be debating something; after a moment, he gave a shake of his head.

"What?" she asked.

"I was just trying to associate the word *humble* with you. It doesn't work." Turning back, he settled his gaze on the two bowls on the coffee table. "You have company."

"Just my sister. She's upstairs."

"You should have told me I was interrupting your dinner."

She moved past him and went to sit in the armchair, picking up the bowl as she passed. "Salad hardly qualifies as dinner. *I* wanted hamburgers or steak, but Cassie's a vegetarian," she said crabbily as she picked a piece of turkey out and ate it. "Sit down, present your case, ask your questions, and I'll tell you no again. Then you can tell your boss that you tried but I was totally uncooperative."

"Which won't surprise Alexander one bit," he replied with a chuckle. "You do have a reputation for being uncooperative."

He had gorgeous eyes, she thought, that reflected his emotions. They were a pretty blue—she would have expected brown to go with his hair—and they laughed when he was amused, scowled with annoyance and turned soul-numbing cold when he was angry.

She wondered idly how they looked when he was aroused; then, realizing that there was nothing idle about her body's response as her temperature climbed a few degrees, she banished the thought. This was business, she reminded herself. With a man like Smith, it would never be anything *but* business.

"All right," he agreed, settling on the sofa. "First off, I'm here because it was the only way to keep Shawna from having you picked up and taken in for questioning."

"Interrogation, you mean," she corrected him dryly. "She takes her job seriously, doesn't she?"

"Yes, she does. Kind of reminds me of you."

Jolie didn't appreciate the comparison, although she could see his point. She and Shawna Warren did have a lot in common. They both cared about their jobs, and they were both pretty single-minded when it came to doing them right. They were both considered—unfairly so, in Jolie's mind—less than feminine by a number of the men they worked with, because they were ambitious, they had drive and determination, and they wouldn't settle for anything less than best. In a man it was considered assertive; in a woman it was aggressive, with all its most negative connotations.

But sharing a number of traits didn't mean she had to like the other woman.

"So...you don't care to come forward with the identity of your source."

She shook her head.

"Obviously it's someone in Falcone's organization."

"Or maybe someone who's merely watched him closely."

He considered that for a moment, then shook his head. The action made a strand of hair—brown, preppy short and

perfectly casual...or should that be casually perfect?—
feather across his forehead. "The only people who get that
close to him are those who work for him."

"A lot of people work for him."

"But not that many are close to him."

She didn't respond. She wasn't going to be drawn along
on a fishing expedition. Smith was too good, too clever. At
her best, she could hold her own with him...but tonight she
was at less than her best. The setting was too intimate—this
was her home, after all—and some stubborn part of her was
as interested in making personal observations about him as
the reporter part of her was in business.

From upstairs, the music grew louder as the guest room
door opened. Cassie had traded the soft, relaxing CD—the
language was Gaelic, Jolie thought but wasn't sure—for
something with a salsa beat and lyrics clearly recognizable
as Spanish.

"Am I keeping your sister from her dinner?"

"Cassie's getting dressed for a date. She'll wander down
whenever she's ready, which could be any time in the next
two hours."

"You were no better when you were dating." Cassie came
quietly into the room and settled on the arm of Jolie's chair.
"You do remember dating? Back before you started college? Before you decided that everything else in life had to
go on hold until you'd won your Pulitzer?" Without waiting for a response, she leaned forward and extended her
hand to Smith. "I'm Cassie Wade, the youngest of Jolie's
many siblings."

Smith introduced himself as he shook her hand. There
was a note of distinct male appreciation in his eyes—not interest, the protective Jolie was relieved to note, but simple
appreciation. Cassie inspired that in most men. She wasn't
beautiful, not breathtaking or heart stopping, but she was
undeniably, sweetly, purely lovely. With dark hair that
reached straight and smooth past her waist, dark eyes and
pale golden skin, she was striking—and her taste in clothing made her more so. Her dress this evening was black, as
usual, but instead of brushing around her ankles, this one

ended inches above her knees. With it she wore a crocheted vest, textured hose and funky, chunky suede heels, all in black. Only the vest was even remotely stylish, but Cassie didn't mind. Some women got their style from their clothes, she insisted, while her clothes got their style from her.

It certainly worked for her, Jolie thought with more than a hint of pride. The girl never went anywhere without drawing admiring looks.

"Sorry about dinner, Jolie, but Trevor's here. I saw him pull up."

"He's not coming to the door?"

Cassie gave her a long, level look that was gently chastening. "Don't wait up for me."

"What time is curfew at home?" Jolie asked as her sister rose from the chair.

"I'm practically eighteen now, Jolie."

"Uh-huh. And what time is curfew?"

Cassie sighed softly, but with enough force to make her annoyance—and acceptance—known. "One o'clock. I'll be home then. Mr. Kendricks, it was nice meeting you. Later, Jolie."

She left as quietly as she had come—left Jolie alone with Smith, a Spanish ballad she didn't understand and a conversation she didn't want to have. He wasn't eager to have it, either, she suspected when he remained silent for a time.

Or perhaps he was simply gathering his bearings after being exposed to Cassie. Men often needed to do that.

"She's a lovely girl," he remarked after a moment.

She smiled that he had used exactly her own description. His next words made the smile disappear.

"Now that the vegetarian is gone, why don't you quit picking at that salad and let's go find a steak?"

Chapter 2

Smith would have recalled the words if he could. The last thing he needed tonight was anything even remotely resembling a date with Jolie Wade—and taking her out to dinner hit too close to the mark. Since taking back the words was impossible, his next best bet would be to cancel the invitation as soon as he'd offered it, but that would be rude, and Clarice Kendricks hadn't raised her only son to be rude.

Maybe Jolie would turn him down.

Or maybe, he thought, considering the prospect of having dinner and spending the rest of the evening with her... maybe, if he was lucky, she wouldn't.

"Dinner," she said tentatively, as if not quite sure she'd understood him. "You want to have dinner."

Jolie Wade unsure in a situation. That was a first.

"I do it most nights around this time." His smile felt as hesitant as her voice sounded. "It'll be my treat."

"Because this is business." She said it as a foregone conclusion, but there was a slight lilt at the end that turned it into a question. It was a tough one to answer, because he didn't know what answer she wanted. Hell, he didn't know what answer *he* wanted. The wisest thing would be to agree that, yes, the time they spent together this evening would be strictly business.

But wise wasn't necessarily true.

He wound up giving no answer at all. "Go on, get some shoes."

She hesitated, then got to her feet, setting the salad dish on the table. "I'll just be a minute."

While he waited, he gave the room another long look. If he had ever given any thought to the place Jolie called home, he wouldn't have chosen this. He would have placed her in some place relatively new, some place contemporary, streamlined, stripped-down. He could have easily imagined her in one of those places, like his own, that were routinely featured in decorating magazines: walls of glass, an expanse of marble floor, all white or black or gray, the only furnishings a crimson futon and her trusty laptop computer.

With her blond hair and creamy golden skin, she would look damned tantalizing on a crimson futon.

Swallowing hard, he forced his gaze to focus on the opposite wall, forced his attention to return to a more appropriate line of thought.

The last place he would have expected to find her living was in a little yellow house in a middle-class neighborhood, with flowers blooming in the yard and a swing on the porch. He hadn't thought of her as a cozy-tidy-house sort of woman, a woman who collected books and little cobalt blue bottles, a woman who framed crayon drawings and bits of old lace for her walls.

He hadn't thought of her as a sister, particularly to a pretty girl half her age. Frankly, he hadn't thought of her as having family at all. She was so independent, so ambitious. Relationships took a back seat to ambition like hers; Smith knew that from his own experience. For years, he had shared the same sort of drive to prove that he was a damned good prosecutor, that he'd earned his position based on hard work and a high conviction rate, that his family name, money and privilege had nothing to do with his career success.

He had achieved those goals, but at the cost of his personal relationships. He'd rarely made it back home to Rhode Island to visit his family. His sisters' husbands were merely names attached to vaguely familiar faces, and his nieces and nephews were virtual strangers. He hadn't managed to maintain a steady, ongoing relationship with any woman in longer than he cared to recall. What little bit of himself he'd had left over from his job he had invested in his friendships with Michael and Remy.

But Jolie hadn't reached her goals yet. It was common knowledge that she had her sights set on a hell of a lot more than New Orleans could offer. There were bigger and better markets out there—Chicago, New York, Washington— and she intended to work her way into one of them. She wanted to be famous. She wanted to be one of those rare journalists whose names were household words in households where her particular paper was never read.

And she wanted that Pulitzer. What was it her sister had said? That everything else in her life had to go on hold until then.

But, despite that ambition, that drive, she still had roots. She managed to be a sister to young Cassie. She framed drawings done most likely by her nieces and nephews and hung them on the walls. Just as he'd always made time for his best friends, apparently she made time for her family.

She came down the stairs then, interrupting his thoughts. She had changed from shorts into wheat-colored jeans, from a T-shirt promoting a recent 10-K run to a dressier, round-necked T-shirt that looked like rusty-hued silk. She had drawn her hair off her neck with a tortoiseshell clasp, fastened a watch around her narrow wrist and slipped into a pair of rubber-soled huaraches. Such simple changes for such maximum effect. Ten minutes ago he would have said she looked comfortable, lazy, even cute. Now conflicting words came to mind, words like pretty. Wholesome. Alluring. Innocent. Sexy as hell.

As he rose from the sofa, she picked up her purse, brightly colored straw woven in a wave pattern, and slung it over her shoulder. "I'm ready."

He went outside, holding the screen while she locked the door behind her. "I have overnight bags smaller than that purse," he remarked as they started across the porch to the steps.

"I need a big purse."

"For what? The tools of your trade?"

"Precisely. A notebook, pens, a tape recorder, extra tapes, extra batteries and a power cord."

"Just in case you happen to run into a story on the way to dinner."

"Hey, would a cop leave home without his gun and badge? Would you go out without your pager and cellular phone?"

"That's hardly the same," he teased even as he automatically checked to make sure the pager was securely in place on his belt.

"It's exactly the same. We all like to be prepared." She came to an abrupt stop where the sidewalk that crossed her yard met the driveway. "Is that your car?"

He took an exaggerated look around. "There's only you and me here. Is it yours?"

"Of course not."

"Then it must be mine." Pulling his keys from his pocket, he circled to the opposite side of the Blazer and unlocked the door. "Let me guess. You expected a Mercedes or a BMW or—no, I know—a Lexus."

"Well . . . yeah." The step up that was perfectly easy for Smith was more of a climb for seven-inches-shorter Jolie. From his vantage point a few feet back, he discovered that her snug jeans and the silk top that conformed to her curves made it an appealing process to watch.

After closing the door, he returned to the other side and climbed in himself. "Then you were wrong," he replied. He didn't tell her that he had, at one time or another, owned each of those three cars, that it was a Lexus he had traded in when he'd bought this. "I bet my guess is more accurate than yours. I'd say you probably drive something a lot like yourself—a Corvette, maybe. A red one." Starting the engine, he flipped on the headlights, and the twin beams lit up the low-slung red 'Vette parked beside the house.

"Guess, hell," she muttered. "You cheated. You've seen my car before."

"I've ridden in your car before," he reminded her with a chuckle. "Back in January, when we went to a meeting with Michael, Remy and Valery, remember?" He backed out of the driveway, then headed toward downtown and one of his favorite restaurants, waiting all the while for her inevitable question. It didn't come until they had gone more than a half dozen blocks, and even then she asked it only grudgingly.

"How?"

He knew exactly what she meant, but pretended not to. "How what?"

"How is a red 'Vette a lot like me?"

"You're both little and flashy." She scowled, as he knew she would. Of course, she was entitled. After all, what woman appreciated being compared to a car? Still, he continued. "You're both sleek and classy. And I daresay you've both inspired more than a few male fantasies." He certainly had a few of his own.

There was a moment's hushed silence, as if his response had taken her totally by surprise, and then she laughed. "Oh, yes, I know the kind of fantasies I inspire in the men I come in contact with. Most of them deal in some variation with my disappearing off the face of the earth."

He opened his mouth to tell her she was wrong, then closed it again. This was business, he reminded himself. Small talk was perfectly acceptable; it was even advisable. Personal observations—personal feelings—weren't.

Tightening his hands around the wheel, he forced his wayward thoughts back to a more acceptable subject. "Your sister said she was the youngest of your many siblings. How many kids are we talking about here?"

"There are thirteen of us—nine girls and four boys. I'm the oldest, and Cassie's the baby." He saw her smile in the dim light. "My parents are good Catholics. When the Lord said multiply, they took him seriously."

"I have an older sister and a younger one. Growing up, I thought the younger one was one too many. What was it like for you with so many kids?"

"Loud." She smiled again, not the brash, confident smile he usually associated with her, but a gentler one. "There were lots of advantages. Being the oldest, I had to help out with the others, so I learned responsibility at an early age. I learned to do what I was told when I was told—with thirteen kids, Mama didn't have time to repeat herself. I learned to concentrate in the midst of chaos, since that's all there ever was in our house." Her voice grew softer as she gazed out the window. "There were times when I wanted to be an only child, to have a room all to myself, to have my parents' attention all to myself. There were times I wanted less responsibility and more childhood."

Then she sighed and her voice returned to its normal, straightforward tone. "It wasn't a bad childhood. My parents loved every one of us, and we all got along well. With so many of us in such close quarters, we had to."

"Do you see them often?"

"Reasonably so. Everyone's grown up now. They have jobs, families, lives of their own. But they all still live in the area, except Meg. She married a soldier and moved to Germany. I see Cassie the most, and Mama and Daddy." She barely paused before continuing. "Where does your family live?"

"Rhode Island. Newport."

Jolie gazed through her reflection on the window as houses gave way to businesses. She had asked the question only to be polite; she already knew the answer, just as she already knew a number of things about him. For instance, he was from Rhode Island, he'd gone to college up in Baton Rouge, then had returned back East for law school. She knew he had never married but would; everybody would eventually, it seemed—everyone except her.

He lived in one of those riverside condos that was three times the size of her little house and about twenty times as expensive. He dated frequently—much more so than *she* managed to get out—and the women he dated were beautiful. In her own paper she had seen photographs of him at one social function or another, all dressed up in a tux, and he was always with another lovely New Orleans belle.

Yet, for all his advantages and family wealth, he wasn't a snob. He had never been less than polite to her in a professional situation, never less than friendly in a social setting. Besides Remy Sinclair, whose background was close to his own, his best friends since college had been Michael Bennett—son of a small-town preacher and a housewife—and Evan Montez, also small-town, small-time. He was loyal to his friends—had stood by each of them as they married and had been there last year when Evan was buried.

He was, when all was said and done, a very nice man.

A very nice man who just happened to be heir, along with his sisters, to millions.

"How did you manage to get a Friday night free?" she asked, turning to look at him. Now that they were in the business district, there was enough light to see his face clearly, to see his smile.

"Actually, I had plans for the evening, but some hotshot reporter ran a story in this evening's paper that got under my boss's skin, so I had to cancel." Then he relented. "I was supposed to have dinner with Michael and Valery and Remy and Susannah. When I got tied up with Alexander and Shawna, I bowed out."

"Let me guess. Warren wanted to have me arrested, and Marshall..." She thought about it a moment, considering what fate Alexander Marshall would most like to see befall her. "He probably wanted to have me exiled to a deserted island."

"Actually, *Remy* wanted to have you arrested—he and Michael dropped by to bring me a copy of the paper. Shawna wanted to slap you into jail for contempt and throw away the key. You're probably right about Alexander, though. I think the idea of you totally incommunicado on a deserted island would make him very happy."

"Lucky for me you're so reasonable. I'd hate to be spending the night in jail."

His laughter surprised her. "I don't believe that for a minute. If you had no other choice, you would go, and you would go knowing that every major newspaper in the country was writing about it. You would enjoy it."

"You're wrong," she quietly disagreed. "I don't want to make the news, and I don't want to *be* the news. I just want to write about it."

He didn't respond to that until they were parked in a lot just down the block from the restaurant that bordered the central business district and the French Quarter. After getting out, he came around to meet her and, for a moment, simply studied her. When he finally spoke, his voice was soft, his tone regretful. "You know, we could charge you if we wanted."

She knew that, but she challenged him anyway. "With what?"

"For starters, you have knowledge—and proof—of a crime, and you haven't reported it."

She looked past him to one of the high-rise hotels looming overhead. Of the entire folder of documentation Nick had given her, she had used maybe one-fourth of it for today's story. How reasonable would Smith be if he knew all the secrets she was saving for next time?

Not very, she suspected. Had he known, he probably would have voted with Remy, Shawna Warren and Alexander Marshall. He wouldn't have given her the courtesy of tonight's visit. He sure as hell wouldn't be taking her out to dinner.

And even if it *was* just business, in months to come it might be nice to look back and remember this one dinner with Smith.

"In the end, Smith, we both have the same goal," she remarked as they began walking toward the restaurant.

"Are you sure of that?"

"We both want to see Jimmy Falcone punished."

"I know one of us wants that. I wonder if the other doesn't see one hell of a career-advancing opportunity."

Although his words carried a bit of a sting, she looked up at him and smiled brightly. "Aw, Smith, you shouldn't

doubt yourself that way. Your career's advancing just fine.
You know you'll be a full-fledged U.S. Attorney with or
without convictions in the Falcone case.''

His smile came reluctantly, then disappeared. ''You say
you want to see him punished. Prove it.''

''How?'' She asked it casually, as if she didn't already
know what his answer would be. As if she didn't already
know what *her* answer would be. What it *had* to be.

He waited until they were inside the restaurant, then until they'd been seated at a courtyard table, before he replied. ''Tell me who your source is.''

''I can't do that. Next request.''

''Ask him to talk to me.''

She leaned back in the wrought iron chair and gazed
around the courtyard. It was large, enclosed on two sides by
the restaurant itself and on the other sides by the neighboring buildings. Ivy grew across the brick facade, a fountain
gurgled in the center, and the paving stones that unevenly
supported the iron and glass tables were ancient and
chipped. The place was old and charming, similar to any
number of French Quarter courtyards.

She remembered when it used to be a parking lot.

Ask Nick to talk to Smith. She could do that. She could
call him— No, she couldn't. He had contacted her through
Jamey O'Shea last time because he'd known that the FBI
had a line ID—and possibly a wiretap—on his phone. At the
very least, they knew the numbers of every outgoing call,
along with the number from which every incoming call was
made. With a wiretap, they would be recording every conversation.

So she could go by Jamey's place. He and Nick had been
friends forever, had grown up together on the streets and at
St. Jude's. When Nick had gone off to college, Jamey had
gone off and joined the army. After a time they had both
come back home, Jamey to take over a shabby little bar on
Serenity Street, Nick to work for Falcone. She didn't know
whether Jamey had played it straight the last ten years or
whether he'd shared Nick's taste for criminal activity. If so,
he certainly hadn't shared Nick's talent; judging from the

condition O'Shea's was in, the years hadn't been prosperous ones for him.

But apparently he'd kept in touch with Nick. He could pass on Smith's message for Jolie.

For whatever good it would do.

"I can ask," she said, plucking a rose petal from those that had fallen to the table from the center bouquet. "But it's pointless, just as your asking me is pointless. His answer will be no."

"You don't know that."

"Smith, if he were interested in cooperating with your office, he would have gone to you, not me."

"Maybe he could be persuaded."

There had been a time when she would have given all she had and everything she might ever have to persuade Nick. She hadn't wanted so much of him at that time—just to be a part of his life. To continue seeing him. To continue believing he loved her the way she loved him. It wouldn't have cost him so very much to give her that.

But what Smith was asking could cost him his life.

"Not by me," she said flatly. When he started to protest, she went on. "I'll talk to him. I'll ask him if he'll talk to you. But I won't try to convince him. If his answer is no—and, I promise, it will be—then that's the end of it."

He still looked as if he wanted to argue, but instead he nodded once. "Fair enough."

"Now you be fair with me. Is Warren going to be watching me?"

It was his turn then to scrutinize their surroundings. When he finally looked back at her, there was regret in his eyes. "I can't answer that."

"You call that fair?"

"You're following your conscience, Jolie, and that's fine. But I have to follow the law. If I give you information regarding a federal investigation, then I'm as guilty as everyone else in this mess. I can't do it."

Jolie picked up the menu with a faint sigh. Pointless questions, predictable answers. Smith couldn't break the law, she couldn't betray a source, and Nick ... Hell, no one could make Nick do anything.

Then, after choosing an entrée, she laid the menu down and smiled slowly at Smith. "You know what one of the good things is about living and working here for so long?" When he shook his head, she went on. "I know everybody. I know all the cops, everyone in the sheriff's department, everyone in your office." Her smile grew more smug. "I know everyone in the FBI office. So if Shawna wants to keep me under surveillance in the hopes that I'll lead her to my informant, tell her to borrow someone from another office. And give her one other message."

Looking mildly amused now, he waited.

"Tell her he'd better be damned good at what he does. Because I'm the best at what I do."

Saturday was sunny, the sky filled with puffy white clouds that cast fleeting shadows as they crossed over Jackson Square. The moments they blocked the sun were too brief to lower the temperature even one degree, but it felt as if they did, and that was as good as an actual cooling, Smith decided.

He was standing on Michael's balcony, three stories above the square, looking down on a crowd of tourists and residents alike and listening to the mélange of voices, music and traffic. This was the French Quarter at its best—loud, chaotic, a million things happening at once and people everywhere. They had become more than a group, more than a crowd, but a mass, now moving in rhythm to the music, now yielding to the enervating drain of the lazy summer heat.

But there was also much to be said about the Quarter at midnight. Maybe that was its best time, when most businesses had closed for the day, when Bourbon Street still seethed with life but most other streets slept for the night. There was a quiet then that wrapped itself around you, disturbed only by distant echoes from other streets, from other lives.

And a damp, foggy dawn in the square held its own appeal, when the humidity was so heavy that you could see it swirling about your legs when you walked, when St. Louis Cathedral rose, solid and enduring, out of the insubstantial mist. That was the Quarter at its most peaceful, its most serene.

He had lived in New Orleans for twelve years now, in Louisiana for sixteen. He had moved to Baton Rouge when he was eighteen, fresh out of school and ready for college. Just as it was family tradition that he would become a lawyer and go into public service, it was also family tradition that he could earn his undergraduate degree wherever he chose, and he had chosen Louisiana State. It was a university he'd known little about in a city he'd never visited and a state where he knew no one. It had been his first chance in eighteen years to be entirely on his own.

It was a decision he'd been grateful for every one of the nineteen years since.

No one at LSU had known or cared about his family background. For the first time in his life, he had been accepted as just one of the guys; he had been treated no differently from anyone else. There had been no special favors and no proving himself, and he had made the best friends a person could ever ask for. Michael, Remy and Evan had become his family. Evan's death some fifteen months ago— a cop, he had been killed by a kidnapper while helping Michael rescue the man's eight-year-old victim—had been the most painful loss he had ever suffered.

He had come South nineteen years ago for four years of college and to temporarily escape the burden of being a Kendricks. When he had returned seven years later after finishing law school, even though it had been to a different city, to one he barely knew, it had been like coming home. This was where he belonged.

It was where he intended to stay.

Behind him the French door opened and feminine voices drifted out. Susannah Sinclair and Valery Bennett. Susannah was a midwesterner, a transplant from Nebraska, but in her short time here—a half year, maybe a little longer—her accent had already started fading, giving way to the softer, rounder Southern sounds. Valery was a native Louisianan, born in New Orleans, growing up first here and then in the tiny town of Belclaire, up the river halfway to Baton Rouge. To his New England ear, she sounded typically Southern with her languorous drawl and words that flowed slowly but effortlessly, musically, one into another.

When the door closed again, their voices vanished, but they were replaced by Michael's. "Anything interesting going on out here?"

"There's *always* something interesting going on out here." He rested his palms on the iron-lace railing, feeling the day's heat, sharp and uncomfortable, seeping into his skin. Gazing out over the square, he made the request he had come here for. "Care to discuss work?"

Michael's chuckle was dry. "I'm a cop."

And cops were always ready to share cop talk. That was something Smith had learned early on. "Tell me what you know about Jolie Wade."

Moving to stand beside him, Michael offered one of the cans of soda he carried, then popped the top on his own. "She's fair. Trustworthy. If she makes a promise, she'll keep it."

Although those were interesting points, they weren't what he wanted to know. He wanted to know things like what men she had been involved with, even temporarily. He wanted to know whether she ever got involved with anyone she had to deal with through her job. He wanted to know what it would take to compete with that damned job of hers.

But those were personal questions, and he *had* specified business.

"You've known her a long time, haven't you?"

"Thirteen years. The day she started at the paper, she came down to the station and introduced herself to a bunch of us—said we'd be seeing a lot of her in the future and that she hoped we would work well together. That was long before she started covering crime for the paper."

"She didn't waste any time, did she?"

"She still doesn't." Michael paused to drink deeply, then leaned forward to brace his forearms on the railing, cradling the can in both hands. "I don't know much about her upbringing, but I get the feeling it wasn't easy."

"In what way?" Smith's interest sharpened. Michael was a damned good cop and the best judge of character that he knew. His instincts were always right, his judgments dead center on target.

"I don't know," he replied with a sigh. "But ambition like that has to come from somewhere."

"*I* was ambitious like that, and my upbringing was perfectly normal."

Michael grinned. "Normal for rich folks, you mean. Normal for living in a fifty-room cottage on a twenty-acre estate and flying off to Europe in the family jet for spur-of-the-moment weekends. Normal for having an entire staff of servants to do everything from dress you in the morning to tuck you into bed at night." Then he grew serious again. "You were ambitious because you had something to prove. You wanted to show everyone that you could succeed not because of, but in spite of, the money your family had. Maybe Jolie wants to prove that she can succeed in spite of the money her family *didn't* have."

"Do you know anything about her family?"

Michael shook his head. "Just that they lived down here when she was a kid."

"I know she's got twelve younger brothers and sisters."

"Jeez. Her folks never hear of birth control or did they just not believe in it?" He didn't expect a response and didn't wait for one. "Jolie's hungry. She always has been. When we met, she was just out of college, twenty-two years old and didn't have a dime to her name, but she knew exactly what she wanted and how hard she was going to have to work to get it. Thirteen years later that determination is still there. She still knows what she wants, and she's still working hard for it. She hasn't got it yet, but she's a hell of a lot closer."

"She's not going to change her mind and cooperate with us, is she?"

The look Michael gave him was wry and chiding, a silent chastisement for asking a dumb question. "They don't give

Pulitzers to reporters who sell out their sources." With one
hand he gestured toward the crowd below. "Speak of the
devil..."

Smith didn't need anything more specific than that broad
wave, no directions, no pointing out. He looked down into
the crowd and immediately picked out a head of silky blond
hair, fastened in back with a ruffly red band. Her back to
him, she was facing the street performers on the opposite
side of Decatur Street, but he knew well that with her height
disadvantage, she wasn't seeing much other than the backs
of people taller than her.

Movement at her side caught his attention—Cassie—just
as Jolie abruptly turned and tilted her head back to look up
at them. Big dark glasses hid her eyes and half her
face...but not her slow, lazy, incredibly smug smile.

Leaning on the rail, Michael greeted her with a good-
natured gibe pitched loud enough to carry over the noise of
the crowd. "You'd be easy to lose in a crowd, Wade. Sur-
round you with normal-size people, and you can't see a
thing."

"I've never been lost yet, Bennett," she called back
sweetly. "What are you guys doing up there?"

"Enjoying today's festival."

"You can't enjoy it from up there. You have to be down
here in the middle of it. Come on."

"Not for me, thanks."

Her gaze slowly shifted sideways to Smith. He swore he
could feel it when it made contact, more intense than the sun
and more potent than the heat. "What about you?"

He was a reasonable man—she had commented on it
herself last night—but sometime in the past few seconds,
reason had deserted him. He knew he'd spent enough time
with her last night. He knew he certainly didn't need to be
spending part of his afternoon with her. He knew he sure as
hell didn't need to be sharing a French Quarter festival on a
powerfully hot, humid and lazy day with her.

Still, when he opened his mouth to decline, the wrong
words came out. The wrong ones for what he wanted.

But the right ones for what he needed.

"I'll be down in a moment."

Her smile changed—softened, sharpened—and her voice, even from this distance, seemed throatier. "I'll wait here."

Smith watched her turn away, watched her touch Cassie's arm and direct her attention elsewhere, and still he remained exactly where he was.

At least, until he realized that he was receiving the same sort of steady scrutiny from someone a lot closer at hand. He looked at Michael but didn't quite meet his gaze. "What?" he finally asked, aware that there was a question in his friend's expression, also aware that his tone was far more snappish than Michael deserved.

"You said work," Michael replied mildly. "Business. You want to know about Jolie? She's a nice woman. She's sweet. She's funny, smart and stubborn as hell. You push her and she's going to dig her heels in. She has about a million friends, from the bag ladies on the street to the mayor's office, and there's nothing she wouldn't do for any of them as long as it doesn't compromise her principles. As far as personal relationships, I've never known her to go out with the same guy more than once, and even that doesn't happen often. I always thought maybe there'd been some guy in her past, someone who'd hurt her, but I don't know."

Smith walked as far as the door before looking back. "Thanks, Michael."

"He's kind of cute."

Under other circumstances, Jolie would have winced at anyone, even Cassie, referring to a thirty-seven-year-old man as "kind of cute," but in Smith's case, it applied. While *she* considered him flat-out handsome, there *was* something kind of cute about him... in a straitlaced, buttoned-down, preppy sort of way.

"I think he likes you."

After losing sight of him in the crowd, she turned to her sister. "Of course he likes me," she bluffed. "Everyone likes me."

"Except a number of the people you work with. And half the cops in town. And two-thirds of the politicians. And Father Francis."

The impudent response Jolie had been prepared to make died unspoken at the mention of the priest. She'd had what she supposed was a typical association with him all the years she was growing up, but that had ended when she was eighteen. Although St. Jude's had long ago shut down, he was still in New Orleans. She still occasionally ran into him at some function or in connection with some story, but she had nothing to say to him. She had disappointed him, but he had disillusioned her. She had been a frightened teenage girl, but he had been an adult, a priest, a man of God. Whose was the greater sin?

"Oh, yeah, like I care what any of them thinks of me," she responded at last, but her tone wasn't as sarcastic as she had intended.

"Anyway, Mr. Kendricks is different." Cassie removed her hat, a broad-brimmed straw tied up with a gauzy black streamer that matched her skirt, and fanned herself with it. "It's a different kind of liking."

"You know, Cassie, he's only a couple of years older than me. I don't think he would object if you called him Smith."

"You're changing the subject."

Jolie didn't admit or deny it. Truth was, Cassie was right. Smith's feelings for her—if he even *had* feelings for her—were a little too important to discuss with a seventeen-year-old, no matter how mature Cassie was. Besides, the idea that she wanted a man—any man—to be interested in her was still new enough to Jolie, still scary enough, that she didn't feel comfortable even thinking about it.

Even though it was almost all she'd thought about since he'd taken her home last night.

"Michael was right." Smith sidestepped a stroller built for two before finally joining them. "You *are* easy to lose in a crowd. Fortunately, I could follow your sister's hat. Hello, Cassie."

Cassie gave Jolie a sweet smile, then very politely smiled at him. "Hello, Mr. Kendricks. Jolie, I'm going down to listen to the band. Why don't you head that way and meet me there later?" Before Jolie could respond, she drifted away, making her way effortlessly through the crowd.

"You don't often see a teenager with her presence," Smith remarked.

"No, you don't," Jolie agreed, still gazing after her. Abruptly, she swung around to face him. "I didn't mean to interrupt whatever you and Michael were doing."

"You didn't. I just stopped in since I couldn't make it to dinner last night. Susannah's there—she's teaching Valery about quilts for the shop—so we went outside to talk."

Valery and Michael were in the process, Jolie knew, of buying the antique clothing shop where Valery had worked since moving back to New Orleans. Along with gorgeous old clothing, the shop carried evening bags, jewelry, shoes and shawls and a growing collection of decades-old hand-pieced quilts. Jolie loved to go in and browse, although she had neither the height nor the style to carry off many of the old dresses. Still, she *had* found a lovely shawl that was now spread across her bed as a coverlet, and the ecru-shaded lace handkerchiefs that were mounted on velvet, framed and hanging on her living room walls had also come from there.

"What do you think of the festival?" she asked as they moved away from the tall fence that encircled the park and slipped into the throng of wanderers.

"You people down here certainly know how to throw a party."

"And we don't need an excuse for it, either. Surviving yet another day is reason enough." Moving with the flow of the crowd, she sneaked a quick but observant look at him. He was dressed about as casually as he ever got, wearing khaki trousers and a short-sleeved polo shirt in pale blue. While there was no denying that the subdued shades were flattering to him, she would like to see him in some real color— magenta or fuchsia, emerald green or electric blue or rich, royal purple.

But she doubted he owned anything in bright, vibrant colors. She would bet next Tuesday's paycheck that his closet was filled with very expensive suits in very traditional fabrics, cuts and colors, that his dress shirts were mostly white or blue, that the rest of his clothing came in shades of gray, khaki, black, brown and blue. There might be a pair of sweatpants, maybe some old forgotten jeans, but no vivid colors, nothing ratty or worn-out, nothing designed or made for pure, unadulterated comfort.

"So..." He looked down, his eyes meeting hers. "Have you had a chance to talk to your informant yet?"

She looked away, fixing her gaze on the ground ahead. She didn't need to watch where she was going, at least not literally. She knew Jackson Square intimately. For years it had been her playground, practically her backyard, a place where she and other Serenity Street brats had roamed freely. Even if she tried never to go back to Serenity, she still came often to the square. She knew the grounds and the sidewalks, knew the cracks and the bumps and fissures that might trip an unsuspecting person.

On the other hand, in a more figurative sense, she *did* need to watch exactly where she was going. For a moment she'd forgotten that her business with Smith was strictly that—*business*. She had let herself forget that he wasn't suddenly spending time with her out of the generosity of his heart or because he liked her, as Cassie suggested. He wanted something from her, and it wasn't her company, her charming conversation or her Saturday afternoons.

He wanted her source.

Nick.

"No, I haven't." But that *had* been one of her reasons for coming down to the Quarter today with Cassie. She had figured that before the afternoon was out, Cassie would run into a group of her friends or possibly good old Trevor and would ditch her; their outings often ended that way. Then she could stroll on over to Serenity and Jamey O'Shea's bar—stroll, she had decided, even though the short walk from here to Serenity led her through streets that were sometimes less than safe, because then she would be out in the open and moving slowly. The farther she got from the square, the more obvious it would be if someone—like an FBI agent—was following her.

"You really don't think he'll cooperate, do you?"

"No more than you thought I would."

"Can you tell me if it's someone the grand jury has already indicted?"

She forced a grin. "How many indictments were handed down in this case? How many defendants do you already have awaiting trial?"

"Enough to keep me busy for a long time," he admitted ruefully. "But maybe if your guy was on my side, I could get a few guilty pleas and skip a few trials."

"Oh, right," she scoffed. "Jimmy Falcone has never admitted guilt, not once in his entire life. He's the most brazen liar you've ever prosecuted. You could place him at the scene of a shooting, put the gun in his hand, present a thousand unimpeachable witnesses who saw him pull the trigger *and* show a videotape that captured the killing from beginning to end, and he would still insist that he was innocent. And you know what? People would believe him. He has that talent."

"You're right. That's why I need whatever the hell I can get to help strengthen my case against him. That's why I need your guy."

She choked back the impulse to tell him to quit calling Nick *her* guy. If it hadn't once been true, maybe she wouldn't mind so much. Then again, considering how Nick had turned out, maybe she would. He was hardly the kind of man a woman fantasized about taking home to meet Mama and Daddy. He certainly wasn't the sort of man a woman would want to spend the rest of her life with...unless she didn't mind high walls, armed guards and conjugal visits behind bars.

They had at last reached the opposite end of the square. The benches between the park and the cathedral were filled, as was most of the small plaza there. In a clearing a band was set up and filling the air with the Dixieland jazz so closely associated with New Orleans. Pushing her hands into the pockets of her shorts, Jolie tapped one foot in tempo while searching the crowd for Cassie.

It was Trevor she located first, his arm draped over her
sister's shoulder. He was unshaven, his black hair looking
as if it hadn't seen a comb in days, a small gold stud glint-
ing in his ear. As a woman who remembered being seventeen and in love with an unsuitable man, she could
understand Cassie's attraction to him. He was handsome in
a narrow-eyed, rebellious sort of way, and he possessed a ton
of the bad-boy allure that Nick had practically exuded.

But as a mature, responsible adult, she could also understand why her parents didn't approve of him. They remembered all too well her own heartache with Nick. They had
already lived through this scenario once, and they didn't
want to go through it again. Who could blame them? The
results the first time had been disastrous. They'd thought
Nick had ruined her life.

Truth be told, *she* had thought so, too, for a very long
time.

There were still times, usually late on hot summer nights
when the moon was full and birds were singing, when the air
was heavy with the scent of roses, that she still thought so.
Times when she knew she could never get back what he had
taken from her. Times when she feared she could never put
right what he—and she, for she had played a part, too—had
done wrong.

"Is that Trevor?" Smith asked, so close beside her that
her skin rippled.

"How do you know his name?"

"She mentioned it last night."

And she had, in passing. *Sorry about dinner, Jolie, but
Trevor's here.* Jolie gave a shake of her head. Smith was very
observant and paid attention to small details. She needed to
remember that. "He's the reason she spent last night at my
house. Our parents don't like him and have forbidden her
to go out with him."

"But you help her break their rules. Hardly the actions of
a responsible adult...but exactly what I would expect from
a good sister."

"Putting him off-limits doesn't help. Doesn't forbidden
fruit taste all the sweeter precisely because it *is* forbidden?"

Upon a gruff request from the people behind them, Smith laid his hand on her back and shifted her closer to the rail fence and the stones that supported it. Her skin was warm through the cotton of her T-shirt. He was warm, too, uncomfortably so, but it had nothing to do with the day's heat.

And everything to do with Jolie.

"Trevor's probably not as bad as he looks," he remarked, hoping his voice sounded steadier to her than it did to him.

She gave him something of a surprised look, then burst into laughter. "Honey, he *looks* pretty damn good."

He looked at the young man again, but what he saw hadn't changed in the past few minutes: a sullen punk who needed to grow up, clean up and shape up. It took a woman to fully appreciate Trevor, he supposed, which obviously was completely outside his realm of experience—but he didn't have to be a father to imagine Mr. Wade's dismay at seeing his pretty baby girl with someone like that.

"So that's your type, huh? Teenage rebels."

"Used to be." Looking past him, she gestured down Chartres Street, a few yards away. "Let's get out of the crowd. It'll be easier to talk."

He let her make a path and followed along close behind. It gave him a chance to appreciate something else outside his realm of experience: Jolie herself.

The farther they went from the square, the less crowded the sidewalks were. Within a block and a half, they were walking side by side in relative peace. He took up the conversation where they'd left off. "So what is your type now?"

"My type? I'm not sure I have one." After a moment's consideration, she went on. "Living and breathing would be nice. On the right side of the law would be a plus."

"If your parents didn't already have gray hair, I bet you and Cassie have given it to them. She's in love with a young James Dean, and you're on a first-name basis with half the criminal element in the state. Is that the life they envisioned for their eldest and youngest daughters?"

For a moment her expression turned sad, deeply sad, and Smith remembered too late what Michael had said. *I always thought maybe there'd been some guy in her past, someone who'd hurt her...* His theory had sounded reasonable enough on the balcony. It was looking stronger every minute.

When she finally replied, the sadness was hidden... but not gone. "My family was very traditional. Men worked and supported their families, and women had those families and took care of their men. Since it worked for my parents, they thought we should all live just like them. It wasn't easy for them to understand that I didn't want that kind of life. They thought that, in rejecting the life-style, I was rejecting them, and it wasn't that at all. I just wanted more. *I* wanted to make decisions—more important decisions than what I would cook my husband for dinner or whether I would do laundry on Monday, the way Mama did, or on Saturday, like Granma. *They* wanted me to be an obedient wife and a good mother, and *I* wanted to go out into the world. I wanted to support myself. I wanted a career—not a job, not work, but a profession."

Her smile was a few watts less bright. "I imagine my parents sound terribly old-fashioned to you."

"Actually, no. My family is also very traditional. Neither of my sisters has ever held a job or had any interest in a career. Initially my parents supported them, then they each came into some family money when they turned twenty-one, and now their husbands take care of them."

"I'm not knocking it. A number of my sisters are full-time housewives and mothers, and some of the others would like to be if they could afford it. If it makes them happy, that's all that matters. I just wanted a different life for myself."

At the corner of Ursulines, she turned right, and he automatically followed her. "But does having a different life—being independent, having a career—mean you can't also be a little traditional?" he asked, aware that her answer interested him more than was wise. "Don't you ever feel the urge to give the wedding march a spin? Don't you ever hear your biological clock ticking?''

"Never," she replied flatly.

"Never? Not even after you have a Pulitzer or two?"

She repeated the answer with the same certainty. "Never. I helped raise the last nine or ten of my mother's children, Smith. I've changed diapers, mixed formula, fed, burped, bathed, rocked and walked more babies than you can imagine." She looked up at him, her expression earnest, determined and not the least bit regretful. "I won't ever have any of my own."

Chapter 3

It wasn't such a big deal, Smith told himself.

It wasn't as if they were contemplating marriage or anything long-term and serious like that. Hell, he hadn't even contemplated asking her for a date—last night, being business, didn't count—although he *had* contemplated making love to her. He had acknowledged that that would surely be a fine way to pass an evening . . . a weekend . . . *a lifetime*, a traitorous voice whispered.

So what did it matter if she hadn't merely delayed marriage and a family for the sake of her career, but had done away with the possibility altogether?

What did it matter if she sounded like a woman who most definitely knew her own mind?

What did it matter if she absolutely, positively, without doubt, did not want children?

What did it matter that *he* did?

They were just acquaintances. Associates of a sort. Two people who knew a little bit about each other and liked that little bit enough to spend a summer afternoon together.

But it *did* matter. The disappointment that reached deep inside told him it did. The regret and lack of understanding repeated the message. The feeling that something that might have been very special had ended before it even started confirmed it.

Smith Kendricks did not take on losing battles. He didn't involve himself in fights that couldn't be won. He didn't invest his time and his self in relationships that were doomed from the start. He didn't believe people could be changed. Crooks remained crooks no matter how many second chances they were given. A man who treated a woman badly before they were married still treated her badly after they were married.

And a woman who never wanted to have children, a woman who had changed diapers, mixed formula, fed, burped, bathed, rocked and walked ten baby brothers and sisters, wasn't going to yield to any sudden and unwanted maternal urges.

"What about you?" she asked, her tone easy and conversational again. "When are you going to get married and present your parents with an heir?"

"My sisters have three children each. My parents have plenty of heirs."

"Ah, but you're the only son. Your sisters' children are probably perfect little grandchildren, but only your children will carry the Kendricks name. Unless you rich folks are significantly different from us commoners, that's still important to a man. It was certainly important to *my* father."

"No," he admitted with a sheepish smile. "My father's not that different. He wants a grandson first—"

"A daughter-in-law first," she interrupted teasingly.

"Of course. There have been no illegitimate births in our family for at least two hundred years. Anyway, after a grandson to ensure that the name lives on, then he figures we can have all the daughters we want."

"Who is the feminine half of this 'we'? Does he have someone eminently suitable in mind? Some virginal, young, blue-blooded lass?"

He scowled at her. "You make it sound as if she would be offered up as a human sacrifice to appease the gods. Trust me, Jolie. Marrying me wouldn't be a hardship for any reasonably intelligent woman."

"Such modesty." Her teasing was gentler this time; so was her smile when she looked at him. No losing battles, he reminded himself. "I'll concede that. Considering what's available for marriage these days, you're a reasonably good catch. So... does Dad have a blushing bride awaiting your return to Rhode Island?"

"Not that I'm aware of," he replied, "although I have no doubt that if I asked him to find one for me, he would. Mergers are his corporate specialty. I'm sure he could locate a fortune or two to merge our family with."

Beside him, her steps slowed until she was standing motionless in front of a tiny restaurant. Smith had to retrace his last few steps to reach her again.

"Are you hungry? I'm hungry," she said, never pausing for his response. "Come on, let's split a sandwich."

He followed her inside and back to a corner table. She didn't bother with a menu; before he was even settled in a chair, she had ordered a muffuletta, onion rings and iced tea for both of them. "You come here often?"

"Often enough," she replied.

"Does your family still live around here?"

Her gaze narrowed as she twisted and pleated a paper napkin into a crude flower, then smoothed it again. "How do you know my family used to live around here?"

"I work for the government." He lowered his voice conspiratorially. "We know everything."

She wasn't amused. "You checked?"

"That was a joke, Jolie."

"So what was it then? A lucky guess?"

He leaned back in his chair and studied her. He'd never seen Jolie on edge. He'd seen her laughing and teasing and sarcastic; he'd seen her at her most professional and, on occasion with Valery, at her most relaxed. He had even seen her angry. But not edgy like this. Not this kind of suspicious, almost paranoid nervousness.

"Michael told me," he finally admitted.

"So you had him check."

"No. We were talking. We talk about business, about his cases and mine. I asked him what he knew about you, and one of the things was that you'd grown up in the Quarter."

He watched as the tension slowly drained away. It was a physical thing—the color returned to her face, the tightness eased from her jaw, the stiffness left her body. He brought some of it back when he covered her hand on the tabletop with his own. "Jolie, if you've got something to hide, then you'd better think twice about what you're doing. We need your cooperation, and if we don't get it, I won't have to ask someone to check on your background. The FBI will initiate it on their own—and, honey..."

He broke off as the waitress served their tea, then grimly finished. "They won't leave you any secrets."

Two hours later Jolie was wandering through the open market, occasionally stopping to examine a piece of jewelry, a display of sunglasses or a T-shirt. She'd been keeping a close watch on the crowd around her, searching for familiar faces, for anyone who seemed too intent on going where she went. She had been exaggerating last night when she'd warned Smith that she knew all the cops, all the deputies and feds in the parish—not by much, but exaggerating just the same. There were surely a few faces that were unknown to her.

But no one seemed unusually curious about her this afternoon.

No one except Smith.

After lunch they had walked back to the square. They had talked about the weather, the festival, about Mardi Gras and the Quarter and life in general in New Orleans. They *hadn't* talked about his job or hers, and they hadn't continued the conversation they'd dropped at the restaurant, although she had sensed that he wanted to.

Jolie, if you've got something to hide...

Sighing, she replaced the brooch she had been examining on its cotton bed and shook her head politely when the vendor offered her a half-off discount. Weaving around tour-

ists, she exited at the end of the building, stood in the bright
sun for a moment, then started toward Serenity Street.

It wasn't fair.

It was blackmail, truly, it was. Tell us what we want to
know, Smith was saying, or we'll dig up and reveal all your
darkest, most intimate secrets. Cooperate with us or we'll
punish you.

She couldn't cooperate with them.

She couldn't betray the trust Nick had placed in her.

But, even more, she couldn't have the FBI snooping
around in her past. For one thing, doing so would most
likely give them Nick's identity. Shawna Warren wasn't
dumb. Somewhere in their file on Nick was the information that he'd grown up on Serenity Street. Somehow she
would find someone who remembered him, who remembered Jolie. Somehow she would connect them, and then she
would know.

For another, Jolie *did* have something to hide. Only a few
people knew—her parents, her grandmother and Father
Francis, among others—but she couldn't be sure that
Shawna wouldn't somehow stumble across it. She couldn't
take that chance.

She had to make some sort of deal to get them off her
back.

She had to give them something.

Hands pushed into her pockets, she crossed the street to
the shady side, taking the opportunity to look casually behind her. There was no one closer than two blocks, and that
was a young girl playing hopscotch on a chalk-drawn grid.
Still, she walked past Serenity, around an extra block, then
came back. Satisfied that she wasn't being followed, she
headed toward O'Shea's halfway down the street.

Four sets of double doors stretched across the front of the
bar. Faded black shutters were folded out against the brick
wall, and grimy French doors were propped open inside.
The bar had been there as long as she could remember, always bearing the swinging sign that proclaimed it O'Shea's,
but Jamey was the first O'Shea in her memory to do anything more than drink there. The doors she walked through

never closed, except from 2:00 a.m. until 10:00 a.m. and when the occasional hurricane blew through. They provided fresh air to combat the haze of cigarette smoke and the smell of booze. Along with the ceiling fans overhead, they offered a slight cooling breeze in summer and let in light and a little of the sun's heat in winter.

Inside, the floor needed sweeping and the tables needed washing, but that didn't matter to the patrons drinking away their afternoon. Business was never booming—O'Shea's was too far off the tourist path, Serenity too rough a neighborhood for sightseers—but it was steady. Jamey would never get rich, but as long as the liquor didn't run dry, he would always get by.

He was behind the bar, a towel in hand, lazily drying a glass and watching her, his customers and the baseball game on the corner-mounted television all with equal interest. When she climbed onto one of the stools that fronted the bar, he finally forgot the rest and gave his attention to her. "It's a long time since you wandered in here."

She acknowledged that with a nod and a shrug. "How've you been, Jamey?"

"I can't complain."

To some degree, it seemed that had always been true. She had been ambitious, Nick had been bitter and driven, but Jamey... He'd been the good-natured one. The accepting one. The one who understood that his father was an alcoholic who couldn't help getting drunk and spending his entire check before he even made it home on payday. The one who understood that Margie O'Shea had gotten married too young, that she'd gotten pregnant too young to be a decent mother to him. He hadn't resented going hungry or being locked out of the apartment for hours on end because his mother needed to be alone. He hadn't resented being forced to accept charity from the neighbors and the church because neither of his parents was willing or able to take care of him themselves.

More than either her or Nick, she thought, Jamey deserved a better life. He deserved to escape Serenity Street.

But he was satisfied to stay there.

Sometime she might wonder why, but not today.

"Can I have a beer?"

Reaching under the bar, he pulled out an icy can of soda and set it in front of her. "You don't drink beer, remember? It makes you sick."

She gave him an exaggerated scowl. "That was twenty years ago, Jamey. I've grown up since then."

"Not much, you haven't. So, L.B., are you here about Nicky?"

In spite of herself, his nickname made her grin. They'd had plenty of nicknames for her when they were growing up: L.B.—short for little bit—half-pint, shrimp, baby. That last had belonged to only Nick, and he had used it only under the most intimate of circumstances.

She wondered what sort of endearments a man like Smith would use in circumstances like that. No likely candidates came to mind.

"I need to get in touch with Nick. Do you have a way to do that?"

"Yeah, I can do that."

"Would you ask him to meet me tomorrow night?"

"Same place, same time?"

She thought about returning to the park at midnight, and a little shiver danced down her spine. Reluctantly she shook it off and nodded.

"Is it safe to call you and let you know what he says?"

"I think so. Just be discreet. Oh, and Jamey? If anyone comes around asking questions about me . . ."

"I've covered for you and Nicky since you were fifteen years old. I'll cover for you now."

"Thanks," she murmured.

He subjected her to a long, steady gaze before asking, "How much trouble are you going to get into over this?"

"I don't know. It seems that's mostly up to Nick."

"Maybe this time you'll get something out of your association with him."

She smiled bitterly. She'd gotten something out of it last time—a broken heart, which Jamey knew about, and some mighty big losses, which he didn't.

Sliding to the floor, she pulled a crumpled dollar from her pocket and laid it on the counter. "Thanks, Jamey." Taking the can of soda with her, she left, replacing her sunglasses when she stepped out of the dimly lit bar into the relentless sun. Her first impulse was to turn back toward Decatur and to leave the area as quickly as possible, but on second thought she turned toward the end of the street. She took a stroll down memory lane.

Serenity had never been much to look at—even a hundred and fifty years ago, it had been a place where the Quarter's less fortunate lived—but in the past thirty years it had gone into a significant decline. Most of the businesses she remembered—a corner grocery, a couple of family-owned restaurants, a small drugstore, a five-and-dime—were gone, and their buildings were abandoned or taken over by bars. When she was a kid, it had been possible to live life within the twelve blocks or so that made up the neighborhood. Except for medical care and schools, everything a family needed was located within that small area.

Everything except decent jobs. Decent lives.

She wasn't sure exactly when she had realized that things were better for other people. That not all families lived in cramped apartments without air-conditioning, where the only heat came from the kitchen stove. That not all little girls wore hand-me-downs collected from the church or various cousins and friends, that not all of them slept two or three to a bed, four or five to a room. That not all fathers worked two jobs just to put enough food on the table, that not all mothers struggled as hard as hers did.

At some time, though, realization did hit, along with the determination that, when she was grown, *she* would have a better life. Her children would have a better life. Her parents, when they retired, would have a life easier than anything they'd ever known, and *she* would make it all possible. Hard work and goals were all it would take. She would be the first person, she decided, in either her father's or her mother's families to go to college; because she needed scholarships, she applied herself to her schoolwork. She studied hard, made straight *A*s and studied even harder. She didn't allow anything to distract her from her plans…until the summer she was fifteen and Nicky Carlucci changed everything.

Realizing that she had stopped walking, she looked up and saw an all-too-familiar house across the street. Their house—or, rather, the house where the Wades, the O'Sheas and, for a time, the Carluccis had lived. Victorian in style, it had once been a reasonably nice place, though not in this century. Built to house only one family, its three stories had been subdivided into eight apartments—if calling the Carluccis' single corner room an apartment wasn't being too generous.

She didn't remember much about Mrs. Carlucci, except hearing her aunt tell a gathering of friends that the Mrs. was really a Miss, that there'd never been a Mr. and that Carlucci was the woman's family name. At the time, Jolie had been too young to understand the significance of it, and by the time she'd been old enough to understand, she'd had too big a crush on Nick to care.

They had played together, studied together, grown up together—and the summer she was fifteen, they'd done a whole lot more together. The boy who had always been brash and confident about everything had been sweetly nervous that sultry night, only a little more experienced than she was. It had been the scariest, most important thing she'd ever done.

It had also been the biggest mistake in her life.

But she wouldn't undo any of it if she could, not what had happened then, not what had come later.

Although maybe she *would* alter it.

Just a little.

Sighing heavily, she turned away from the house. Away from the memories.

Away from the regrets.

Smith stood on the levee behind the Café du Monde, staring down at the Mississippi River as it flowed sluggishly toward the Gulf. It looked pretty much the way he felt— relatively calm on the surface, but with eddies and currents underneath. This was the way he felt after a long, frustrating day at work.

And this afternoon he had Jolie to thank for it.

He had come to the river after she'd left him at Jackson Square. He hadn't been prepared to bring their afternoon to an end just yet, but she apparently had. It was just as well. After his warning to her, things had never quite gotten back on an even keel.

What mysteries were hiding in Jolie's past? he wondered as he tracked the progress of the ferry as it made its return trip from the west side of the river. Would she ever trust him enough to confide in him? Was there anything he wouldn't do to find out?

Yes. He wouldn't misuse his authority. He wouldn't take advantage of his position to delve into her background, not unless it was official. Not unless she became the subject of an active investigation.

For her sake—for his own sake—he hoped it didn't come to that.

"Mr. Kendricks?"

He'd heard little from that soft, melodic voice that flowed as smoothly as the river, but he recognized it immediately. Turning, he saw Cassie Wade standing a few feet away. "Hello, Cassie."

"Hi. I was looking for Jolie when I saw you up here. I trust you didn't succumb to temptation and throw her in the river."

He smiled at her choice of words. If he was going to succumb to temptation and throw Jolie anywhere, it sure as hell wouldn't be the river. A bed would be his first choice, although a sofa, the ground or the back seat of his car would make acceptable substitutes. "I swear, I haven't drowned anyone today. The last I saw of her was at Jackson Square about an hour ago. I assumed she was going looking for you."

"She probably did." She moved a few steps closer, then leaned against the piling there. Settling comfortably, she removed her hat and let the slight breeze rustle through her hair.

As he'd told Jolie last night, Cassie was a lovely girl, but on first look—and second—he had found no family resemblance. Where Jolie was short, Cassie was tall. Jolie, though slender, gave an impression of strength, of toughness, while Cassie looked delicate enough to break. While Jolie was fair—blond-haired, golden skinned, green-eyed—Cassie's complexion was pale, her long hair was brown and her eyes were calm, deep brown.

But there were a few similarities, after all, he decided, though nothing so obvious as coloring, height or build. They both had this measuring, evaluating way of looking at a person that left him feeling unprotected. Although Jolie's grins were usually quick and bright enough to blind, her smiles, like her sister's, were sweet, almost shy. Their voices fell into the same range, and their accents were virtually identical. If Jolie ever got serious and calm, or if Cassie ever became excited, brash or angry, they would be difficult to tell apart sight unseen.

"What happened to Trevor?" he asked, more to break the silence than because he cared.

"He had to go to work."

"He works?" He tried not to sound too surprised, but it came through anyway, making Cassie smile indulgently.

"Yes, he works. I know my parents don't approve of him, but it's only because they've refused to get to know him. They remember what it was like with—the others, and they're determined not to give me a chance."

She'd been about to say *with Jolie*—Smith was sure of it—but she'd covered so smoothly that anyone less interested wouldn't even have noticed. He wanted to question her, wanted to ask exactly what it was that her parents remembered about Jolie. She had admitted that teenage rebels like Trevor had once been her type. What had happened? How serious was it that, fifteen years after she'd made the passage from teens to twenties, her parents remembered well enough to try to keep their youngest daughter from repeating her sister's mistake?

But if Jolie had gotten irritable about his finding out from Michael that she'd grown up in the Quarter, she would be out-and-out furious over him pumping her sister for information on something that had likely happened before Cassie was even born.

And while there were many ways he would like to see Jolie, furious wasn't one of them.

"You can't blame them for worrying," he said, referring back to Cassie's parents. "You *are* their baby."

Smiling broadly, she replaced her hat, throwing a loosely woven shadow across her face. "I'm *their* baby—and Jolie's. And Meg's. And Theresa's, Allison's, Susan Marie's, Mary Kay's… They all helped raise me, and they all feel that entitles them to a say in how I live my life."

"Families are like that."

She gave him a look that was much too wise for a teenager. "To say that so acceptingly, Mr. Kendricks, either you must be an only child or you live very far away from your family."

"I'm the middle of three, and they're in New England. And I'd prefer it if you would call me Smith." After her nod, he went on. "Would you like some help finding your sister?"

"No, thank you. I'm going to leave a note on her car, then catch a cab home."

He looked across the river, hoping the offer he was tempted to make would somehow disappear before it made its way into words. Of course, he couldn't be that lucky—or that smart. "I'm ready to go. I'll give you a ride."

"That's not necessary."

"I know."

"I hate to impose…"

"You didn't ask. I offered." Even though he shouldn't have. Even though it didn't mean he was likely to see Jolie again today. Even though being nice to her sister wasn't going to earn him any points with her. In spite of all that, he turned away from the river and asked, "Where is Jolie's car?"

* * *

As it turned out, he was half wrong, half right. He did see Jolie again, and being nice to Cassie wasn't going to earn him anything more than suspicion from her.

He was sitting on the porch swing, discussing movies with the younger Wade, when the squeal of tires around the corner nearly a block away made her stop in midsentence. "Here comes Jolie now. Daddy says she drives like a bat out of hell, but Jolie swears she hasn't earned even one of all those speeding tickets she's gotten. She insists cops are just prejudiced against people who drive little red sports cars."

Smith had heard that theory before, although he'd never seen any data to prove it. However, if he were a cop, he imagined the combination of a flashy red 'Vette driven by a beautiful little blonde just might be more than he could resist.

To say nothing of the attention-getting squeal of the tires, he added with a grimace, as she brought the car to a sudden stop in front of the house.

She'd already seen—and recognized—his Blazer in the driveway. Now she crossed the yard to the porch, stopping at the top step. Although she was wearing those big glasses again, he swore he could see through them to the suspicion and wariness that were clouding her eyes. "What are you doing here?"

Cassie rose from the swing. "Don't be rude, Jolie. I left you a note saying I'd found a ride home."

"You didn't say it was with the assistant U.S. Attorney."

"I didn't feel it was necessary. Smith, thanks. I'll see you around."

After she disappeared inside, Jolie moved one step closer. "So why are you still here?"

"We were talking." That was true, and it sounded better than the rest of the truth: *I was waiting for you to come home so I could see you one more time.*

"And what can you find to discuss with a seventeen-year-old girl?"

"Music. Movies. Books. Our tastes are very similar."

"That figures," she mumbled.

He raised his right hand as if being sworn in to testify. "I didn't ask her a single question about you, I swear."

She was so silent for a time that he found himself wishing she would remove those glasses so he could see what was in her eyes. Even if he couldn't read her thoughts, gazing into her green eyes was a pleasure in and of itself.

When she did finally break her silence, her tone was serious, her manner cautious, and her words left him momentarily speechless. "I know she seems older, and she *is* mature for her age, but she's still just a child, Smith. You do understand that, don't you?"

His stare of surprise slowly gave way to a scowl. "Of course I understand that. Hell, Jolie, I'm old enough to be her *father*. You know I wouldn't . . ." Breaking off, he finished with an impatient gesture.

"No, I don't." She pulled her glasses off and settled them on top of her head, the earpieces gliding through her hair, then came to sit at the opposite end of the swing. "Yes, I do. What can I say? I'm the oldest, and she's the baby. I tend to be overprotective." Turning to face him, she lifted her feet to the seat and leaned back against the arm. "So what *are* you doing here?"

"You want the truth or an excuse?"

He expected, at the least, a smile—at most, one of those devastating grins of hers. What he got was utter seriousness.

"I guess that's one of the few things you and I agree on. I generally prefer the truth."

Drawing a deep breath, he gave it to her. "I was waiting to see you."

Her expression didn't change. "Why?"

"Damned if I know." With a wry smile, he decided to try some of the directness she was famous for. "I like spending time with you, Jolie."

For a moment she simply looked at him, too calm, too serious; then, bit by bit, amusement began lightening her eyes. "Yes, I'm such a refreshing change from all those proper society belles you normally spend time with."

"You're definitely more interesting."

"Uh-huh. I bet you haven't once threatened to have the FBI arrest or conduct a background investigation on one of them."

"Not necessary. I can find out whatever I want about them through the Social Register."

"A place where no mention of the French Quarter Wades will ever be found," she said flippantly.

"A fact that you are undoubtedly proud of." He chuckled at her smug grin, then turned serious. "I wasn't threatening you, Jolie. It was a warning from one friend to another. I don't want to see you get in over your head on this one. I don't want it to cost you more than you're ready to pay."

For a moment Jolie didn't know what to say. On one level she was touched that whatever might happen to her seemed to matter to him. On another, she was suspicious, uncertain whether she could trust this unexpected concern. And on a third level, she was worried; he sounded as if the matter of her coming under FBI scrutiny was a foregone conclusion.

Maybe it was. She was stubborn and unwilling to turn Nick over to the government, and she knew too well that the FBI wasn't known for its reasonable treatment of anyone who stood in their way. Unless Nick volunteered to come forward, chances were pretty good that she would be seeing Smith in a courtroom—and she *wouldn't* be there to cover the proceedings.

God help her, she didn't want it to come to that. She didn't want to push Shawna Warren until the agent felt she had no other choice. She didn't want, as she'd said last night, to *be* the news. She didn't want to face Smith in court, didn't want him to treat her in that cool, impersonal, slightly derisive way that he had with defendants. Even though he would simply be doing his job, a job in which she and Shawna would leave him no choice, she suspected that it would hurt to have him look at, speak to and speak about her in that way. And even though *she* wouldn't take it personally, she couldn't help but think he would. Prosecuting her inside the courtroom, she thought, would change the way he felt about her outside, and that would be a loss she would regret.

Most of all, though...

Most of all, she didn't want that background investigation.

"I appreciate the warning, Smith," she said quietly.

"Not that you're going to heed it." His expression was regretful.

"I told you I would talk to him, that I would ask him to talk to you. That's the best I can offer."

"Convince him, Jolie. Because I don't want to see you in court for any reason other than to cover Falcone's trial." Rising from the swing, he walked to the top of the steps and stopped there.

"Thank you for bringing Cassie home," she said, forcing a smile as she joined him.

"My pleasure." After a moment, he glanced at her. "Under the circumstances... you wouldn't... it wouldn't be wise for me to ask you to dinner, would it?"

She shook her head.

"I didn't think so."

Jolie watched him walk down the steps, then start toward his car. Before he'd gone far, she called his name. "Smith? For the record... I liked spending this time with you, too."

He gave her one last smile before climbing into the car. Long after he'd driven away, she was still standing there looking where he'd last been, his final question replaying in her head. *Under the circumstances... you wouldn't... it wouldn't be wise for me to ask you to dinner, would it?* Smith Kendricks—handsome, richer than God, well-bred and excruciatingly well mannered—sounding hesitant and unsure about asking a woman out. Who ever would have believed it?

Not Jolie, not if she hadn't heard it for herself.

Especially when *she* was the woman.

Behind her the door opened just an inch or two, then wide enough for Cassie to slip out. "Is Smith gone?"

"Yes." She returned to sit on the swing, pleased when Cassie joined her there.

"He doesn't quite know what to do with you, does he?"

"What do you mean?"

"Whether to arrest you or romance you."

She should laugh off the comment, Jolie knew, or respond with sarcasm or cynicism, but none of those things would come. All she wanted, all she really wanted to do was to ask for reassurance. *Do you think he really likes me? Do you think he's really interested? Do you think I stand a chance?* Fortunately, for the sake of her pride, none of those questions would come, either.

"What if they do arrest you, Jolie?"

The uncustomary worry in Cassie's eyes reminded her of the point that she'd foolishly made clear to Smith: Cassie seemed older and *was* mature for her age, but she was still just a seventeen-year-old girl. Not grown-up. Not mature enough. Not old enough yet that she should be worrying about Jolie.

"If they do," she began, her tone lighter than her spirit, "then I'll probably go to jail. I'll become something of a celebrity. Reporters locked up under these circumstances generally do." After a moment, she glanced at the girl. "Will it embarrass you if they do?"

Cassie gave her question careful consideration before answering. "No. I can't imagine anything you would do that might embarrass me. But it will worry Mama and Daddy."

"Well, look at it this way, kiddo, if I get locked up, they'll be too wound up over that to nag you about Trevor. It'll take the heat off for a while."

That earned her one of those older-than-her-years chastising looks. "I can handle Mama and Daddy and Trevor." After another moment's quiet thought, she went on. "You know they're proud of you... but they don't understand you. They don't understand why you want to do what you do, why you hang out with criminals, why you're so often at odds with the police. Daddy, in particular, doesn't understand why you won't get married and be a wife and mother like the others."

Jolie redirected her gaze to the zinnias that grew right next to the porch. Occasionally one of the tall, spindly stalks was strong enough to stand up under the weight of its flower, but most of them leaned against the railing for support, and one or two had broken, their vividly colored blossoms resting upside down on the mulch. Most of her life she'd been like the plants that needed support, and she had taken it where she could—from her family, her friends and, for a time, from Nick. On a few occasions, like the weaker flowers, she had bowed under the burden of her life and her choices, had bowed and damn near broken, but today she could stand alone. She didn't need marriage. She didn't need a man in her life.

And she would never let herself need children.

"Frankly, Jolie, I don't understand it, either. I intend to go on to college and to have a career, but I also intend to get married and have a family. There's no reason why a woman shouldn't have it all."

Her throat tight, her jaw strained, Jolie smiled in Cassie's general direction without meeting her clear dark gaze. "If you can manage all three, sweetheart, fine. Go for it. But *I* can't. I have the energy for only one major commitment in my life, and I've chosen my job. It's more important to me than the options." Forcing a laugh, she gestured to the emptiness around them. "It's a pointless discussion, anyway. Do you see any prospective suitors lined up waiting for a chance to change my mind?"

"No. But just a little while ago, I heard one asking permission to ask you out, and you turned him down."

The tension inside her knotted a little tighter. "I can't go out with Smith."

"Why not?"

"You were partly right earlier. He doesn't yet know whether he's going to have me arrested. Call me silly, but I try to avoid going out with men who are holding the threat of jail over my head."

"You also try to avoid going out with men you might come to care for," Cassie said quietly. "I think Smith falls into that category, as well." She got to her feet, then bent and gave Jolie a hug. "I'm meeting friends this evening for dinner and a movie. I'm going to start getting ready."

Jolie murmured something agreeable, then stretched out on the hard wooden bench, staring up at the porch ceiling. For a woman who prided herself on telling the truth, on being direct and plainspoken, she felt remarkably like a liar this afternoon.

She didn't need marriage. She didn't need a man in her life.

And she would never let herself need children.

Those were statements she'd made the better part of her adult life, rules she had lived by. She would never get married, would never let herself get caught in the trap that could keep her from fulfilling her potential, from meeting her goals, from being the best damn reporter the country had ever seen.

She would never need a man. Nick had taught her a few lessons there—about love, hatred, intimacy and betrayal. He had shown her how weak he was and, worse—far, far worse—he had taught her how weak *she* was. They were lessons she needed to learn only once.

It went without saying that, without marriage, without a man, there would never be children. Once she had wanted babies. Three—a boy and two girls, she had thought—was a nice round number. With three kids, the entire family could fit in one car. A family of five was so average, as opposed to her family of too many. Three mouths weren't impossible to feed; hand-me-downs, if they were necessary, weren't so handed down. Three names were easy to remember; the girls wouldn't find themselves answering to any girl's name she shouted out, as she and her sisters had been forced to do when family, friends and teachers alike couldn't connect the proper name with the proper face.

Once she had wanted babies—one baby—so badly that she had thought she would die from the pain.

Now she was past that. Of the last five or six babies born to her sisters and in-laws, she hadn't wanted to even hold them. She had bought gifts, admired them from a distance and walked away without feeling as if her heart had been wrenched out.

She had lived by those decisions, had dedicated herself to her career, and for seventeen years, she hadn't—except in the rare weak moment—regretted it. Nothing had changed.

So why did she now feel like such a liar?

Because something *had* changed. She wasn't sure if it was Smith or if the changes came from deep inside her. Maybe it was because they'd never spent any real time together, not alone, not away from their offices. Somehow, though, in the past twenty-four hours, she had begun seeing him in a totally different light. He was no longer just a casual friend with whom she had little in common, but a man. A potentially special man. A man who could make reality of dreams she hadn't yet dared to dream.

A man she still had little in common with.

Maybe it was the summer heat or a combination of other factors, but she had to be crazy to even think about Smith that way. She still didn't need a man in her life...even if lately she found herself thinking that maybe it would be nice to have one. She certainly didn't need a man like Smith, who was everything she'd never been, who had grown up in a world that she could never relate to.

And Smith—who dealt with the rich and powerful both in his job and in his personal life, who was on a first-name basis with people the reporter inside her could only fantasize about meeting someday, whose influence ran deep in the city and throughout the state...

A man like Smith certainly didn't need her.

The condo was quiet, cool. Filling half of the eighteenth floor of a twenty-story building that loomed over the Mississippi River, it had cost a fortune to buy and a smaller fortune to furnish. It was beautiful, impressive and offered breathtaking views from every window—of the river, the city and the Quarter.

And all in all, Smith thought, he would rather be in an unremarkable neighborhood in a little yellow house with crayon drawings framed on the living room walls.

He'd brought case files home from work with him Friday evening, but they seemed a pretty poor way to spend a sunny Sunday afternoon. He had thought about calling Michael and Remy and inviting them over, then had remembered Valery mentioning plans for Sunday dinner at Belle Ste. Claire. If Remy's parents had invited Valery and Michael to the family home, then they had surely invited Remy and Susannah, too. That—the Bennetts and the Sinclairs—exhausted his list of people he would call on short notice and say, "Let's get together and do something."

Except for one.

Turning from a view down Poydras Street, he glanced at the phone. He had looked up Jolie's number several hours ago. Like a normal person, she was listed in the phone book, quite likely the only person he knew in town who *was* listed. Of course, most of the people he knew were cops, federal agents, lawyers and prosecutors. Considering their line of work and who they dealt with, it wasn't a good idea to be too accessible. Granted, Jolie dealt with many of the same people, but her line of work made accessibility important.

He had memorized her number, but he hadn't yet gone so far as to dial it. Hadn't she made it clear yesterday that she wasn't interested in a date with him?

But hadn't she also said that she had enjoyed the time they'd spent together?

He sighed, feeling alone and more than just a little lonely. Everything had changed in the past fifteen months. Evan had died. Michael had married Valery. Remy had almost gotten killed twice and had married Susannah. The four best friends were reduced to one.

Of course, Evan had been married for years—nine or ten, Smith couldn't recall—before his death. His wife Karen had accepted them as a package deal—if she wanted Evan, she took the rest of them, too—and she'd done so graciously. She had made them all welcome at their house, had invited them for Thanksgivings and Christmases, had cooked birthday dinners and baked birthday cakes. She had mothered them all, had been a friend to them all. But, after Evan's death, she had drifted away from them. It was easier for her, Smith suspected, to escape the constant reminders they provided of her husband. As far as Smith knew, no one—with the possible exception of Michael—had much contact with her these days.

Evan's marriage hadn't brought many changes into their lives. Michael's, followed so quickly by Remy's, had. There were no more three, four or more weekly get-togethers, no more long hours spent talking shop, just the three of them. The friendship was as strong as ever; Michael and Remy—and now Valery and Susannah—were still family. It was just that the focus had changed. They each had a wife to go home to, a wife to plan a future with, a wife to have children with.

And Smith still came home to a quiet, cool, empty condo. Smith still had no one.

He was beginning to discover how lonely that could be.

Listlessly he walked over to his desk, a sleek contemporary piece chosen by one of New Orleans's top interior designers. She'd been a lovely woman, a few years older, divorced and well aware of his standing on the eligible bachelor list, and she had understood absolutely nothing about what he'd wanted in a home. He had given her free rein, and she had given him, he suspected, what *she* liked. The rooms were monochromatic—black, white and shades of gray—with an occasional touch of yellow, crimson or royal blue. There was a great deal of leather, of tile, marble and stone, of highly polished surfaces that required three-times-a-week visits from his housekeeper to maintain their gleam.

And there was the furniture. Every piece, it seemed, had been chosen for form rather than function. After all the thousands of dollars he'd spent on the few pieces the designer had chosen for the living room and his den—less was better, she had thought, except when it came to price—there wasn't a couch in the place worth stretching out on.

It was his own fault. Do whatever you want, he'd told her. He spent so little time at home that he hadn't wanted to be bothered by determining exactly what it was he wanted.

So this was what he got.

From the right-hand desk drawer, he removed his address book, then seated himself in one seriously unattractive leather-and-steel chair. As he settled in, he glanced around the office. The gray was charcoal in here—steel in the kitchen and bathrooms, dove in the master bedroom—and the one accent the designer had allowed was a textile piece, a wall hanging in crimson and glittery gold. The realization struck him that this—ultramodern, minimalist, visually stunning and cold as hell—was exactly what he had envisioned for Jolie.

Except Jolie, with no more than her mere presence, would have made it sizzle.

Turning his attention back to the address book, he thumbed through the pages. If he would settle for just anyone's company, there were dozens of people he could call, ranging from people he worked with to those he knew socially. A large number were women he had dated, most of them proper society belles, as Jolie had called them. He rarely ended a relationship on a bad note; he could claim to still be friends with virtually every woman he had ever been involved with. Granted, the friendships were casual—except for Remy and Michael, *all* of his friendships were casual—but there wasn't a woman out there who didn't think as well of him once an affair ended as she had while they were still together. He could call any one of them and, unless she was involved in a new relationship, make plans for later this afternoon or evening.

Muttering a curse that echoed in the still room, he tossed the address book onto the desk. He didn't want to spend the afternoon or the evening with anyone listed in those pages. He was going to call Jolie. To make her feel more comfortable, he wouldn't call it a date; he would simply ask if she wanted to have dinner. They could meet someplace public, and she could bring Cassie along. What could be less intimate than being baby-sat through dinner by her baby sister?

Just as he stood up to reach for the phone, it rang, one soft electronic trill. He picked it up, grateful for the distraction, for the delay that just might bring him to his senses before he actually carried out the plan to call Jolie. Recognizing his boss's voice at the other end of the line, he lost a little of that gratitude.

"Have you talked to Wade?" Alexander Marshall asked without wasting time on greetings.

"Yes, I have."

"And?"

And he had enjoyed damned near every moment of it. But his boss wasn't interested in hearing that—not that he was going to be too thrilled to hear what Smith was going to tell him, either. "I told you Friday, she's not giving up her source."

"So turn Warren loose on her tomorrow."

"Wait, Alexander. Jolie did offer to talk to him, to ask him if he would meet with me. At least give her a chance to do that before you alienate her any further."

"Before *I* alienate *her?* I'm not the one breaking the law here. I'm not the one interfering in a federal investigation. I'm not the one keeping crucial evidence from the FBI and the U.S. Attorney's office. Yet you think *I* should worry about alienating *her?*"

Smith focused his gaze on a metallic gold coil in the center of the wall hanging. He'd never been able to figure out what the piece represented, if anything. He'd been too appreciative of the color it gave this gray place to care.

Taking a deep breath, he began pacifying his boss. "Turning Jolie over to Shawna isn't going to tell you who the source is. She's good at this, Alexander. Do you think she doesn't know that you and Shawna want her head on a platter? That you're both just waiting to make her an active part of the investigation? She's not going to have the guy's name and number in her desk or at the paper or at home. She's not going to leave evidence lying around for the FBI to find with a search warrant."

"So what do you suggest? That we do nothing? That we sit on our hands and wait for her next story? That we let her make the government look foolish?"

"Basically, yes." He restrained the urge to point out that Jolie wasn't deliberately making anyone look foolish. She

was just proving that she was better at her job than Shawna
Warren and her entire team of FBI agents were at theirs.
"Let's give her the time she needs to contact the guy, to see
if he'll talk to me."

Marshall was silent for a moment. "She just offered to do
that, huh? All on her own?"

Not exactly. Smith recalled that part of the conversation
Friday evening in the restaurant courtyard. The dusty red
brick and the ivy growing across it had provided a subdued
background for her blond hair and green, green eyes, and
the splash of the fountain a muted counterpoint for her
Southern-soft voice. *Tell me who your source is,* he had
asked, and she had immediately replied, *I can't do that.
Next request.*

Ask him to talk to me.

I can ask. But it's pointless ... His answer will be no.

"Out of the kindness of her heart," he said lightly.

"Jolie Wade doesn't have a heart," Marshall responded
with a gruff snort. "All she cares about is headlines and
bylines and abusing her position as a reporter."

That last part made Smith's jaw tighten. Jolie believed
too much in the responsibility of the press and in the public's right to know to ever misuse her authority. She bene-
fited from her work, true, but only because she put so much
of herself into it, because she was so damned good at what
she did.

"She's willing to make an effort," he pointed out, keeping his voice level, his tone mild. "All we have to do is give
her a chance."

Marshall's tacit agreement was given grudgingly. "When
is she supposed to get back to you?"

"We didn't set a time. If I don't hear from her by tomorrow afternoon, I'll call her."

"You think her source will go for it?"

"I don't have any idea. Maybe he will, maybe not." Jolie, he recalled, was sure the answer would be no. Maybe he
could be persuaded, he had suggested. Her answer had been
flat, emotionless. *Not by me. If his answer is no—and, I
promise, it will be—then that's the end of it.* "I want him

whether he comes to us on his own or because the bureau gives him no choice. But you know as well I do that we'll get more out of a willing witness than one who feels coerced.''

"Do you trust her to actually contact him? How do you know she won't say she did and that he refused when, in reality, she's done nothing?''

"I trust her.''

"How can you be sure—''

Smith interrupted. "Jolie's been at the paper longer than I've been working for you. This isn't the first time we've been at cross-purposes. She said she would do it. Believe me, she'll do it.''

"Then let me know as soon as she gets back to you. She's got about twenty-four hours." Ill-tempered humor became audible in his voice. "Then we feed her to Shawna.''

Chapter 4

Jolie drove past Serenity to the next street over, turned left and drove all the way to the end. It was fifteen minutes before midnight; she had come early, as was her habit, to her meeting with Nick, but unless she was wrong, he had come earlier.

She was guessing that the Lexus with the tinted windows sitting curbside in front of an abandoned old house—the house that backed up against the park a block over—was his. In some neighborhoods, it wouldn't be safe to leave a car like that parked on the street. In this neighborhood, the young punks who might be inclined to vandalize such a car knew better. They understood that a person who could afford a car like that and who had business in a neighborhood like this *wasn't* someone they wanted to anger.

A Lexus. It was exactly what she had expected of Smith—and exactly the sort of car the Nick she'd grown up with would have snickered at. Like all teenage boys, he'd had fantasies about cars, but it hadn't been leather seats, individual climate control and tinted windows that had stirred his blood. He had wanted *power*, something fast and wicked. Her 'Vette would have been more to that Nick's taste.

Briefly she considered parking behind the car and entering the park as he most likely had, through the back gate. And if he slipped off again? Did she really want to make two trips totally alone through the midnight-dark yard of that empty, spooky old house?

No way. She drove past the Lexus and around to the end of Serenity, parking the 'Vette underneath a streetlamp near the iron gate.

Unlike last time, the street wasn't deserted tonight. A group of teenage boys hung out on the corner nearly a block away, gathered underneath a streetlight. They had watched her drive past, and now they turned as one to watch her get out of the car and walk toward the park entrance. Although none of them made any unusual moves, there was something threatening about them.

It was their stillness, she realized. She'd spent enough time in rough neighborhoods to become accustomed to the tough talk and the crude suggestions that aimless young men tended to make to solitary young women. But not one of these young men made a sound. They simply watched her, and she cautiously kept an eye on them as she left the sidewalk for the park's crooked, uneven path.

As before, she ventured only as far as the light from the street. Although she saw no sign of Nick, she could already smell the smoke from his cigarette, its scent thinned by the heavy night air. She had complained long and loud about his habit twenty years ago, but he had never paid attention. She had even repeated the pop slogan that kissing a smoker was like licking an ashtray—and, with a devilish grin, he had proceeded to prove her wrong. No matter how he tasted, kissing Nick had been her teenaged idea of heaven.

Thank God she had grown up.

"Nick?"

He didn't come forward, but he finally spoke. "Over here."

She followed his voice and, soon enough, the glowing tip of his cigarette to a distant corner. There was a bench there, a regular little park bench with wooden slats and wrought iron supports, just like you might find in any real park in the city. This one, though, was set in concrete, she remembered, to keep someone from walking off with it.

It took a moment for her eyes to adjust to the darkness. When they did, she saw Nick leaning against the wall, looking casual and relaxed, although she knew he was neither. One ankle was crossed over the other, one hand—the one not needed for the cigarette—was in his pocket, and the bricks were probably warm against his back. She wondered briefly if that was how he felt comfortable these days—with something solid and unyielding protecting his back.

"You got my message."

He didn't respond to that, but she grimaced. Of course he got it; how else would he know to be here?

She sat down on the curlicued arm of the bench farthest from him. "Do you by chance have a group of sixteen- or seventeen-year-old kids standing watch on the corner?"

"Maybe."

That meant yes . . . but it didn't mean she could feel safe when she left. If Nick had paid the kids to warn him of anything suspicious, they would do that—and nothing else. They wouldn't raise a ruckus if someone messed with her car—or with her—unless he had specifically instructed them to.

Somehow, she didn't think he had been so gallant.

"I saw your story. Not bad."

"Gee, thanks," she replied sarcastically. He never had been much on offering praise . . . but maybe that was because he'd gotten so very little of it himself when he was a kid and it mattered.

If her sarcasm touched him—she doubted it—he didn't let it show. "What do you want?"

"I'm here to deliver a message."

With an impatient gesture, he waited for it.

"Smith Kendricks wants to talk to you."

"No."

"You didn't even think about it," she protested.

"I don't need to. I don't want to talk to him."

"You've put me in a difficult position, Nick."

A sardonic smile came through in his voice. "Honey, I've had you in all sorts of difficult positions. As I recall, you enjoyed every one of them."

Clamping her jaw shut, Jolie clasped her hands tightly together. At that moment, she hated him. Regardless of the past that tied them together, she *hated* him. But that was no reason to let him get to her. She despised an inordinate number of the people she dealt with, but she still managed to remain civil and to get her job done. She wouldn't let Nick Carlucci be the one to change that.

When her temper had cooled a degree or two, she spoke again, carefully forming the words. "If you would talk to Smith, just once, it would certainly make things easier on me."

"Smith?" he echoed. He ground out his cigarette after lighting another one, then came to sit, as she was, on the opposite arm of the bench. "You're on a first-name basis with the assistant U.S. Attorney who's planning to send me to prison?"

"You made it so easy for him, Nick," she said sweetly. "You made a big mistake when you tried to use Susannah Duncan to get to Remy Sinclair. You didn't count on her falling in love with him, did you?"

"I didn't count on her doing anything. I didn't count on her at all."

Her gaze narrowed on the shadowy planes of his face. "What do you mean?"

"Nothing. Is that all you want?" He sounded impatient. Weary.

"Will you at least think about meeting with Smith?"

"What would you get out of it if I do?"

"I escape FBI harassment and possible charges, for contempt among other things." She paused. "I don't want to go to jail for you, Nick."

His shrug was as callous as his words. "That's a risk you take in your line of work."

"They're going to find out about you anyway," she said quickly as he started to rise from the bench. "If I don't come up with your name, the FBI's going to investigate *me*. They're going to find out that I grew up on Serenity Street, and they're going to start interviewing people. They'll look at our school yearbooks. They'll talk to anyone down here who still remembers me. They'll track down people who have moved away."

"So?"

"Don't play dumb, Nick. And don't pretend the feds are dumb, either. Don't pretend they won't find it interesting that I—with a highly placed source in Falcone's organization—used to run around with Nicky Carlucci, who just happens to be Falcone's own personal lawyer."

He sat still for a long time, ignoring her, ignoring even the cigarette that burned close to his fingers. Then, abruptly, he moved, getting to his feet. "I'm not talking to Kendricks."

Jolie stood up, too, moving to block his way. "I *don't* want them snooping around in my background."

For a long time they stared at each other. His face was as utterly expressionless as anything she'd ever seen, as if there were life inside…but no soul. Finally, as if he'd let her look long enough, he took a long step back. "Are you ashamed of where you come from, Jolie?" he asked softly. "I always heard you wore your poverty-stricken background like a badge of honor, proof of how far you've come." His voice softened even more and took on a shiver-inducing slyness. "But maybe it's not the poverty part you're ashamed of. Maybe it's the running-around-with-Nicky Carlucci part. That wouldn't set too well with some of the people you're trying to impress, would it?"

"I'm not ashamed of anything, Nick," she said quietly. But it was a lie. She *was* ashamed—not of growing up poor, not of him, but of herself. "Please. Just let me arrange a meeting for you with Smith."

He raised his hand as if to touch her. When she involuntarily stepped back, he gave a dry, bitter little chuckle and lowered his hand again. "I can't, Jolie. But give them the documents when you're done with them. Maybe that'll hold them off for a while."

"Can they use them?"

"Right now their only value is investigative. To be admissible in court, Kendricks would have to prove where they came from. Until then, though, there's plenty of information there to justify expanding their investigation to cover a few dozen more people."

"What about fingerprints?"

He grinned. "They won't find mine anywhere except on the folder, so kindly put everything in another folder and destroy the original."

"Isn't that destroying evidence?"

He shrugged. "Then keep the original. Just hide it away where they'll never find it. And remember, they'll think to look everywhere."

"And what if that's not enough, Nick?" she asked, a challenging tone in her voice. "What if they still want *you?*"

For a long time he was silent, gazing off into the darkness. She would like to think that he was caught in a moral dilemma—his desire to protect himself by retaining his anonymity somewhat weakened by his desire to keep her out of trouble—but she was kidding herself. The man he had become was bothered by neither morals nor dilemmas. He was looking out for himself.

Finally he looked at her again. "Make up your mind, Jolie. You can be the hotshot crime reporter who risks life and limb and investigation by the FBI for a story, or you can fold at the first threat. I brought the stuff to you because you know Falcone and because you're good at what you do, but if you don't want it anymore, if you can't handle the responsibility, I think I can find someone else who can. The decision is yours."

She wanted to defend herself, wanted to point out to him the times she *had* put herself at risk for a story. But unless she could explain why this time was different, any defense would be pointless.

And the last thing she ever wanted to do—especially to this man—was explain.

He was waiting impatiently, as if he had better places to be and better things to do than stand here with her. After a moment, she quietly responded. "I can handle it."

He nodded once in acknowledgment, then started to walk off. A few feet away, he turned back. "Consider this, Jolie. Maybe the FBI's not so good at what they do. They've looked into *my* background, and they haven't come up with you."

It was small comfort, but she would take whatever she could get.

"When will your next story show up?"

"I'm working on it now. It'll be a couple of days."

"I'll be looking for it." With that, he spun around and walked away.

Jolie sank down onto the bench behind her, her legs suddenly feeling weak. Nick had always had a way of cutting through to the heart of an issue, and he was right this time. She could be a hotshot crime reporter, or she could take care to never do anything that might stir up interest in herself. She could go after the important stories, the hard-hitting ones, and occasionally be forced into defending her principles, or she could avoid ever having to defend herself and her beliefs, avoid ever putting herself on the line.

And if she chose the latter, she might as well give up her beat and switch over to the society pages. If she had no more courage than that, she deserved to be stuck in reporter hell, covering nothing more important than garden parties and teas.

Somewhere on a nearby street, a gunshot sounded, reverberating in the still night. A voice shouted, a dog began barking, and Jolie rose from the bench. This was neither the time nor the place to be debating her courage. She had it— how else could she have conducted some of the interviews she'd done?—but this was a better time to be smart.

And smart people didn't venture out alone on Serenity Street after dark.

She hurried through the park to the gate. A quick glance to her left showed that the young men were still there, still silent, still watching her. Pulling her keys from her pocket, she crossed the sidewalk, circled around the car and inserted the key to unlock the door.

It was already unlocked.

Even though she knew beyond a doubt that she had locked it when she got out.

Standing very still herself, she looked at the boys again. She had nephews their age, but she clearly understood that age and gender were *all* Meg's and Theresa's sons had in common with these young men. These guys, typical of Serenity Street, were troublemakers, punks. Their families either couldn't control them or didn't care or, worst of all, were just like them. Their neighbors and teachers—assuming they bothered to go to school—were likely afraid of them. Every one of them, she would bet, had had an arrest record before they turned fourteen. She had probably written about some of their crimes in the paper.

And one of them had been inside her car.

There was nothing to steal—a few cassette tapes of classic rock, a five-dollar bill clipped to the sun visor and a few bucks in change in the ashtray. This time she had left her purse, with her ID, cash and credit cards, at home. No need to tempt someone to smash a window or jimmy a lock.

But someone had done it anyway.

Turning her attention away from the boys, she opened the door and slid inside. The stereo was still in the dash where it belonged. The cassettes were still in the passenger seat, the five was still clipped to the visor, and the leather seats were intact. Nothing had been taken. Nothing had been damaged.

On the contrary, her uninvited visitor had left something behind on the passenger-side floorboard: an accordion pleated folder in bright green.

She started to reach for it, then, remembering the boys, drew back. Slamming the door, she locked it, started the engine and made a one-eighty across the potholed street. Instinct told her to floor it, to make a loud and very quick retreat from Serenity to the safety of her own neighborhood, but she ignored the impulse and drove down the block at less than twenty miles an hour.

The group followed her progress, including one boy standing directly under the streetlamp. As she slowed even more, he raised a match to the cigarette in his mouth, cupping his hands to shelter the flame, drawing her attention to the thin black gloves he wore on this sticky warm night.

She got only an instant's look at him—not too tall, thin, dirty blond hair and unshaven jaw—but she committed the image to memory. If she ever saw him again—this being Serenity Street and her job being crime, she was sure she would—she wanted to remember him.

And if, in breaking in, he had left so much as a scratch on her precious 'Vette, she thought, annoyance creeping in to replace fear, she damned sure wanted to remember him.

Monday morning Smith was contemplating having lunch at his desk when the intercom buzzed. At the secretary's announcement that he had a visitor, the idea of a take-out sandwich and canned soda gave way to thoughts of a quiet restaurant, a secluded table, the outstanding food New Orleans was famous for and an intriguing guest.

All business, of course.

He agreed to see the visitor—who didn't have an appointment, his secretary had needlessly informed him—and rose from his desk just as Jolie came through the door. She closed it behind her, then came across the room and tossed an envelope onto his desk. It landed with a thud and slid an inch or two before coming to rest on the yellow pad he'd been making notes on.

He looked from her to the envelope. It was thick, about ten-by-twelve inches, and had seen better days. A tear across the front had been reinforced with clear tape, and the top layer of the heavy kraft paper had been torn off along with whatever mailing label it had once carried.

After a moment he looked back at her. She was wearing dark green trousers, a rose-hued shirt and a tapestry vest woven through with both colors, and she was standing between the two chairs, one hand on her hip, wearing a brash, smug smile. She was the prettiest sight—and the most welcome—his office had seen in a long time.

"Good morning to you, too," he said in dry greeting without reaching for the package. He knew what was in it— knew from that smile, knew from the way her mind worked.

"Aren't you even interested?" she asked, gesturing toward his desk.

He didn't bother telling her that he was already studying what was most interesting to him in this room. It would probably make her smile fade, would send a wariness into her eyes. It would most likely make her uncomfortable, and he wanted her to learn to be very, *very* comfortable with him.

Slowly he shifted his attention to the envelope. Reaching for it, he sank back into his chair. A flimsy metal clasp secured the flap; when he straightened the prongs, one broke off and landed without a sound on his desk pad. He grasped the envelope by the opposite end and tilted it, letting its contents slide out onto the desk, giving it a shake to dislodge them when they got stuck. When the envelope was empty, he surveyed the gift: a stack of papers, a few photographs and two tape cases containing eight microcassettes.

Her source's material.

He didn't touch any of it. Shawna Warren would want to process it for fingerprints. Naturally, they would find Jolie's, but there was no need to add his own. Not that he expected there would be others. If Jolie was voluntarily turning the data over, then it was a safe bet that hers were the only prints on it.

And it was an even safer bet that her informant had turned down Smith's request for a meeting.

"Are these originals or did you make copies?"

"That's what I was given."

He gestured toward the chairs, and she slid in a comfortable sprawl into the closest one. She looked at-home comfortable. Leaning forward, his hands clasped on the desk top, he felt stiff and formal. "Are you giving this to me free and clear, or are you here to deal?"

"Deal?" she asked innocently. "I'm a law-abiding citizen, Smith, with evidence that a crime's been committed. I'm simply turning it over to the proper authorities."

"And what do you get in return?"

"An exclusive on the Falcone case would be nice, but I know I'm not going to get that." She grinned once, quickly, before turning serious. "Actually, I thought maybe we *could* deal." While he waited for her to go on, she straightened in the chair, settled both feet firmly on the floor and lost her amused edge. "I was hoping maybe you could cut me some slack."

"Go on."

"There's a lot of information there. Records of payoffs. Photographs of very private meetings with very prominent politicians. Tapes of some of those meetings. Most of the documentation is very detailed. There's enough there to allow the FBI to broaden the scope of their investigation to include a number of people a whole lot more important than one reporter."

"I assume some of this documentation incriminates your source, as well as Falcone and those politicians."

She simply shrugged. It was no answer at all, and the answer he preferred. If she had said yes, it would have given the FBI a field of possible suspects to begin weeding out. If she'd said no, she would have been lying, and he really didn't want to hear Jolie lie to him.

"He refused to meet with me, didn't he?"

"Yes."

"Why?"

She shrugged again. "I don't claim to know how men think—crooked ones in particular. I don't know what's going through his mind. I don't know why he won't cooperate with you. I don't even know why he *is* cooperating with me."

"Haven't you asked him?"

She nodded.

"What did he say?"

"He said he wants justice."

"And you believe him?"

She hesitated before answering, but her voice revealed no doubt. "Yes, I do."

Justice. It was probably the last answer Smith would have expected. What did Jimmy Falcone or any of the people

who worked for him know of justice? These were people
who thought they had a God-given right to kill, to threaten,
to destroy. Nothing mattered to them besides money, power
and more money. Jimmy's idea of justice was to try to kill
Remy for getting too close in his investigation. He and his
disreputable lawyer had kidnapped Susannah Duncan's
brother and used him to blackmail her into betraying Remy
so they could make yet another attempt to kill him; to them,
that was justice.

"One of Jimmy's people out for justice. That paints quite
a picture, doesn't it?" He made no effort to control the derision in his voice. "Revenge is a more likely motive. Or
maybe he's looking to make a deal. Before his trial date,
he'll show up, claiming the material and wanting special
consideration."

"I don't think so."

So her informant *was* one of those already indicted. He
had asked her Saturday afternoon, but she had sidestepped
the question. Granted, though, that bit of information
didn't narrow the field any. The grand jury had returned
indictments against a substantial number of defendants in
this case, including everyone he might suspect as Jolie's
source.

"Okay," he said, returning to the earlier subject. "You're
passing on the information he gave you. I'm supposed to
give it to Shawna and convince her that you're cooperating
with us—at least, as much as you're capable of—and so she
should leave you alone."

Jolie nodded.

"You know Shawna. You know how she feels about you.
You're asking a lot."

"There's some good stuff there, Smith, and there will be
more to follow. I'll see that you get everything I get. I think
that deserves a little special consideration."

He didn't doubt that. What little he could see with his
hands-off approach—a ledger sheet that appeared to doc-
ument payoffs, including payments to a number of highly
recognizable names—was alone worth the consideration
Jolie was asking for. While he already knew he would ar-

gue the point on her behalf, his wasn't the final say. The bureau could make life miserable for Jolie without his approval or backing. "What if she refuses?"

Her expression changed, growing subtly harder, less generous. "Then you won't get anything from me. You'll have to read the paper like everyone else."

"There won't be anything to read if you're in jail," he pointed out.

"Oh, there would be plenty to read, just nothing that would help you. It would be stuff about the First Amendment, about the freedom of the press, about the right of a reporter to shield the identity of a source."

For a moment he turned away, swiveling his chair around so he could see out the window. It was one of those rare clear days when everything radiated heat, when the very air seemed to shimmer with it. It was a day for lazing in the shade or floating down the river. He wondered idly if Jolie had a talent for lazing. She *did* have that porch swing, a definite point in her favor.

When he turned to face her again, it was with a rueful smile. "Tell me something, Jolie. Isn't life tough enough on its own? Do you have to go and complicate everything?"

She smiled, too. "It keeps things interesting."

He didn't bother agreeing. "Let me get this clear. Your source will probably supply you with more records. If we leave you alone, you'll use the information to write your articles and then you'll hand everything over to us. If we don't, you keep it to yourself, in which case Shawna would insist on getting a search warrant to find it. Do we agree so far?"

Jolie nodded.

"Of course, being prepared for that eventuality, you would make sure that there wasn't anything to find."

"In which case Shawna would probably have me arrested. And even if the assistant U.S. Attorney is ordinarily a reasonable man," she said with a slow, teasing smile, "he would still stand up in court opposite me and ask a judge to find me guilty of contempt and to give me a little time in a jail cell to contemplate the consequences of my actions."

She had been in court with him a time or two too many. Those were exactly the words he had used on more than one occasion. "If it counts for anything, he wouldn't be happy about asking."

"If it's worth anything to you, I wouldn't be happy about going to jail."

It was worth something, but he didn't acknowledge what. At least he knew for sure that she wasn't looking for a way to gain some notoriety, preferably nationwide, for herself. "If you go to jail," he pointed out, "the stories stop."

"So does the information. You think this guy's going to drop off packages of evidence with the jailer?"

"So if we leave you alone, we eventually get everything except his identity."

"And if you harass me, you wind up with nothing."

"All right." At her questioning look, he shrugged. "I'll talk to Shawna and Alexander. I'll convince them that it's in our best interests to let you handle this your way. I'll remind them that a little cooperation is better than none at all."

He expected one of her flashing triumphant smiles, but all she did was nod as she got to her feet. "I appreciate it, Smith."

Without considering the wisdom of what he was about to do, he also stood up. "Then prove it."

The look she gave him was undeniably wary. "How?"

"Have lunch with me." Before she could turn him down, he went to work persuading her. "It's the middle of the day, Jolie. We'll be in a public place surrounded by other people. We're both on a tight schedule. What harm could it possibly do?"

She laced her fingers together. "You just agreed to argue my case with Shawna and your boss. They'll give a lot more weight to your opinion if they think you're speaking from a strictly professional point of view. They wouldn't be so impressed if they thought that friendship was possibly influencing your position."

"Then we can go someplace very private where there won't be anyone else around." Certain that she would refuse, he spoke in a voice that was part persuasion, part resignation.

A long, still moment passed. He was about to accept that, once again, silence would be her answer when she replied. "All right. Where?"

There were a number of restaurants where privacy could be had, from secluded tables to private rooms to discreet entrances. He didn't consider any of them. "My place." Reaching for a pen, he wrote the address on a slip of yellow paper, ripped it off and held it out to her.

Jolie looked at the ragged edge of the paper. Part of her wanted to snatch it out of his hand before he could change his mind. Part of her wanted to change *her* mind before she could take the paper. In the end, though, she reached out and, without touching him, slipped the address from his grasp. "When?" she asked, wondering if her voice really sounded huskier than normal or if it was just her imagination.

"Give me forty-five minutes to take care of this." He gestured without looking to the papers and tapes on his desk. "Have you ever been fingerprinted before?"

She shook her head.

"They'll need to do that, to compare your prints against the ones they find on this stuff."

"They'll have to call me. I'm not volunteering anything else." She gave a slight shake of her head. It felt odd discussing business as if she hadn't just agreed to go to his condo for a very private lunch. "If they ask, tell them I'll be in the office most of the afternoon." Sliding the thin strap of her purse over her shoulder, she started toward the door. "I'll see you soon."

He nodded once, but already his attention was elsewhere. As she let herself out, he reached for the phone and began dialing.

Jolie closed the door behind her, then started toward the elevator, passing the stiff-necked secretary who had tried to stop her earlier. She didn't look at the woman, didn't speak to her, didn't do more than vaguely recognize her presence.

Alone in the elevator, she looked down at the paper she had crumpled in her hand. She knew the address, knew exactly where the building was. She had never been there before, had certainly never been inside any of the condos, and she shouldn't be going there today. She had to be out of her mind, agreeing to have lunch with him at all, agreeing to do it in such a private place. If she had to be an idiot, she should at least do it publicly or maybe at her own house. There was something so much safer, so much less intimidating, about her house.

Once she got to her car, she climbed in and simply sat there a moment, the engine running, the chill blasting from the air conditioner dispelling the heat that had gathered during her short absence. She could return to the paper and work on the next Falcone article for a half hour, or she could go for a drive. She wasn't far from the interstate. She could drive across Lake Pontchartrain and back. That was always a soothing, high-speed way to relax.

Or she could run an errand that she should have taken care of before coming to Smith's office.

With a resolute sigh, she backed out of the parking space and headed away from the central business district.

Her parents had finally managed to leave Serenity Street thirteen years ago, right about the same time she had graduated from college. It had been a toss-up at the time as to which event was more important to her. She still couldn't quite decide.

The new neighborhood wasn't impressive, but it wasn't inner-city poor, either. The houses were older, built before the forties. Most of them were white, had broad porches and were flanked on one side or the other by a narrow driveway. Every house had a yard, and most of them had a detached garage out back that bordered the alley. It would have been a nice place to grow up, she thought wistfully as she slowed to a crawl before turning into the driveway. While none of them had escaped Serenity Street entirely— Cassie had been four years old at the time of the move—at least the younger kids had gotten to balance it out with life on everyday-average Oak Street.

Wide stone steps led to the porch and the front door, painted black to match the shutters. Knowing that, as a concession to the rising crime rate, her mother kept the door locked these days, she knocked, then pushed her hands into her pockets. A set of wind chimes occasionally tinkled in the corner, and the fragrance of her father's flowers drifted on the slight breeze. From a few blocks down came the toot of a car horn, and the sound of a television was muted through the door, but other than that, the block was quiet. Peaceful.

Serenity Street, in spite of its name, had never been quiet *or* peaceful.

God, she was forever grateful to be free of it!

Opening the door, her mother greeted her with a surprised smile. "What are you doing out this way?"

"Running errands. How are you, Mama?"

Rosemary Wade brushed back her graying blond hair. "I'm fine, honey, just trying to stay cool. I was taking a break from the laundry and watching my soaps."

"I won't keep you from them. I just—"

Before she could go on, her mother interrupted her. "Don't worry about it. I can call Joanne across the street and catch up on what I miss. Come on in where it's cool. You can sit down, have a little lunch with me."

Jolie let her draw her inside into a small entry that led to the living room on one side, the dining room on the other and the kitchen and stairs straight back. "Thanks, Mama, but I can't stay. I have an appointment for lunch." Or was it a date? "Listen, I was wondering if I could store some things over here for a while. I've been doing some clearing out, and I'd like to get them out of the way until I'm finished." The words she had prepared this morning came out easily, naturally, and—as far as they went—they were true. But they felt like a lie. They felt shameful.

"Of course you can. Do you want to put them out in the garage or in one of the closets upstairs?"

"The garage will be fine." She would prefer to leave the box in the closet, where the air-conditioning and cooler temperatures would somewhat offset the effects of humid-

ity, but she knew her parents' garage. As far as she could
recall, no car had ever been parked inside it, because the day
the family had moved into this house, her folks had immediately started filling it with items unneeded in the house but
too good or too important to throw away. After thirteen
years, it was almost full except for a few narrow paths between stacks. It was also the perfect hiding place.

"Let me get the keys," Rosemary volunteered. "You get
your things and I'll meet you out back."

With a nod, Jolie left through the front door as her
mother disappeared into the kitchen. She hurried down the
steps and removed the box from the passenger side of the
car. She had packed most of its contents at home this
morning, then added a few things from her desk at the
newspaper office. On the bottom were all but the last of her
high school yearbooks; the blank pages, front and back,
where her friends had written sometimes funny, sometimes
sentimental and occasionally outright vulgar notes, con-
tained a number of references to Nick. Her senior year-
book, though, was still on a shelf at home. By the time she'd
received it, he had already removed himself from her life.

On top of the annuals was a stack of stenographer's
notebooks, filled with notations and information from previous stories and other informants. Her address book, slim
and pocket-size and *very* private, was sandwiched between
them. She had tossed in a few letters from the two sisters
closest to her in age, Meg and Theresa—letters that had been
written the summer after high school when Jolie had moved
to Mississippi to live for a time with her mother's family—
along with the journals she had begun when she was fourteen but had given up on at eighteen. The last thing she'd
added was a photograph—small, blurry, the colors fading
and distorting with age. She hadn't wanted to part with the
picture, not even temporarily, but she felt she had no choice.

All of those last items—the notebooks and the address
book, the letters, the journals and the photo—were secured
inside two folders.

Green accordion-pleated folders, wrapped with rubber
bands and stacked one on top of the other.

Pushing the door shut with her hip, she carried the box along the side of the house, where hydrangeas bloomed, to the lush backyard. Maybe it came from living all their lives in apartments, first as children themselves, then raising their own thirteen kids in one, or maybe it had something to do with those kids growing up, getting out on their own and needing less of their parents' time, but her mother and father had thrown themselves into yard work with total commitment. Their grass was greener and thicker than any of the neighbors'. Their flowers were healthier and produced bigger blooms. Their roses were of blue-ribbon quality, their azaleas had topped six feet and their vegetable garden could feed the entire block for the entire summer. The yard was a lovely place and particularly satisfying, Jolie knew, after the bare-dirt parcels of Serenity Street.

Rosemary was waiting beside the garage, a key ring in hand, testing various keys in the lock. Jolie watched patiently as she tried, then discarded, a half-dozen keys. "If you don't know what they go to, then maybe you should get rid of some of those keys."

But her mother had heard the suggestion before. "If I threw them out, then I'd find out what they went to," she said matter-of-factly. She gave her daughter a triumphant smile as the next key she slid into the padlock turned the tumblers.

As Rosemary opened first one wide wooden door, then the other, sunlight edged inside. The garage was as orderly as a room full of junk could be. Finding anything in there would be like finding the proverbial needle in a haystack. Jolie wouldn't want to be given the job.

She fervently hoped Shawna Warren wouldn't take it upon herself.

While her mother waited at the door, Jolie went inside, turning this way, then that, looking for the perfect spot.

"Since you'll be picking it up again soon," her mother suggested reasonably, "why don't you leave it near the door?"

"I want to put it where I know it'll be left alone. I've got some stuff in here I don't want disturbed." She didn't explain any more than that. Her mother didn't need a better explanation. She understood.

About halfway back along the far wall, she found the spot she was looking for. Boxes were stacked in a single row against the wall, some reaching over six feet high, some only four or five. One particular box was empty, its contents needed and reclaimed. There were water stains down the side, the corrugated cardboard was wrinkled and misshapen, and a thin layer of dust coated the flaps, two open, two folded down.

Setting her own box down, she carefully raised the folded flaps only as far as necessary to slide her smaller box inside. Just as carefully, she folded all four flaps into place, then gently blew across them. Dust lifted, swirled, then resettled, coating the top of the box evenly.

It wasn't a perfect hiding place, she acknowledged as she stepped back. If Shawna Warren did get a search warrant and turned up nothing at the newspaper or Jolie's house, she would know that Jolie had hidden everything elsewhere, and her parents' house would probably come first to the agent's mind. Then it would be a simple matter of asking Rosemary. As much as she loved her daughter, she wouldn't lie to the government to protect her.

But a search warrant had to be confined to specific places. While Jolie had no doubt that a federal magistrate would give the FBI free rein to search *her* property, she thought—hoped—he would require some sort of compelling reason before unleashing them on her family. She would have liked to confirm that with Smith before coming here, but she wasn't sure he would tell her, and she hadn't wanted to give him any hints about her plans.

"Are you sure you can't stay for lunch?" her mother asked as Jolie walked out into the sunlight again. "I have roast left over from Sunday dinner and a fresh-baked loaf of bread."

"I really can't, Mama. Thanks for the offer, though." Impulsively she gave her mother a hug. "Thanks for the use of the garage. I'll get that stuff out of your way when I'm all finished at home."

"Don't worry about it." Bypassing the back door, Rosemary walked to the car with her arm around Jolie. "Tell me something, sugar. Are you going to be the first of my children to land in jail?"

"Anything's possible," she replied with a lightness she didn't feel. "I *am* trying to avoid it, though."

"I wish you would. It would really put a crimp in my schedule if I had to make time for visiting day down at the jail." Then her mother's smile faded, and she became as serious as Jolie had ever seen her. "This involves *him*, doesn't it?"

The first *him* that came to mind was Smith, who would be waiting for her at his condo in less than fifteen minutes. Then she remembered all the times she'd heard that simple little word from her mother in that disdainful, derisive tone.

You're going out with him, aren't you?

I'm asking you to quit seeing him.

I'm not going to stand back and let you throw your life away for the likes of him.

She swallowed hard. "Mama, I can't tell you—"

Rosemary's smile was sad and distant. "You don't have to tell me. You're protecting Nicky Carlucci. You're risking jail for *him*."

"I can't discuss this, Mama."

"Didn't he hurt you enough eighteen years ago? Do you have to give him a chance to do it again?"

Jolie gave her another hug, then pulled away and opened the car door. Before climbing in, though, she hesitated. "Don't bring this up with Daddy," she insisted, then softened it. "Please."

The look Rosemary gave her was haughty. "I would never mention Nicky Carlucci's name in your father's house. He despised Nicky as a boy and he despises the man even more. This is between you and me."

"Thank you."

"And between you and me, Jolie, you'd have to be a fool to go to jail to protect Nicky, and I didn't raise you to be a fool."

Jolie grinned as she slid into the seat. "Being foolish is something else I try hard to avoid. Mama, I've got to go, or I'll be late for lunch. I'll talk to you soon. Give my love to Daddy."

As she backed out of the driveway, she returned her mother's wave, then headed back toward downtown. If only Smith knew to contact her mother, the questions of cooperation, the First Amendment and jail would all become moot points. Rosemary Wade knew where her loyalties lay—with family, God and country. She would have no misgivings about telling what she alone had guessed, not if it meant saving her eldest daughter from the indignity of a jail cell.

Not if it meant repaying Nick, after eighteen long years, for a little of the trouble he had caused.

Not if it meant finally seeing *him* pay. Rosemary would take great pleasure in that, in knowing that for once he was in as hopeless a situation as he'd left her daughter.

And sometimes, Jolie had to admit...

Sometimes so would she.

Chapter 5

Smith had been right. By doing no more than walking into his condo, Jolie had changed the entire character of the place. She did more than make it sizzle. For the first time since he'd moved in, it felt like a home and not a showplace. For the first time, he *knew* someone lived there.

She was standing near the glass wall in the living room, gazing out. It provided the best view: the Mississippi, wide and brown, winding on out to the Gulf; the high-rise office buildings and hotels of downtown New Orleans; Jackson Brewery sprawled between the river and Decatur Street; and the trees and ages-old rooftops of the French Quarter.

"This is a great place," she said, turning to smile at him as he unpacked the take-out lunch he'd brought with him at the beveled-glass-and-stone table in the breakfast nook between kitchen and living room. The nook was raised six steps above the living room, was big enough only for the table and four chairs, and achieved some measure of separateness from the lush potted plants that were placed along the edge of the curving floor.

"It meets my needs."

Still smiling, she rolled her gaze heavenward. "The man owns a chunk of prime riverfront property, and it meets his needs. Please, Smith, what more could you ask for?"

He could think of several answers that he was certain she wouldn't like—starting with someone to share the place with—but settled for one that was equally true. "Grass. A hammock. Windows that open. Not having seventeen stories of parking garage and other people's homes underneath me."

"If you wanted a house, why did you buy a condo?"

He shrugged. "It was easier." Easier to choose, easier to maintain, easier to not get attached to. Buying a house was a complicated decision—a family sort of decision. He would have wanted something that he was comfortable with, something that his wife, when he eventually married, would like, something that would suit his children, when they eventually had them. Every aspect of house buying would have been important, while the condo had been simple. He had paid for it, the designer had decorated it, and he had moved in.

He could move out tomorrow and never miss the place.

Climbing the steps, she chose to sit in one of the side chairs where she could still catch the view. "The easy decisions are rarely the best ones," she remarked. "You, of all people, should know that."

"Why me?"

"Because of your line of work. You see firsthand what taking the easy way out does for a lot of people—the ones who believe it's easier to steal than to struggle, easier to get rich dealing drugs than to work for minimum wage, easier for a witness to keep his mouth shut and stay healthy than to come forward and testify."

"So why aren't you taking the easy way out?"

She grinned. "Because I'm not like those people. Easy's no fun."

Sliding into the seat across from her, he began dishing out food. Aware from previous accidental meetings that they shared a taste for Chinese food and a preference for the same tiny little restaurant, that was what he'd chosen for lunch. "So that explains your choice of careers and your particular specialty within the career. Cloak-and-dagger meetings, impending court appearances, the threat of jail... It's not easy, but it's fun, right?"

"I didn't exactly choose the career," she admitted as she reached for the sesame chicken. "When I started college, I didn't have much of an idea what I wanted to do. I just wanted to learn. I wanted to escape."

"Escape what?" He tried to keep his tone casual, tried not to reveal how interested he was in the conversation, tried not to give any hint that his interest was purely personal.

"The way I'd grown up. The neighborhood I grew up in."

He didn't pursue that line. Her reaction Saturday afternoon when they had talked briefly about where she'd grown up had been enough to warn him that it was a particularly sensitive point with her. "Where did you go to school?"

"Mississippi. Ol' Miss. I had a full scholarship, and I worked full-time in summer and part-time the rest of the year. That's the only time I've ever lived away from New Orleans."

"And now you can't wait to go elsewhere. Won't you miss it when you're gone? No family and friends, no Mardi Gras or Jazz Fest, no Christmas bonfires on the river?"

Was her laughter a little strained or did it merely seem so to him because he wanted it to? "I'll make new friends. It may surprise you people in the government, but I *am* considered a likable person. As far as family and the rest, that's what they have cars, trains and planes for."

"But it won't be the same. Visiting your family two or three times a year can't begin to compare with living nearby. Sometimes I wonder what kind of relationship I would have with my family if I hadn't left home when I was eighteen."

"Do you regret it?"

He considered it for a long moment before shrugging. "Sometimes. Don't get me wrong. I'm reasonably satisfied with my life here. I like New Orleans, and I intend to stay. I like my job, I have good friends, and I feel as if I belong here. At the same time, it would be nice to be more than casual acquaintances with my family."

Her smile was as dry as her tone. "There's nothing casual about the relationships between any of the Wades. Of course, when fifteen people share a four-bedroom apartment, they get to know each other very, very well."

He thought about that—fifteen people in four bedrooms. Allowing one room for her parents and another for the four brothers, that meant Jolie had shared her room with three or four sisters. From the time he was three or four years old, he'd had his own private suite of rooms at his parents' home—a bedroom, a sitting room and bath—while Jolie had been lucky to get a private moment to herself. No wonder she had been eager to escape. No wonder she had worked hard to earn a scholarship, then had worked even harder to get through college. She had seen it as a way out, a way to a better life for herself.

But how much better did it have to get before she would allow herself to quit pushing?

"So you went away to college without any specific plans," he said, returning to their earlier subject. "What drew you to journalism?"

"One of my part-time jobs was with the local paper. I walked in my first day, and it was as if a light bulb had come on over my head. I knew right away that that was what I wanted to do. I wanted to write the news. I wanted to inform the public." Her smile was self-deprecating. "I wanted to make a difference."

"You've accomplished those goals. What more, besides a Pulitzer, do you want?"

"To be the best." She answered simply, unequivocally. It wasn't about money—although money was always nice, Smith acknowledged, especially to someone who'd grown up without it—or respect, also nice. She wanted to be the best.

And she couldn't very well do that in New Orleans, Louisiana.

"What about a family? Does that figure into your plans anywhere?" When she started to reply, he raised one hand to stall her. "Not kids. You made your feelings quite clear about that Saturday. What about a husband? Aren't you ever going to get married?''

She cut the last egg roll in half, dipped it in sweet-and-sour sauce and took a bite, chewing slowly before finally swallowing and dryly asking, "Didn't we cover that Saturday, too?"

The snatch of conversation she was referring to echoed in his mind. *Don't you ever feel the urge to give the wedding march a spin? Don't you ever hear your biological clock ticking?*

Never.

Never? Not even after you have a Pulitzer or two?

Never.

But she had followed up that last flat response with more—with talk about helping to raise her brothers and sisters, about never wanting children of her own. She hadn't made any specific references to the marriage part of his question.

"Not exactly. You kind of got hung up on the kids. You didn't get around to rejecting marriage as thoroughly as you rejected motherhood."

She finished the egg roll, wiped her hands on a napkin and settled back in the chair to study him. "Interesting that you should ask, considering that you're older than I am, about as ambitious and still single yourself."

"But I haven't ruled it out. Marriage has always been part of my plans. I just haven't met the right woman yet."

"Maybe you haven't met her because she doesn't exist."

He shook his head. "I don't believe that." He had a damned good reason for not believing it, and she was sitting across the table from him. "Besides, we're not talking about me or the existence of a Ms. Right—or Mr. Right—for every one of us. We're talking about you and your narrow-minded refusal to even consider the possibilities."

She stared at him, irate astonishment bringing a spark of green fire to her eyes. "Narrow-minded?" she repeated, her gaze sharpening, her voice harder and tighter. "You're calling me narrow-minded? *You*—a lawyer, a *prosecutor*, who lives by the book, who sees right and wrong, black and white and no shades of gray—are calling *me* narrow-minded?"

"Yes," he replied mildly. "You're also stubborn, hard-headed and just a little hot tempered, too."

"And you're a chauvinist," she retorted. "You just can't quite accept the idea of a woman who doesn't need a man to be happy."

"That's not what we're talking about, either—and by the way, several of my aunts have lived long, independent, adventurous and very fulfilling lives without ever marrying."

Her features settled into a scowl. "Then what *are* we talking about?"

"Chances. You're afraid to take them. And I'd like to know what mine are."

For a long, still moment, she simply looked at him. The scowl was gone, and so was the annoyance. There was wariness in her eyes, though, and a soft residue of surprise around the edges.

Then the moment passed, and she left the table and descended the half-dozen steps to the living room. He remained where he was, using chopsticks to pick shrimp out of the remaining rice while he watched her. She stopped in front of a large sculpture that dominated one wall and stood there, hands in her pockets, studying it.

A minute crawled by, then another and another, and yet he waited patiently. At last she spoke, her voice too cheery to be genuine. "I have no class when it comes to art. I like to know what I'm looking at without having to ask someone to explain it to me. I like the pretty paintings of the French Quarter that Michael does and portraits of people with all the parts in their proper places. I like pictures of big-eyed kids and sad-eyed clowns." Her tone shifted, and even though her back was to him, he knew she was smiling at least a little. "I'm sure this piece was obscenely expensive and the sculptor is universally admired, but to me it still looks like just a few glass rods, some pieces of steel and some rocks. So...what is it supposed to be?"

Smith pushed his chair away from the table and leisurely walked over to stand behind her. "A few glass rods, some pieces of steel and some rocks," he teased. "Do you like it?"

"I'm sure I'm supposed to, but no. Not particularly."

"I'm sure I'm also supposed to like it—especially since I signed the check that paid for it—and you're right. It was expensive. But I don't care much for it, either."

She glanced over her shoulder at him, then moved a step or two away. "Then why did you buy it? And why do you have it displayed so prominently in your home?"

"I bought it because Lily Andrews told me to buy it, and it's displayed here because that's where Lily had the men put it when it was delivered. Since it weighs about five hundred pounds, it'll probably stay there forever."

"Lily Andrews did all this, huh? That explains a lot."

"Such as?"

"Her work is very contemporary, very avant-garde. I would have guessed that your tastes were more refined. More traditional. Antiques and rich colors, lots of wood and very little metal."

"You would be right." Because she kept edging away from him, he moved a step closer. "I do have one painting that you might like. It's in the hall. Want to see it?"

She responded with an open shrug, and he led the way to the hall. Down past the kitchen to the right were two guest bedrooms and baths. To the left was his room. The painting he had referred to hung over a table only a few feet from his door.

Jolie backed up to the opposite wall and turned her attention to the framed painting. The subject was the St. Louis Cathedral in Jackson Square, and the artist, although the work was unsigned, was undoubtedly Michael. It wasn't one of his pretty Quarter paintings that she had referred to earlier. This one was dark, despairing, filled with sorrow. The cathedral rose, distorted and unwelcoming, from ghostly mists that drifted through the square. Instead of comforting, it threatened. Instead of sanctuary, it offered menace.

It was a strong piece. An unsettling one. A powerful one.

"Michael in his post-Evan period," she murmured; then abruptly she turned to meet Smith's gaze. Evan had been his friend, too; although he had handled Evan's death far better than Michael had, it had to have been difficult for Smith, too. "I'm sorry. I wasn't being flippant."

"You're right. He painted it about four months after Evan died. Valery won't have it in the house, and Michael wasn't interested in keeping it anyway, so I asked if I could have it."

"Why?" She couldn't stop herself from asking. "Do you like it?"

"'Like' isn't the right word for it. I have a gut-level reaction to it every time I see it." He glanced down at her. "That's what art is—not trying to please everyone, or confuse or confound them. It's having the power to touch them, to make them feel. That piece in the living room doesn't succeed at that. This one does."

There was no doubt about that, Jolie thought, looking at the painting once again. She could easily understand why Valery didn't want it around, why Michael had been willing to get rid of it after all the work, all the anguish, he'd put into it.

She could also understand why Smith had asked for it, why he had hung it here where he would see it every time he walked down the hall. It wasn't a pretty picture or, like the sculpture, something a person could remain indifferent to. It wasn't an easy painting to look at, particularly for Smith, she imagined—knowing the artist as he did and sharing the grief that had inspired it.

But *easy*, they both seemed to agree, wasn't the way they wanted to live.

Except, of course, for this condo. It was probably the first, and the only, easy choice Smith had ever made.

After a moment, aware that she was being nosy and not caring, she took the last few steps that brought her to the open doorway beyond the painting. It was a bedroom, the master bedroom judging from the size of it.

Smith's bedroom.

Like the rest of the condo, the furnishings were contemporary and lacking in color and warmth. The headboard on the king-size bed looked like a rising sun in a world that had been leached of all color but the softer, thinner shades of gray. The walls were textured gray, the floor covered with thick gray carpet, the ceiling a slick, gleaming version of the same color. The dresser and night tables, the chairs in one corner, the armoire against one wall, the vertical blinds gathered at the corner of the windowed wall—all were bland, lifeless, colorless gray. From her place in the doorway, she saw only three touches of real color: the black telephone on one night table, a gold watch left on top of the dresser and the quilted burgundy comforter that covered the bed.

The part of her that appreciated the absence of clutter and the gleam of sunlight on vast dust-free surfaces thought it was beautiful.

The part of her that imagined Smith sleeping in this empty, cool, colorless room found it almost as unwelcoming as Michael's church in the hallway.

Turning, she gave him a long, steady look. "Lily Andrews?"

He nodded.

"Before you handed her a check that would make most people's eyes pop out, didn't you bother to discuss your tastes?"

"No. I told her that I didn't want to be bothered with the details." He looked past her, his gaze sweeping around the room, then shrugged. "It's not what I would have chosen, but it's not so bad once you get used to it. Besides, it's temporary. Except for Michael's painting, I'll leave it all behind when I eventually move into a house."

No, she silently agreed, it really wasn't bad. She appreciated the clean lines, the starkness, the texture, and there was a certain soothing quality to the absence of colors. She imagined that when he was tired from a tough day in court, these sleek, sophisticated rooms were very easy to relax in.

Still, she would take her battered and scarred wood, unevenly stuffed couch and crayon drawings over this any day.

With a glance at her watch, she started down the hall, sliding past Smith without coming too close. "I'd better get back to work."

"You still owe me an answer."

His tone was conversational, his expression benign, but she knew immediately what he was referring to. *Then what are we talking about?*

Chances. You're afraid to take them. And I'd like to know what mine are.

She waited until they were back in the living room to respond. Even then she postponed the discussion with a gesture toward the patio. "Can we go out?"

He unlocked the door and slid it open, then followed her outside. To the east the clouds were fat and puffy, but all that remained overhead were the thin, stretched-out tails that allowed wisps of pale blue sky to show through. Back to the west another bank of clouds was building, these darker, more ominous. Summer in New Orleans with its relentless heat and enervating humidity was a marvelous place for thunderstorms. When she was a kid, she had loved the drama of them—the great claps of thunder that made the old house reverberate, the lightning that forked across the sky and the rain that came in sheets to wash Serenity Street clean. She had weathered countless storms huddled on the porch, getting wetter with every gust of wind and anticipating every rumble of thunder.

This condo would be a great place to witness a really powerful storm.

Smith's bed would be even better.

She walked to the railing, big fat posts painted dark gray to better blend with the architecture of the building, and rested her hands on it. It was hot, and the air was impossibly still. She swore she could feel the coolness draining right out of her body, pushed on its way by the perspiration being drawn to the surface, just like condensation forming on a glass.

Down below, the river was busy with tugboats and cargo ships, with the ferry full of cars and riverboats loaded with tourists. Years ago, she, Nick and Jamey had spent many summer hours by the river, concocting stories about distant ports, envying tourists with the time for vacations and the money for a two-hour trip to nowhere and throwing rocks at the occasional rats.

To this day she never let a summer pass without at least once staking out an empty spot along the rail on the *Natchez,* propping her feet up and enjoying a Bloody Mary as they sailed an hour to nowhere and an hour back again.

And she felt a little more kindly toward rats than any sensible person should.

Aware that Smith was waiting—he was so damned patient—she finally turned to face him, hooking her arms around the top rail, leaning back against it. "I'm not afraid to take chances," she said evenly. "Remember me? The one making nasty accusations about Jimmy Falcone in the newspaper? The one slipping off to middle-of-the-night clandestine meetings with New Orleans's finest crooks? The one facing the daily threat of jail?"

He brushed all that off. "That's business. When is the last time you did something risky in your personal life?"

When she agreed to come here for lunch, she wanted to say. When she invited him to come down from Michael's balcony and join her and Cassie at the festival Saturday, knowing full well that Cassie would wander off and leave them alone. When she had accepted his dinner invitation the night before that. She had already risked more to be with him than any man had gotten from her since Nick.

"Pardon me if I don't agree that risk taking is such a great thing," she said airily. "I happen to like being secure and happy and not giving anyone a chance to change that."

"Not even if the change is for the better? Being more secure? Happier?"

"And what if it's not for the better?" She smiled brashly. "Have you ever been in love, Smith?"

He shook his head.

"Well, *I* have."

"Was it such a bad experience?"

"Oh, no. Being in love was great. It was exhilarating. It was wonderful." Her tone went flat. "While it lasted."

"So you got hurt. And that's it? No more chances?"

She held back an exasperated sigh. She couldn't make him understand unless she told him everything, and she couldn't tell him everything. She *couldn't*. "No," she replied, searching for the right words. "It's not that simple. It's not about getting hurt again. I don't need to get married. I don't need a man in my life. My job—"

"Career," he interrupted, his tone softly mocking. "You have a career, remember? Not a job and not just work."

She changed the word but ignored his taunt. "My career is more important to me than a husband or children." The claim felt as phony, as untruthful, today as it had Saturday when she'd made it to Cassie. But it *was* the truth. She'd made it the truth—with a little help from Nick Carlucci— half a lifetime ago. "Feeling as I do, it would be wrong of me to begin any sort of relationship with any man. It would be a waste of time. It would be unfair."

She recognized the way he was looking at her, a studying sort of look that she'd seen him subject witnesses to in court. It made her uncomfortable. "So you're saying that my chances of changing your mind are slim."

"Nonexistent." A twinge of shame rippled through her. Other things she'd said had felt like lies. That answer *was* a lie, not so pure and simple.

He came closer, still studying her, still searching her face for something, but, judging from the slow shake of his head, not finding it. "I don't believe you, Jolie," he said at last, his voice gentle enough to almost make her overlook the fact that he was calling her a liar. "Call it my prosecutor's instinct, but I don't believe you."

She inched away. "I'm not one of your suspects, Smith. I don't have to prove myself to you."

"Do you think you're the only person afraid of getting hurt?" He shook his head again. "Frankly, you scare the hell out of me. You're not like any other woman I've ever known."

There was a world of truth in his last statement. Most, if not all, of the women he'd been involved with were just like him. They shared the same upbringing, the same social status; they had more money than they knew what to do with, and if you cut them, they bled blue. *She*, on the other hand, was common, average, church-mouse poor most of her life and just finally, after years of hard work, approaching middle-class comfortable.

Feigning another bold smile, she said, "I'll take that as a compliment."

"I meant it as one." After a moment's silence, he offered her a tentative smile. "Want to make a deal with me?"

"What kind of deal?"

"You don't want to fall in love, don't want to get married and have kids. That doesn't mean you can't have a relationship."

"But why bother—"

He cut her off with a gesture. "Since you're utterly convinced that there's nothing I can do to change your mind, since you've clearly warned me of that and we both understand the limitations that imposes, there's really no reason why we can't proceed from there."

"You mean have an affair," she said flatly.

"That's one way of putting it." He moved to lean against the rail a few feet away, gazing out over the river while she studied their reflections in the glass doors. "You do enjoy sex. You do indulge from time to time, don't you?"

"From time to time," she agreed, her mouth barely moving from its tightly compressed grimace. As it happened, so much time had passed since the last time that she'd quit counting, had almost quit remembering. She had almost convinced herself that physical intimacy was something else she didn't need in her life.

But not quite.

"Exactly what is it that you're proposing?" she asked stiffly. "That we sneak off twice a week for an hour of wild, passionate sex in an anonymous hotel room somewhere?"

"Not at all." He turned to face her, but she didn't look at him. What she could see in her peripheral vision was enough. "I'm proposing that you have a relationship with me. That we talk. Spend time together. Go out to dinner. Get to know each other better. I'm proposing that we date, Jolie. You don't have to worry about getting hurt, because you don't need a man in your life and you're not interested in ever getting married and there's nothing I can do to change your mind. And I won't have to worry about getting hurt, because I know going in that there's no future...." He smiled just a little. "Unless, of course, you've underestimated both yourself and me and I *do* manage to change your mind."

"And if that does happen? Then what?"

"Who knows?" He shrugged. "Maybe—horror of horrors—we'll live happily ever after."

Down on the river a boat whistle sounded, filtering up through the heavy air. She automatically glanced down, then looked at him. "I've got to get back to work," she said quietly. "I imagine Shawna's just itching to get my ten little fingers in her ink. Thanks for the lunch."

He let her get as far as the glass door before he spoke. "So what do you say, Wade? Do we have a deal?"

She looked back and smiled a troubled smile. "I'll let you know."

"Well, that was a wasted afternoon," Shawna Warren announced, disgust evident in her voice. "I knew the moment I saw that smug little smile of Jolie's that we weren't going to find anyone else's fingerprints on the evidence. The lab confirmed it. That means what she gave us is likely copies, not originals at all."

"Or," Remy broke in, "whoever put it together was smart enough not to leave his fingerprints, which would mean that he really planned ahead. He never actually touched any of it—from the time he tore the wrapper off the printer paper, opened the package the cassette tapes came in or removed the photographs from the processing envelope."

Smith sat behind his desk, the chair swiveled to one side, his legs stretched out and crossed at the ankles. He'd been about to leave the office when Remy and Shawna had shown up. He wasn't even annoyed that they were keeping him late. He had nowhere to go. No one to see. Nothing to do.

Except think about Jolie.

He wondered what her answer to his suggestion would be. He wasn't being rude this afternoon when he'd told her that he didn't believe her about not wanting a relationship; he was simply telling the truth as he saw it. He didn't believe she was really as sure of herself, as sure of what she wanted, as she claimed. He didn't believe she was so sure of *him*.

He didn't believe for a moment that, given time, opportunity and the right incentive, he couldn't change her mind. Arguing was what he did for a living, arguing passionately, logically and rationally to sway a judge or to win a juror to his side. Any prosecutor worth a damn was persuasive as hell.

And Jolie just needed a little persuading.

The first thing he had to do was persuade her to give him the time and opportunity.

She provided the incentive by merely existing.

Slowly he became aware of the stillness in the room. Shifting his gaze from the bookcases he'd been staring at, he slowly looked at Remy and Shawna. They were sitting in silence, watching him, Remy's expression vaguely amused, Shawna's annoyed. What part of their conversation had he missed out on, he wondered, and how important had it been?

"It's been a long day for all of us," Remy said evenly, providing him with an excuse for not paying attention.

"Yeah, well, the days are going to get a hell of a lot longer if the Falcone trial starts and we still don't have Wade's informant," Shawna snapped. "Do you think you can pay attention for five minutes more, Smith, or should I take this up with Alexander?"

He straightened in his chair, turned to face them and folded his hands on the desk pad. "I'm paying attention," he said coolly. "What is it you want?"

"I'd like to put a couple of people on Jolie, and I'd like to get a line ID on her home phone."

"No."

"Come on, Smith. It's procedure."

"No," he repeated stubbornly. "Not as long as she's cooperating."

"Falcone's trial starts in a couple of weeks," she reminded him. "I agree, the stuff she gave us is good. It opens up a whole new arena of investigation. But it's not admissible in court, not without being able to prove where it came from. We *need* her informant for the trial."

"We made a deal with her. *I* made a deal with her. Do you know what she would do if we reneged? She would use the front page of the newspaper to tell everyone who can read— every crook, every informant, every law-abiding citizen— that the U.S. Attorney's office isn't to be trusted. That they made promises and didn't keep them. Do you know what kind of damage that could do?" He paused, but not long enough for a response. "No one would deal with us again— no suspects, no informants, no lawyers. We would be screwed, and we'd have no one to blame but ourselves."

Her expression argumentative, Shawna asked, "What about once the trial starts? How are you going to handle this then?"

Smith made a conscious effort to hide the discomfort her question caused. He knew exactly what she wanted to hear, what Alexander Marshall would expect to hear: that he would subpoena Jolie. That he would put her on the witness stand and question her about the evidence, about its source. That he would attempt to force her to respond and that, when she refused, he would ask the judge to find her in contempt.

That was what Shawna wanted, what Alexander wanted, and it was exactly what he would do.

Even if it was the last thing *he* wanted.

"I'll handle it, Shawna."

"How?"

He gave her a long, warning look. "I have a better conviction rate than anyone else in this office. I know how to handle my trials. I don't have to explain my strategy or my intentions to you. Now...is there anything else you want to discuss this evening?"

With a tight shake of her head, Shawna gathered her jacket and briefcase, muttered a cross goodbye and left his office. After a moment's silence, Remy asked, "Does that invitation to leave include me, too?"

Smith sighed. "No."

"You got problems?"

"Life without problems would be easy, and easy's no fun," he murmured.

There was a moment of puzzlement in Remy's expression, then he shrugged it off. "Michael says you spent most of Saturday afternoon down in the Quarter with Jolie." He paused. "You've got a hell of a sense of timing, pal. The biggest trial of your career is coming up in a couple of weeks, and she's going to be right smack in the middle of it."

"Maybe not."

"She's not going to roll over on her source."

"No. But maybe we can figure out who he is by then. Maybe he'll come forward on his own. Maybe his lawyer will persuade him to make a deal."

"Uh-huh. And maybe Jimmy will save us all the trouble by pleading guilty to everything and avoiding a trial." Remy fell silent for a long time. When he did finally speak again, he looked troubled. "This one's important, Smith. After what Falcone did to Valery and to Susannah . . . this one's damned important."

"Don't forget what he did to you." Smith drew his fingertip back and forth across the fine grain leather that covered his desk pad. "It's important to me, too. I've never wanted a conviction the way I want this one. I promise you, Remy, I'll do whatever it takes within the limits of the law to get it."

"Even if it causes problems for you with Jolie."

"I've never let my personal life interfere with how I do my job," he replied stiffly. But that wasn't exactly true. His personal feelings for Remy, Valery and Susannah had certainly influenced his professional desire to send Falcone to prison. When Falcone had threatened them, he had made the case intensely personal for Smith. And, on a more minor level, he had sat here a few minutes ago and let a portion of a work-related discussion slide right by him while he was preoccupied with thoughts of Jolie and the arrangement he had offered her.

"I know that. But until now your personal life has never included Jolie Wade."

"You don't like her much, do you?" It was Michael who got along well with her, Michael who openly admired her. Remy, Smith recalled, had always tolerated her. They rarely carried on conversations but traded insults and barbed taunts. Michael and Jolie were friends. Remy and Jolie were adversaries.

"For a smart-mouthed, hotshot, overconfident reporter, she's not so bad." Remy grinned unexpectedly. "She certainly knows how to get Shawna stirred up. All she has to do is smile, and Shawna's blood pressure shoots off the charts."

I knew the moment I saw that smug little smile of Jolie's . . . Smith grinned, too. He knew exactly the smile Shawna had been referring to. It was the same one that usually made Remy scowl—the same one that, personally, *he* found amusing. Of course, he wasn't competing directly against her in any way, which, in a very real sense, the FBI agents were. He could afford to be amused.

"Come on. I'll walk out with you." Remy got to his feet and stretched. "You want to come over for dinner?"

Smith pulled on the suit coat he'd removed when the agents had arrived, straightened his tie and picked up his briefcase. "I'm sure Susannah appreciates you inviting guests over without asking."

"You're not a guest. You're family. Want to come?"

He considered it a moment, then shook his head. "I'm kind of tired. I'll go on home."

As they walked down the quiet hall to the elevator, Smith noticed that his friend was favoring his right leg. The first time Falcone's people had tried to kill Remy, he'd been shot three times at close range—in the arm, the chest and the thigh. A bulletproof vest had saved his life, and the arm wound had been minor, as minor as a gunshot wound could be, but the bullet that had gone through his thigh had done some serious damage to the femur. The cast had been off since March, and he no longer needed crutches or a cane to get around, but he still had a titanium plate screwed into the bone for support, and he still had occasional aches.

"Been overdoing it lately?" Smith asked softly.

Remy's grin was wry as he stepped into the elevator. "I didn't think the limp was so noticeable anymore."

"It's not."

"My granddaddy used to tell me that he always knew when it was going to rain because he could feel it in his bones. Now I know what he meant. Those clouds building off to the west may not bring any rain, but they're sure increasing the humidity."

Downstairs, they stepped outside, then parted, each heading for his car. As he drove, Smith considered stopping somewhere for dinner, then decided to go on home. Remy was right about those clouds. The humidity was unbearably high, the air thick and still. The calm before the storm, he thought with a thin smile. He didn't really feel much like eating now, and he certainly didn't feel like being caught out if the storm did break. He could always order something delivered later.

He could, if he got energetic, find something in the freezer to cook.

Or he could finish off the leftovers from his and Jolie's lunch.

When he walked in the door of his condo, the scent of perfume, as elusive as the woman who wore it, greeted him. It was in the living room, hovering over the dining table, weaving down the hall and drifting faintly in his bedroom. She had spent barely an hour there, and yet she had left her mark.

As he pulled off his jacket and tie, the first rumble of thunder sounded. Seconds later lightning streaked across the sky. The first raindrops were fat, striking the window with audible little plops. As they came harder and faster, they grew smaller, coating the glass, blurring the world outside.

Tired and feeling just a little melancholy, he returned to the living room, put a Louis Armstrong CD in the player, got a cold beer from the refrigerator and went to the patio door. Lightning raced down again, and a flash across the river signaled a strike, probably a transformer somewhere. Immediately behind it, sheet lightning brightened the sky.

He should have accepted Remy's dinner invitation. He should have gone by Michael's or stopped at his favorite restaurant or worked late and had dinner delivered to the office. He should have—

The ringing of the doorbell interrupted his thoughts. For just an instant he thought of Jolie, saw her as she'd looked this afternoon out there on the patio, her arms looped around the top rail, wearing the smile that Shawna hated, and his fingers tightened around the bottle he held. But it wouldn't be her at the door. She wouldn't come over without calling first. She wouldn't have an answer to his suggestion so quickly.

Would she?

At the second ring, he pushed away from the glass and crossed to the door. He was right. It wasn't Jolie standing there when he opened the door.

It was Trevor, Cassie's boyfriend. Like Saturday, he was unshaven, sullen and sulky, but he was also soaking wet. The drenching he'd received made him look more like a harmless kid than the young rebel he wanted to appear.

"Are you Mr. Kendricks?"

"Yes, I am. You're Cassie's friend, aren't you?"

"Yes, sir."

Sir. There was a time the formality would have impressed him, before Michael and Evan had taught him—and he had soon learned on his own—that when the people he dealt with started peppering their conversation with respectful *sir*s and *please*s, they were generally lying through their teeth.

But Trevor wasn't one of those people, even if he did look the part.

"Come on in," Smith invited, stepping back. "I'll get you a towel."

"No, thanks. I've got to get to work. Cassie's sister asked me to deliver this on the way." Reaching inside his leather jacket, he withdrew an envelope and offered it to Smith. It was white, greeting-card size, and his name was written across the front in smeared blue ink. It was also wet. With a slight flush, the young man apologized for that. "Sorry. I couldn't find a parking space nearby. I've gotta go now."

Studying the envelope, Smith murmured his thanks, closed the door and slowly returned to the patio door. Was rejection easier delivered in an impersonal note by a sullen stranger? He didn't think so.

Damn, he really should have gone to Remy's.

With an exasperated sigh that echoed through the room, he set his beer down on the closest table, unsealed the flap and reached inside for Jolie's rejection. Instead, all he found was a ticket for a cruise on the riverboat *Natchez* and, attached to the back, a yellow sticky note. In the same handwriting that had addressed the envelope was a brief note: "Saturday, 1:30."

His smile came slowly, growing until it split into a grin. In her own unorthodox way, Jolie had given him exactly the answer he'd wanted, had hoped for, but honestly hadn't expected. She was giving him another Saturday afternoon and a lazy float down the river. She was giving him a chance.

Sliding the ticket into his shirt pocket, he picked up his beer again and turned his attention back to the weather. Coming on home alone hadn't been such a bad idea, he decided. In fact, he was pretty damned satisfied with where he was and what he had.

New Orleans in July, a summer storm, a cold beer and blues in the air.

And a date with Jolie on Saturday.

What more could a man ask for?

Chapter 6

Jolie wasn't a nervous person by nature. Granted, she had a lot of energy, but she generally put it to good use. She didn't fidget, didn't pace, didn't do anything that might reveal uneasiness. In writing the kind of stories she wrote and interviewing the people she interviewed, impressions were important. Being perceived as brash, bold and tough was good. Appearing nervous and edgy wasn't.

But on this bright Saturday afternoon she was pacing. Her palms were damp, and it couldn't be blamed on the heat.

It *could* be blamed on the fact that nearly a week had passed since her lunch with Smith. Since he'd suggested that they attempt a relationship.

Relationship. As a child, reading to explore the world and to escape her own dreary little part of it, she had learned to treasure language. As a reporter, she had developed tremendous respect for words, their subtle nuances and their power. But *relationship* was one word that she absolutely hated. It smacked of snootiness, of pretension, of imprecision. It was trendy.

However, much as she hated it, she couldn't come up with a better substitute. *Friendship* was too benign, *affair* too intimate. *Romance* was too personal, *liaison* too illicit.

And so relationship it was. Nearly a week since he had suggested it. Nearly a week since she had agreed.

Nearly a week since she'd seen or heard from him.

What if he didn't show up today? What if he had changed his mind? What if he had tried to call this morning to tell her that he wasn't coming? She should have returned home after picking up Cassie this morning, should have checked her machine for messages, instead of going shopping at the secondhand shops that carried her sister's favored styles.

She kicked a stone, sending it skidding across the parking lot and raising a tiny puff of dust, then glanced at her watch. The *Natchez* was already boarding for the afternoon cruise. If Smith didn't show, she decided, squaring her shoulders, she would go without him. She'd done it plenty of times before. It wasn't as if she needed or even particularly wanted company for the cruise. After all, this was a private summer ritual, one she had never shared with anyone else. There was really no reason to start now.

Then she turned, intending to head for the dock, and saw him standing a few yards away, watching her, and she knew that he was a perfectly good reason to start making a few changes in her life.

He was the best reason she could imagine.

Pushing her hands into the hip pockets of her denim shorts, she offered him a smile that neatly disguised every single doubt she'd had. "You're almost late."

"You knew I'd be here."

"Of course I knew," she bluffed. "But I figured you'd be on time."

He glanced over his shoulder. "People are still standing in line to board. I'm not late. I'm never late."

She gave him a long, head-to-toe look. *She* had dressed in her version of casual—denim shorts, a yellow cotton tank top, sandals and a ponytail secured with a yellow band. *He* was dressed in his own version of casual—tailored shorts in olive drab, neatly pleated and belted, a polo shirt in pale yellow, neatly tucked, and deck shoes. Just as she had last weekend, she wished for a shirt in a vivid jewel tone—with his coloring, emerald green would be flattering. And jeans. Soft, faded, snug-fitting jeans.

Not that he didn't look perfectly fine dressed the way he was.

He just looked *too* fine.

Too fine for her.

"We'd better get in line," she suggested. "You don't get seasick, do you?"

He chuckled. "Not since I was about five and learning to sail with my uncles."

She reached for her sunglasses, which dangled by one earpiece from a corner of her shoulder bag, and slid them into place. They shielded her eyes from the glaring afternoon sun, but she had the vaguely uneasy feeling that the dark shades offered little or no protection from the probing way Smith looked at her. "I guess back on the East Coast, you rich folks do that sort of thing, don't you?" she asked.

"I guess we do. I got my first sailboat before I got my first car. It was beautiful. You would have liked it."

Shaking her head, she gestured toward the *Natchez* with its multiple decks looming above them. "This is the only boat I've ever been on, and I have no intention of ever setting foot on anything smaller. I can't swim. I've seen floaters on the job, so believe me, drowning as a means of death holds *no* appeal whatsoever for me."

"I was a good sailor. I never sank a single boat or lost a single passenger." The line moved ahead a few feet, and they moved with it. "How can you not swim? You've lived all your life on the Gulf Coast, surrounded by water."

She had to tilt her head back to give him her driest look. "The Mississippi isn't exactly the most inviting water to jump into—or Lake Pontchartrain. And since my folks never owned a car until I was out of college, family trips to the beach were out of the question."

"There are community pools."

"Not in *my* community." Then she recanted. "Actually, there was a pool in our neighborhood. It had been

built...oh, probably in the twenties or thirties. By the time
I came along, it had long since fallen into disuse and was
about half filled with garbage.''

"Next winter I'll lease a boat and we'll sail down to the
Caribbean. I'll teach you how to swim while we're there.''

Abruptly she looked away so he couldn't see the tension
that made her clench her jaw. Winter was six months away.
She seriously doubted this *relationship* of theirs would survive half that long.

In odd vulnerable moments she wondered if *she* would
survive.

Halfway up the gangplank, they reached the reason for
the slow boarding: a photographer was stationed there,
snapping shots of the passengers. By the time the cruise
ended, the photos would be developed and offered for sale,
a few bucks a print. When he called, "Want a souvenir picture to take home with you?" Jolie smiled politely, shook
her head and started to go on.

Smith had other ideas.

Catching her hand, he pulled her back. "Sure, we do.''

"This is for tourists, Smith," she protested, trying to free
herself without a struggle.

"I've never taken the cruise before. Today I'm a tourist,
and I want the souvenir photo.''

Still she hung back. "Why?''

"To show everyone who knows you and who won't believe me when I tell them that *I* got a date with Jolie Wade.''

"All you have to do is stand still for a moment and
smile," the photographer coaxed.

She gave in only because there was a long line of passengers waiting behind them. Only because it was easier to
stand there with Smith beside her, holding on to her hand,
than to argue. Only because it was less embarrassing to take
off her sunglasses and put on a silly little smile than to cause
a scene.

Only when the photographer snapped the picture, Smith
wasn't beside her anymore; he was behind her. And he
wasn't holding her hand; he had his arms around her. And

if she was smiling, she couldn't tell because suddenly, for reasons she didn't dare examine closely, she felt like crying.

Fumbling, she replaced her glasses, then accompanied Smith to the main deck. Once they reached it, she realized that he was still holding her hand, and she pulled free. Before he could react, she had pushed both hands into her pockets and started off in search of a place to sit, leaving him to follow.

She found what she wanted on a lower deck: two chairs in a rather private corner, close to the rail, warmed by sunshine but with a bit of shade, too. She sat down, settled back and fixed her gaze on Jackson Brewery across the parking lot.

"Are you okay?"

She looked only far enough to her right to see Smith's legs, stretched out long and lean, and his shoes. "I'm fine," she replied; then, hearing the stiffness in her voice, she gave him a slow, lazy smile. "I've done this at least once a year for the last thirteen years, and I usually come alone. Remind me if I forget you're here." Not usually. Always. But telling him that might allow him to read more into the invitation than she had intended. It might make him think that he could, indeed, change her mind.

And if he believed it, he might make it so.

No matter how desperately she didn't want it.

"A Wade tradition, huh? I'm honored to be included." He narrowed his gaze against the sun until only a thin line of blue showed through his lashes. "What other traditions do you have?"

"Besides taking this cruise alone?" She emphasized the last word. "Beignets and café au lait at the Café du Monde on Sunday mornings. Watching the fireworks that close the French Quarter Festival from the promenade at Riverwalk. Running in the Crescent City Classic. Mardi Gras."

"Except for the cruise, those are all pretty general. What do you do for your birthday?"

"Dinner at Mama's with the entire family. Fried chicken, potato salad, baked beans and deviled eggs for a horde.

Carrot cake with cream cheese frosting, thirty-some candles and always one extra to grow on.''

Slouched lazily in his chair, he tilted his head to one side to look at her. "Honey, if you're thirty-some years old, I think your growing days are through." Before she could come up with a retort, he went on. "What about Christmas?"

"The usual. Christmas Eve bonfires, Papa Noel, gifts Christmas morning and a traditional dinner that afternoon."

A blast from the boat's calliope signaled that they were ready to pull away from the dock. Jolie looked down, watching as a narrow strip of brown water appeared, then grew ever wider. Soon they were in the channel and headed at a slow, leisurely pace downriver. There was a bit of a breeze off the river—warm, only mildly refreshing, smelling of pollution, industry and muddy water.

How different would it be on a sailboat in the Caribbean? she wondered as the brewery gave way to the Moon Walk, a pedestrian trail built atop the levee. Soon that view was traded, too, for warehouses along the wharves. In the Caribbean, the water was undoubtedly clearer and cleaner, and wind power undoubtedly quieter than the huge engines that drove the *Natchez*. The quarters would definitely be more intimate—room for two instead of two hundred. She could splurge on a skimpy bikini—thanks to all the thousands of miles she'd run, she had the body for one, if not the daring to wear it—and bake in the sun for hours. They could sail from island to island, and she could really play tourist for the first time in her life.

They could find a deserted island and make love on the beach.

Damn, it was hot, and her thoughts were just making her hotter.

Unable to sit still a moment longer, she abruptly got to her feet. "The invitation includes a Bloody Mary. Is that okay, or would you prefer something else?"

"That's fine. But I can go—"

She was already walking away when she turned him down. "You save our seats. I'll be right back."

Smith watched until she was out of sight, then he settled his gaze on the shore again and slowly, smugly smiled.

Jolie was nervous, which he interpreted as a very good sign. She wasn't sure she could stick to her declarations—that she didn't need a man, that she wasn't interested in having a relationship, that whatever was between them couldn't go anywhere—which meant that those chances she had described to him as nonexistent a few days ago were increasing in his favor. He intended to keep them increasing, until they overwhelmed every deterrent she might throw in their way.

He intended to win.

He hadn't been teasing, while they waited in line, about sailing away with her. It wasn't likely they could do it this winter; a trip like that needed more than the few weeks' vacation time he had coming. Someday, though, he would teach Jolie to swim and to sail. He would show her how beautiful a sunset at sea could be. He would show her the islands. He would take her miles from land, from civilization, from the world. He would make love to her under the hot tropic sun.

When he had made his suggestion last Monday, she had responded in a tight, emotionless voice. *You mean have an affair.* Of course that wasn't all he was asking of her, but yes, *hell,* yes, he wanted to have an affair with her. What man in his right mind wouldn't? She was beautiful, intriguing, passionate, strong. She would be a generous lover, but greedy as well. She would give but would also take. She would satisfy but would also demand her own satisfaction.

And *he* could give it to her, he knew, utterly certain, utterly immodest. More than any other man, more than the man she had once loved, he could give her exactly what she needed. He *was* exactly what she needed.

Someday she would see that.

He assumed from her uneasiness this afternoon that she was already beginning to suspect it.

She returned with their drinks, moving with a runner's grace, dodging other passengers and weaving around chairs and small children. He watched her appreciatively, accepting one of the cups with a murmured thanks. "What prompted the annual Jolie Wade riverboat cruise?" he asked as she settled in beside him again.

"What's prompting all the questions?"

"It was part of our agreement, remember? Getting to know each other?"

"Don't you know of any better way to do that than by interrogating me?"

He took a sip of the spicy vodka and tomato juice before replying in a mild tone. "Well, we could go back to your place or mine, take our clothes off and spend the rest of the weekend making mad, passionate love. I would know you better by Monday morning, but I'd still want to ask all the questions. I just assumed you would feel more comfortable if I asked the questions first and ravished you later."

That almost—not quite, but almost—earned a smile from her. It did earn him an answer to his original question. "When I was a kid, I used to play along the river sometimes. The steamboats and paddle wheelers fascinated me or, at least, their passengers did. All those tourists, all those people, who could afford to leave their homes and travel to another state, to stay in hotels and eat in restaurants and spend their mornings and afternoons cruising up and down the river. I decided then that if I could ever afford it, this was something I would do."

Part of him felt sorry, not for Jolie—never for her—but for the child she had once been. There was something shameful about the disparity in the way they had each grown up—about her sharing a four-bedroom apartment with fourteen other family members while he had grown up in a mansion. About a girl whose idea of extravagance was a two-hour trip on the river, when he had thought nothing of flying halfway across the world for a weekend.

In an effort to lighten the subject, he asked, "What's your favorite food?"

"Steak."

IT'S FUN! IT'S FREE!
AND IT COULD MAKE YOU A

MILLIONAIRE

If you've ever played scratch-off lottery tickets, you should be familiar with how our games work. On each of the first four tickets (numbered 1 to 4 in the upper right) there are Pink Strips to scratch off.

Using a coin, do just that—carefully scratch the PINK strips to reveal how much each ticket could be worth if it is a winning ticket. Tickets could be worth from $100.00 to $1,000,000.00 in lifetime money ($33,333.33 each year for 30 years).

Note, also, that each of your 4 tickets has a unique sweepstakes Number . . . and that's 4 chances for a **BIG WIN!**

FREE BOOKS!

At the same time you play your tickets to qualify for big prizes, you are invited to play ticket #5 to get brand-new Silhouette Intimate Moments® novels. These books have a cover price of $3.75 each, but they are yours to keep absolutely free.

There's no catch. You're under no obligation to buy anything. We charge nothing—ZERO—for your first shipment. And you don't have to make any minimum number of purchases—not even one!

The fact is thousands of readers enjoy receiving books by mail from the Silhouette Reader Service™. They like the convenience of home delivery . . . they like getting the best new novels months before they're available in bookstores . . . and they love our discount prices!

We hope that after receiving your free books you'll want to remain a subscriber. But the choice is yours—to continue or cancel, anytime at all! So why not take us up on our invitation, with no risk of any kind. You'll be glad you did!

PLUS A FREE GIFT!

One more thing, when you accept the free books on ticket #5, you are also entitled to play ticket #6, which is GOOD FOR A GREAT GIFT! Like the books, this gift is totally free and yours to keep as thanks for giving our Reader Service a try!

So scratch off the PINK STRIPS on all your BIG WIN tickets and send for everything today! You've got nothing to lose and everything to gain!

Here are your BIG WIN Game Tickets potentially worth from $100.00 to $1,000,000.00 each. Scratch off the PINK STRIP on each of your Sweepstakes tickets to see what you could win and mail your entry right away. (SEE BACK OF BOOK FOR DETAILS!)

This could be your lucky day – GOOD LUCK!

TICKET 1
Scratch PINK STRIP to reveal potential value of cash prize if the sweepstakes number on this ticket is a winning number. Return all game tickets intact.

LUCKY NUMBER

8Y 559974

TICKET 2
Scratch PINK STRIP to reveal potential value of cash prize if the sweepstakes number on this ticket is a winning number. Return all game tickets intact.

LUCKY NUMBER

2C 559974

TICKET 3
Scratch PINK STRIP to reveal potential value of cash prize if the sweepstakes number on this ticket is a winning number. Return all game tickets intact.

LUCKY NUMBER

5S 559974

TICKET 4
Scratch PINK STRIP to reveal potential value of cash prize if the sweepstakes number on this ticket is a winning number. Return all game tickets intact.

LUCKY NUMBER

9I 559974

TICKET 5
Scratch PINK STRIP to reveal number of books you will receive. These books, part of a sampling program to introduce romance readers to the benefits of the Reader Service, are free.

FREE BOOKS

AUTHORIZATION CODE

130107-742

TICKET 6
All gifts are free. No purchase required. Scratch PINK STRIP to reveal free gift, our thanks to readers for trying our books.

FREE GIFT

AUTHORIZATION CODE

130107-742

YES! Enter my Lucky Numbers in The Million Dollar Sweepstakes (III) and when winners are selected, tell me if I've won any prize. If the PINK STRIP is scratched off on ticket #5, I will also receive four FREE Silhouette Intimate Moments® novels along with the FREE GIFT on ticket #6, as explained on the back and on the opposite page. 245 CIS AS2W (U-SIL-IM-03/95)

NAME _____

ADDRESS _____ APT. _____

CITY _____ STATE _____ ZIP CODE _____

Book offer limited to one per household and not valid to current Silhouette Intimate Moments® subscribers. All orders subject to approval.

© 1991 HARLEQUIN ENTERPRISES LIMITED.   PRINTED IN U.S.A.

FOLD AND DETACH ALONG THIS DOTTED LINE—RETURN ALL GAME TICKETS INTACT.

THE SILHOUETTE READER SERVICE™: HERE'S HOW IT WORKS

Accepting free books places you under no obligation to buy anything. You may keep the books and gift and return the shipping statement marked "cancel". If you do not cancel, about a month later we will send you 6 additional novels, and bill you just $2.89 each plus 25¢ delivery and applicable sales tax, if any.* That's the complete price, and—compared to cover prices of $3.75 each—quite a bargain! You may cancel at any time, but if you choose to continue, every month we'll send you 6 more books, which you may either purchase at the discount price. . .or return at our expense and cancel your subscription.

* Terms and prices subject to change without notice. Sales tax applicable in N.Y.

BUSINESS REPLY MAIL
FIRST CLASS MAIL   PERMIT NO. 717   BUFFALO, NY

POSTAGE WILL BE PAID BY ADDRESSEE

SILHOUETTE READER SERVICE
3010 WALDEN AVE
PO BOX 1867
BUFFALO NY 14240-9952

NO POSTAGE
NECESSARY
IF MAILED
IN THE
UNITED STATES

"Music?"

"Classic rock. The Doors. Jimi Hendrix." She grinned. "Eric Clapton."

"Color?"

She tugged the ribbed knit of her shirt. "Yellow. Your turn. Food?"

"Lobster."

"Music?"

"I like practically everything."

"Color?"

"Your eyes."

When he looked at her, her cheeks were pink underneath the dark shades. "You probably don't even know what color my eyes are," she mumbled.

Smiling, he closed his eyes and tilted his face to the sun. "They're the color of the richest, deepest, finest-quality emeralds from the best mines in Brazil."

She needed a moment to absorb that before she went on. "What's your most favorite place in the entire world?"

"Here. New Orleans."

"You like it better than home?"

"This *is* home. Why wouldn't I like it better? My job's here. Michael and Remy are here." He looked at her. "You're here."

This time she grinned outrageously. "Oh, please, Smith, you're laying it on a little thick."

"If you don't like my answers," he said softly, "we can go back to talking about taking our clothes off."

"Not likely," she retorted dryly.

"Then let's talk about what we're going to do this evening."

"Another Wade tradition. I generally stay in and either watch TV or rent a movie."

"Fine. Your house or mine?" he asked. Then he added, "But let me warn you. My only television is in my bedroom, and the only place to sit while watching it is in my bed."

"Another of Lily Andrews's ideas? She probably hoped to be in bed with you."

"Maybe," he agreed. "There *are* a few women out there who think I might be worth catching."

Jolie paused in the act of removing her glasses, and for a moment her unprotected gaze locked with his. She looked so serious. "I'm sure you are," she said quietly. "I've just never been much of a catcher."

"No. But you're one hell of a runner."

Still looking at him, she cleaned her glasses, replaced them and left her chair to lean against the railing. After a moment, he followed her. "Your house is fine then," he went on as if they hadn't gotten sidetracked from the plans they were making. "You provide the movie, and I'll bring dinner. Let me warn you, though, that I don't like any of those sappy, tear-jerking love stories."

She gave him a look of pure surprise before realizing that he was teasing. "As if *I* would?" she asked disdainfully. "Watch it, or I'll borrow one of Cassie's terribly pretentious French movies with subtitles."

"I speak decent French. I don't need the subtitles."

"You would," she muttered. "And I suppose you've been to Paris."

"A time or two." Maybe that was what they should do this winter, he thought, watching as a sea gull dipped low over the water. A trip to Paris was much easier to arrange than a cruise to the Caribbean and needed far less time. He wouldn't mind visiting a few of his favorite places, renewing old memories and making new ones that included Jolie.

But, while he might well sweet-talk her onto a sailboat for a trip at his expense, he doubted he could persuade her to be so generous about flying off to Paris at his expense. Even if he offered her the trip as a Christmas gift, he had no doubt she would refuse.

But could she refuse such a gift to celebrate their engagement?

Could she refuse such a wedding gift?

As she'd done nearly a week earlier, she turned to lean back against the rail, almost but not quite facing him. "Where else have you been?"

"Most of Europe. England and Ireland. Egypt." He smiled faintly at the memories. "Once I spent a week in Moscow. My uncle was attached to the embassy there."

"All that sounds wonderful. I haven't done any travel at all—at least, none that counts."

"Then what do you do with your vacations? Surely the paper makes you take them from time to time, if for no other reason than to give the rest of the staff a break."

"I generally take a week before Christmas to help Mama get ready. The rest I take a day or two at a time."

"If you want to travel, why don't you? You're single. You don't have the responsibilities of a family. You don't have to match schedules with anyone or worry about kids. All you have to do is go and have a good time."

"Being single doesn't automatically translate into no family responsibilities. I help Mama and Daddy with Scott's college expenses—he's the youngest of the four boys—and Cassie will be starting school this fall."

Smith kept his tone perfectly neutral. "Why don't Scott and Cassie work to put themselves through school the way you did?"

"Scott has a job, and Cassie will get one. Besides..." She smiled faintly. "I remember how hard it was to work and keep my grades up and still manage to graduate in four years. College was a wonderful experience for me, but it wasn't fun. It was very hard work. I want them to enjoy it a little more than I did."

"You're a good sister. A good daughter." He paused. "If you'd give yourself the chance, one day you would make some sweet little baby a good mother."

"Been there, done that," she replied flippantly. "I told you I helped raise all my brothers and sisters. I've done enough mothering for one lifetime."

"You can't tell me that taking care of your own baby wouldn't be different—and just possibly more satisfying—than taking care of your little sisters."

She sighed exaggeratedly. "No, I can't. But I *can* tell you that I was born with a preset tolerance for mothering helpless little creatures, and I used mine up long ago. You no-

tice I don't even have a pet—not even a fish in a tank."
Finishing her drink, she looked around for a trash container. "Let's take a walk. As long as you're playing tourist, you might as well see what there is to see."

They were climbing the stairs to the next deck when she turned to look at him. Several steps higher, she was just about on eye level with him. "We didn't set any rules Monday, and maybe we should have. There's one point I want to be perfectly clear on. If you're looking for someone to spend time with, to go out with, to maybe even have an affair with, fine. I have no problem with that. But if you're looking for anything more serious . . ." She broke off, swallowed hard and looked away, then back again. "If you're looking for someone to have children with, the answer is no. I don't want that. I can't even consider it. Maybe you should give that some thought before this goes any further."

He didn't blink. He didn't flinch away from the directness of her gaze. He didn't let slip with a barrage of questions pertaining to the one part of her statement that hit him hardest: *I can't even consider it.* He simply looked at her for a long time, then nodded. "All right. You've warned me, and I understand. I'll think about it."

Was that disappointment that momentarily flashed across her face? If her glasses were off, if he could see her eyes, he would have known for sure, but even without that clue, he was almost certain of what he'd seen. Even though she claimed to want nothing serious between them, was there some part of her that would have been pleased if he'd said he was more interested in her than in having a family? Did she have some small feminine vanity that wanted to know that, if forced to choose between having her and ever having children, he would take her?

There was definitely a part of him that wanted to say it. He just wasn't sure it would be true. His life had been pretty basically planned for him since he was a child: he would go to college, then on to Harvard Law; he would establish himself in his career, get married and have a family. It was a pretty standard version of the American dream, he supposed. All parents wanted their children to fall in love, get married and have kids. Practically every unmarried person—male or female—he knew had those plans for themselves. It was what he wanted for himself. Over the last thirty-plus years, he had become so accustomed to the idea that, frankly, he just couldn't imagine a future for himself that, somewhere down the line, didn't include a wife and children.

He had never imagined a wife who wouldn't—or couldn't—have kids.

I can't even consider it.

Which was it for her? he wondered. Wouldn't?

Or couldn't?

"What do you do to stay in shape?" Jolie asked as they reached the upper deck.

He gave her a blank look, then remembered that part of their goal in spending time together was supposed to be getting to know each other better. "I play tennis and racquetball."

"Who's your favorite author?"

"I haven't had time to read for pleasure in a long time."

"Then you're too busy. What's your favorite way to spend a day off?"

"With friends." What he did didn't matter. Who he did it with did.

"What's your favorite season?"

"Summer. I like it when it's hot."

"What's your worst character flaw?"

He stopped walking, caught her hand when she would have gone on, and pulled her around to face him. She let him do so, let him continue to hold her hand. "No fair. I asked you easy questions."

"Answers to easy questions are merely interesting. Answers to tough questions tell who you are. Worst flaw. What is it?"

He gave it a moment's consideration. "Don't have one," he replied at last, grinning. "At least, nothing bad enough to qualify for 'worst.' What's yours?"

Jolie didn't need even a second or two to think about it. She'd known for a long time what her worst trait was. "Ambition."

"But ambition is what got you where you are today."

"Yes. But I've had to make some sacrifices along the way." Starting when she was eighteen and brokenhearted. She had made mistakes, sacrifices and bad choices, and she had paid for them. She would pay for some of them for a very long time.

Please, God, she silently prayed, don't let Smith be one of them.

"What's your best?"

This time she did need a few moments to think it over, to search for whatever was best in her. When she finally replied, it was with a shrug and a grin. "Ambition. It got me where I am today, and it's going to take me a whole lot further."

They walked in silence for a time before finally claiming a place that overlooked the giant paddle wheel. She was watching the wheel turn, water splashing in muddy rivulets over the white paddles, thinking how nice it was to waste a sultry hot and sinfully lazy afternoon doing nothing with someone she liked, when Smith's voice, so quiet and cautious, broke the silence.

"What kind of sacrifices, Jolie?"

Her hand, still clasped within his, went limp, but she couldn't pull free because he was holding on too tightly. Struggling to make her voice even, to hide any hint of just how difficult a question that was for her, she stared at the wheel and, just as quietly, answered. "You don't know me well enough to ask that question."

"I'm sorry." He didn't sound as if he really was. "But someday I will, and I'll ask again."

She wondered how he could sound so sure of himself—so sure of *them*—when all she had was doubts. Deciding that just this once, just for this moment, she would have faith in his judgment, she slid her arm around his waist, pulled him into a leisurely stroll along the deck and smiled up at him.

"Someday, Smith, I just might tell you."

*   *   *

Two hours later, Jolie was stretched out in one of her favorite places, the bathtub. Barely warm water covered with a layer of fragrant bubbles reached practically to her chin, one of her favorite tapes was on the stereo with the volume turned loud, and the cool air blowing from the vent overhead raised goose bumps where her wet skin was exposed—her shoulder, one knee and, propped on the faucet, one foot.

It had been a nice afternoon. At the end of the cruise, she and Smith had watched from the upper deck while the other passengers clogged the exits. Tourists were always in such a hurry, anxious to disembark and head for the next attraction. She and Smith had been among the last to leave the boat. Of course, they were fortunate enough to live in New Orleans. They didn't have to cram all its sights and sounds into a few busy summer days. They could enjoy it three hundred and sixty-five days a year.

Although not necessarily the way they had enjoyed the afternoon.

Not together.

The cruise had been different, she reflected, from the twelve or more she had taken in the past. It hadn't been as peaceful, relaxing or lazy. It hadn't been the quiet, solitary journey she had always made before. It hadn't been pensive or melancholy or just a little bit lonely.

For that she could thank Smith.

She could thank him for the souvenir, too. Rolling her head on the folded towel that served as a pillow, she studied the photograph propped up on the counter. After buying the picture, he had ordered a print for himself, then presented her with the original. She had protested, had told him that she didn't need the photo, that it was entirely too touristy a thing for her.

Secretly, she was glad he had insisted. She didn't have many mementos of her life. There hadn't been that many moments that had called for them. But the cruise—their first date, such as it was—had seemed an appropriate occasion for a souvenir. It was a time she would long remember.

The photo was a good one, a study in contrasts. There was Smith, tall, handsome and smiling. Even in the lifeless dimension of a photograph, there was an air about him, a sort of elegance. Her mother would call it breeding. Jolie preferred gentility. Grace. Class.

And then there was Jolie. What she lacked in elegance, breeding and all those other things, she made up for in ambition and attitude. She'd been born with ambition and, over the years, had cultivated attitude. If she had known at some time during those years that she was going to wind up posing for a photograph in the embrace of a man like Smith Kendricks, she would have cultivated a little grace, too. She would have made a serious effort to develop some class.

They were like two horses, she thought whimsically. Smith was the Thoroughbred—lean and long-legged, well-bred and graceful, bred for the purity of its lines—while she was more of the workhorse variety: strong, sturdy and intended for labor.

But workhorses could be valuable, too. Just as much as Thoroughbreds, they, too, could be prized for their lines. They could be pretty to look at and possess a certain grace. You're a pretty woman, Smith had told her after studying the picture, and she had wanted to believe he meant it. She *did* believe he meant it.

The compliment had brought her, still brought her, far more pleasure than it should have. She rarely dressed for effect. Her clothes were casual, her hairstyle simple, her makeup minimal. And she rarely spent more than a few necessary minutes looking at herself in the mirror. She was reasonably satisfied with what she saw and didn't often give her appearance further thought.

But it was nice to be called pretty.

It was nice to believe that Smith thought she was pretty.

The business with the photographer taken care of, they had walked to the parking lot near the Moon Walk where she had left the 'Vette, and they had confirmed this evening's plans. She had been reluctant to leave him, reluctant to bring the afternoon to an end, but finally there had been no reason to delay. The last she'd seen of him, he had been walking toward the Café du Monde. Taking a stroll around the Quarter? she had wondered, wishing he had invited her along. Or maybe he was going to visit Michael and Valery; their lovely old apartment was across the street from the café.

Only six or eight streets farther away was Serenity, and Jolie's old apartment. Only six or eight blocks, but, oh, what a difference those blocks made.

Someday, she thought, reaching for the glass of iced tea resting on the side of the tub, she might do more than tell Smith about those sacrifices she'd made. She might show him. She might take him to Serenity and give him the nickel tour. She could show him the shabby neighborhood that had produced her—the run-down house where she had lived, the grassless yards where she had played, the little park where she had lost her virginity at fifteen and her innocence at seventeen. She could show him the poverty, the aimlessness of Serenity's youth, the hopelessness of the older residents.

Would he look at her differently after seeing where she'd come from? Maybe. Poverty was a foreign concept to someone who'd been born into the sort of wealth the Kendrickses had. It was something a man like Smith could understand intellectually, but not emotionally. For that kind of bone-deep understanding, you had to live it. You had to know what it was like to do without, to want and need but never have, to be ridiculed by the younger kids at school, to be scorned by the older ones.

You had to know what it was like to go hungry.

She had been hungry, in some form or another, all of her life.

On the other hand, though, Smith could surprise her. It was something he'd been doing on a fairly regular basis lately. It would be just her luck, if she showed him Serenity, that it would only serve to impress him. That it would help him more clearly understand just how far her ambition really had taken her.

And if that was the case, if she wasn't already in love with him, she would probably fall right then and there.

Suddenly numbed by the thoughts echoing through her mind, she reached out, hand unsteady, to return the tumbler to the rim of the tub. It slipped and splashed into the water, spilling tea and ice, making her shiver.

She *wasn't* going to fall in love with Smith, she insisted to herself as she opened the drain, got to her feet and pulled the shower curtain shut. She would be his friend, would go out with him and would most likely go to bed with him, but she would not fall in love with him. That was a complication that her life couldn't afford.

But what if she didn't have a choice in the matter?

What if her most stubborn insistences and her best intentions meant nothing?

What if it happened anyway?

It wouldn't.

She wouldn't let it.

Turning the water on, she flipped the lever for the shower and got hit with a blast of cold water before a little heat seeped in. It made her shudder and step back, and it spun the tumbler at her feet in a slow circle before she snatched it up, set it on the shelf next to the shampoo, then stepped under the spray.

After her shower, it didn't take her long to get ready. Just time to dust herself with expensive powder and to spray with cologne in a matching scent. Time to choose between her usual Saturday night ensemble—shorts, a T-shirt and no shoes—and something a little dressier. Time to apply a little more makeup than normal, to dry her hair and secure it with a set of shiny gold combs instead of merely running a brush through it and calling it styled.

Smith was due at seven. At ten minutes till, she stood in front of the cheval mirror in her bedroom. She had opted for an outfit somewhere between casual and dressing to impress—a green silk blouse and a short white denim skirt that would be stunning on someone five foot seven or taller, but was appealing enough on her. She kept her jewelry simple, a delicate gold chain around her neck, a slender bangle around her wrist and earrings curved in graceful gold hoops.

Studying her reflection, she heard again the echo of Smith's compliment. *You're a pretty woman, Jolie.* The words had been simple, his tone matter-of-fact, but she had been flattered. More than that, she had been touched. In an effort to disguise just how deeply touched, she had responded dryly. *I clean up real good. Take me someplace ritzy for dinner sometime, and I'll show you.*

She did clean up nicely, she decided, turning away from the mirror to pull on a pair of loosely woven leather sandals. While she'd never had occasion to dress for something really ritzy, if he took her up on her suggestion, she just might exceed her wildest expectations.

For a few hours, at least.

Just as the tape on the stereo wound to an end, the peal of the doorbell echoed through the house. She hurried down the stairs, giving the living room a glance as she passed to make sure nothing was out of place, taking one quick moment to wonder whether she might have forgotten anything important when she had packed up her papers last week. She couldn't think of anything.

Myriad sensations greeted her when she opened the door. There was the sweet fragrance of the flowers around the porch, rising in the air as the temperature eased down. There was the slash of brilliant sun on the western horizon, turning the sky shades of gold, purple, blue and pink. There was the heat, heavy and breath stealing, easily vanquishing the cool air that seeped out the door. There were the aromas of dinner in the bags Smith carried, enticing and mouth watering, and, more subtle, the scent of his cologne.

And there was Smith himself. How did he manage to look more handsome each time she saw him? she wondered, but she didn't pursue an answer. She was afraid it might be more than she was ready to face just yet.

"That smells wonderful," she said by way of a greeting. "Let me help you."

He shook his head and retained his grip on the heavy bags. "You don't get the food until you show me the movie."

With a laugh, she stepped back so he could enter, then closed the door behind him and went to the coffee table. "For your viewing pleasure," she said with an airy sweep toward the three video cassettes there.

Setting the bags down, he examined each of the tapes. She didn't know enough about his tastes—other than that he didn't like tearjerkers—to make an informed choice, so she had gone for variety. She had picked up last year's megahit adventure movie, something that could be seen time and time again without losing any of the fun, a courtroom drama and a classic romantic comedy from the forties.

"You have good taste," he said. "For your dining pleasure..."

He announced the contents of each container as he removed it from the bags, starting with thick slabs of bread, sautéed in olive oil, flavored with garlic and still warm. Ingredients for a Caesar salad. Thin slices of roasted duck breast with sweet, fruity sauce. Wild rice. Steamed broccoli with brown butter. Chilled wine for dinner and a bottle of champagne to be poured over dessert, a salad of strawberries, peaches, apricots, blueberries and oranges.

Jolie surveyed the dinner covering her coffee table. "Darn. I guess I have to put away the paper plates and disposable cups and use real dishes now." Then she couldn't help grinning. "You do have style, Smith. Let me warn you—if this situation is ever reversed and *I'm* responsible for providing dinner, expect pizza or a bucket of fried chicken."

"I like pizza—no pepperoni, no anchovies, extra cheese. And chicken. Extra crispy." He glanced around the living room. "Want to eat here?"

"I think this dinner deserves the closest to a proper setting I can provide." Picking up the salad containers, she carried them to the opposite end of the long room, setting them on the dining table. He followed with the rest of the food while she went to gather dishes from the kitchen.

Smith poured the champagne over the fruit so the flavors could blend, poured the wine into the glasses she produced and tossed the salad. After dividing it evenly between their plates, he sat down across from her and, for the first time since leaving her in the parking lot a few hours ago, he felt himself relax. In a slow, steady drain, tension that he hadn't even been fully aware of vanished. Forget exercise, aspirin or antacid. All he needed for stress relief was Jolie. If he could come home to her every night, he would be the most even-tempered, unexcitable prosecutor in the Justice Department.

"Tell me something, Jolie," he said, his serious tone earning a quick glance from her. "Why does a beautiful woman stay home alone and watch movies on Saturday nights?"

"I don't know. *I* do it because I like being home. Because there aren't a lot of people I care to spend my free evenings with. Because going out on dates—especially when nothing is going to come of them—is an awful lot of trouble."

"I think you date the wrong men. I think you deliberately choose men you don't like enough to let anything develop. That way you don't have to worry about getting involved."

Her smile was slight and reflective. "Cassie told me the same thing. There's something humbling about getting advice on your love life from your baby sister who's young enough..."

"To be your daughter." Smith finished when her voice trailed off. "Sobering, isn't it? Here we were talking today about wanting babies—"

"And not wanting them." She was flippant again.

"And we're both old enough to be the parents of a young adult. We're both old enough, God help us, to be grandparents." He briefly considered the wisdom of continuing the subject, judged it foolish and went ahead anyway.

"Have you ever thought about that, Jolie? If you don't have children, you'll never have grandchildren. When you're eighty years old, you'll be the most famous female journalist in the world, but your only legacy will be newspaper stories that, soon, no one will care about. Your family will live on, but everything unique and distinctive that went into making you exactly the way you are will be lost. Don't you have any vanity? Isn't there some part of you that wants to believe that your best qualities will live on in your children and their children and their children's grandchildren? Wouldn't you like to think that in three or four generations, one of your descendants is going to give birth to a little green-eyed, blond-haired daughter who's as stubborn, as determined and bright and tough as you are?''

Looking up, she offered him an obnoxious smile. "If I get a vote on our conversation tonight, I'd say that we've said about all there is to say on the topic of babies and kids, and I'd like to suggest that it be placed off-limits for the rest of the night ... if not for the rest of our lives."

Stubborn. Hell, yes, she was stubborn. However, he could interpret her response one of several ways. Maybe she really was tired of the subject. Maybe she was utterly convinced that she had no mothering instincts left; maybe she truly did not want children of her own.

Or maybe she wasn't so sure. Maybe the idea of grandchildren gathered around when she was eighty and slowing down was more interesting than she wanted to admit. Maybe the idea of some future great-great-grandchild who looked like her, acted like her, thought and lived like her held far more appeal than she cared for. God knows, *he* found tremendous appeal in the prospect of children, grandchildren and great-grandchildren who shared his and Jolie's blood.

"All right," he said agreeably. "What would you rather discuss? The Falcone case? Your source?"

"You haven't mentioned it all day," she pointed out.

"It's business. This is pleasure."

"It's business that concerns both of us. And for both of us, business *is* pleasure." She flashed that damned sexy grin. "Besides, I don't believe in keeping the two totally separate. Friends discuss each other's work."

Friends. So did lovers, he wanted to point out. So did husbands and wives. Wisely, he didn't. "Okay. Your article in Wednesday's paper was a good one."

"Thank you. There'll be another tomorrow."

"And another package delivered to my office Monday?"

"Unless you'd prefer that I take it straight to Warren this time."

"Considering that I'm all that's standing between you and Shawna and a judge, I don't think you should cut me out as middleman just yet." Besides, he thought with a moment's private pleasure, it would give him an opportunity to see her tomorrow. "Any chance I can get a preview of the story?"

She shook her head.

"You're still not willing to identify your source."

"No."

"And he's still not willing to come forward."

She shook her head.

"So everything's pretty much status quo." He waited while she removed the salad plates from the table, then he served the main course. "You've met Jimmy Falcone, haven't you?"

"I've interviewed him a number of times."

"What did you think?"

She tasted the duck and made a sound of deep-throated appreciation before answering. "He was kind of charming the first time—in a sleazy, classless, chauvinistic sort of way. He thought it was 'cute' to be interviewed by a 'girl reporter.' He was condescending, amoral, offensive, and yet reasonably polite and nonthreatening. The next time he knew who he was dealing with, and he showed me as much respect as he's capable of giving any woman who isn't paid to follow his orders."

"What about the people around him?" He recited a list of names, ending with the top three: Benson, Cortese and Carlucci. She didn't react in any way to a single name.

"You don't ever see Jimmy alone. He's always surrounded by people—bodyguards, flunkies, advisors, girlfriends. But they're there to protect him and to make him feel important. They don't share his spotlight, and they don't speak at his interviews—except, on occasion, the lawyer."

"Carlucci?"

She shook her head. "He's never been around when I've met with Jimmy. It was always Mulroney."

Which meant she hadn't interviewed the old man in at least two years, because Stephen Mulroney had dropped dead on a country club golf course more than two years ago, felled by a lifetime of bad habits, rich foods and little, if any, exercise. Thanks to his caddy-driven golf cart, even Mulroney's twice-weekly eighteen holes had done less to raise his heart rate than a good argument in the bar afterward.

"Have you heard from Falcone lately?"

"No...but I expect to."

She replied so casually, as if they were discussing the weather or some other insignificant subject instead of a stone-cold killer. Smith couldn't be that casual. He couldn't even try.

"I imagine he or his lawyer will call and request a meeting," she went on. "They'll want to ask all the same questions you've asked—who my source is, et cetera. They may even offer me a deal." She softened that last part with a smile meant to remind him of the deal *he* had offered.

Smith tried but couldn't return the smile. "Dealing with Falcone can get you hurt."

"Dealing with Falcone can get me *dead*," she corrected him, suddenly serious. "I'm no fool, Smith. I wouldn't trust the man as far as I could throw him."

"If they contact you, will you let me know?"

"And what would you do? Order Shawna Warren or Remy Sinclair to protect me?"

"I would send you far away from here. I would remove you from Jimmy's reach." Now he managed a smile, but it was cool. There was nothing pleasant about it. "And don't doubt that I could do it, Jolie. The kind of money I have can buy damn near anything—including your security."

"I wouldn't go willingly."

He shrugged. "You wouldn't have to be willing."

She subjected him to a long, measuring, unwavering look. "I wouldn't forgive you for interfering," she said at last. "I might even hate you for the rest of my life."

His jaw felt tight as he forced his mouth into another smile. "That may well be. But, honey..." He waited until her gaze was locked with his before continuing. "At least you would *have* the rest of your life."

The box telegraphs to her foresta his toupde (12) pp. 264 (128). Using any visible that the rey. At He would calm he cannot to look to with his before eliminated. At least you would face the rest of your life.

Chapter 7

Jolie sat silent for so long that Smith began to wonder if he was about to be treated to a firsthand demonstration of the infamous Wade temper. Whether she had used that time to come up with arguments or simply to regain control, he didn't know, but when she finally spoke, her voice was even in pitch, sensible in tone. The perfect voice of reason.

He wasn't fooled for a minute.

"You can't do that, Smith. You can't take this—" she gestured to the dishes between them "—as permission to interfere with my work. I agreed to have a relationship with you, not to turn control of my life over to you."

"I'm not asking for control. But if Falcone threatens you—"

She interrupted him. "Jimmy isn't going to threaten me."

"What makes you so sure? Do you realize how badly you can hurt him?"

"Do you have a good case against him?"

"Yes, but—"

"So my articles and my source's information don't really affect much, do they? You may not be able to use any of the evidence, but you'll get a conviction anyway, won't you?"

"I don't know."

She smiled slyly. "Oh, come on, Smith. The trial starts soon. Don't tell me you don't have a pretty good fix on how things are going to go down."

He swore beneath his breath. "Yes, I have a strong case. I've got good witnesses. I've got a ton of evidence. The only way we could *not* get a conviction would be if Falcone somehow managed to buy off the judge and every one of the jurors."

"Which is highly unlikely, so he'll leave me alone." Her manner was light, careless. "At this point, the last thing Jimmy needs is to mess with a reporter. He'll ask me who my source is. He'll try to negotiate some sort of payment in exchange for the information. When he realizes that he can't buy me off, he'll back off, because he'll understand that you're not getting the information, either. As long as I keep my mouth shut and don't reveal my informant's identity to anyone, I can't hurt Jimmy where it counts—in court."

"And is that your plan, to keep your mouth shut? Even in court?"

The look in her eyes sobered a degree or two. "Yes, it is."

"Even if I need the information to strengthen our case?"

"You just said you already have a strong case. Good witnesses. A ton of evidence."

"Other prosecutors have built strong cases against Falcone before, and he's gotten off. You said yourself that he's the most brazen liar I've gone up against—that I could place him at the scene of a murder, present a thousand witnesses and show a videotape of him killing the victim, and he would still persuade the jury that he was innocent." He fell silent for a moment, searching for the right words. "I *want* him, Jolie. I want him more than anyone I've ever prosecuted. This is the most important case of my career, but it's not because Jimmy is the biggest crook or because he's involved in the most widespread criminal activity or because it'll be a real boost to my reputation. It's personal, Jolie. He threatened my family. He tried to destroy them. *They* put together the evidence necessary to charge him. Now *I* have to make him pay."

Jolie pushed her empty plate away. He wasn't telling her anything new. From the day last winter when he had gone to Michael Bennett and asked him to help locate Valery Navarre—witness to a Falcone-ordered hit, unwitting pawn in a conspiracy against her cousin Remy, hiding out, afraid and alone—the case had started getting personal for Smith. It had gotten *very* personal on a January Saturday night when Remy had been shot three times by one of Falcone's flunkies. Smith's degree of involvement had intensified a month later when a second attempt—this one orchestrated by Nick Carlucci—had been made on Remy's life.

Yes, this case *was* personal for him. It *was* important.

Important enough to come between *them?*

She didn't know, and she was afraid to ask, afraid of what answer he might give.

But she would find out soon enough. Unless Nick came forward before the trial, she was going to receive a subpoena from Smith's office. She was going to be sworn under oath and placed on the witness stand, and she was going to be asked to identify the source behind her Falcone series.

And she was going to refuse.

She was going to face Smith, knowing how very important this case was to him, and she was going to refuse to help him.

I wouldn't forgive you for interfering, she'd told him a short time ago, but she hadn't really meant it. She would be angry, of course, if he took the action he had threatened, but part of her would be flattered that he cared enough to worry about her, that he worried enough to risk her anger. Part of her would be touched that her safety was so important to him.

But if she refused to help him put Falcone away, if she understood the importance of this case and still turned her back, if she chose to protect Nick Carlucci over helping Smith...

She doubted he would be very forgiving.

Her voice was unsteady, a little bit scratchy, when she spoke. "You'll have to make him pay without me."

The disappointment in his gaze hurt more than she wanted to acknowledge. "Will it bother you, Jolie, if you refuse to cooperate and he gets off and goes back to business as usual? Will you feel any responsibility to the family of the next person who crosses him and pays for it with his life? Will you feel any regret over the lives he'll continue to destroy with his gambling and drug business?"

"That's not fair, Smith," she whispered stiffly.

"It's very fair."

"I can't help you convict him. All I can give you is the name of my source—but if he doesn't want to talk to you now, what makes you think he'll talk to you in court? If you force him to testify against his will, you have no guarantee at all that he'll tell the truth. He could get up there in front of the jury and be the best character witness Jimmy could ask for. What would *that* do for your case?"

"But at least *you* would have done what was right. You would have lived up to your responsibilities. What happened once we got him in court would be a separate issue. He could lie. He could help Jimmy. Or he could single-handedly put Falcone away for the rest of his life."

She shook her head in disagreement.

"How can you be so sure?"

"Because I know him." Nick did what suited Nick, with no excuses, no explanations, no regrets. She had learned that painful lesson eighteen years ago.

Rising from the chair, she began stacking dishes for a trip into the kitchen. She had set the first load on the counter and was filling the sink with hot sudsy water when Smith carried the rest in. He set them down, then moved to stand behind her, resting his hands gently on her shoulders. It was a simple touch to carry such impact.

"Business isn't always such a pleasure, is it?" he murmured, referring to her earlier remark.

"No, it isn't." She leaned back against him, feeling only comfort as his light touch altered into a full-fledged embrace. "I don't like having to make moral judgments of myself. The reporter in me couldn't live with myself if I gave up a source . . . but the person in me couldn't live with the knowledge that, even inadvertently, I did something that allowed Jimmy Falcone to go free.''

"I'm sorry. I was wrong to push you."

She breathed deeply, inhaling the scents and fragrances that were uniquely his. There was something to be said for the concept of aromatherapy, she thought with a faint smile. These particular aromas certainly had a therapeutic effect on her. They made her feel a little more secure, a little easier, a little more relaxed. They made her feel that, somehow, some way, everything was going to be all right.

They made her feel contented in a soul-deep, satisfying, gratifying sort of way that she hadn't experienced since she was a child.

"Let's leave the dishes to soak and watch one of your movies," he suggested, his voice a whisper in her ear that made her shiver. "I'll help you clean up before I leave."

His idea held a certain appeal. But so did simply standing there in the dimly lit kitchen, warm and comfortable in his embrace, thinking very little and feeling—wanting—a great deal.

With a sigh, she drew away from him, slid the dishes into the water, then dried her hands and followed him into the living room. While they watched his pick of the three movies, they shared the sofa, starting at opposite ends but moving together to eat the champagne-soaked fruit straight from the bowl and staying shoulder to shoulder, hip to hip, through the rest of the film. By the time the movie ended, his arm was around her shoulders, she was snuggled close to his side, and her hand rested on his thigh. She was unspeakably comfortable.

Without moving from her position, she used the remote control to stop the videotape, pushed the rewind button, then changed the channel to one featuring music videos. An instrumental was playing, soft, relaxing, a soprano sax backed up by guitar and the sweet melodies of a piano. It was music to relax to. Music to ease your tensions.

Music, she thought with a drowsy smile as he pressed a kiss to her temple, to make out to.

His kisses were sweet, tentative, questing. They stirred a familiar hunger deep inside her and brought to life a need that she had thought forgotten, a desire that she had convinced herself was unwelcome.

She had been a fool.

She moved until she was facing him but still in the circle of his arms. In response he lowered his head to hers, covered her mouth with his. His kiss tasted of arousal, of pleasures promised and satisfaction guaranteed. Of longing and belonging. Of passion and greed.

Oh, yes, greed. She had always been a greedy soul—she had wanted success, recognition, respect, a better life. And now this. She could learn to crave this. She could come to need this—this kiss, this intimacy, this man—to live.

Raising his head, for a moment he simply gazed down at her, drawing her own gaze to him. Something was clearly wrong with the moment, she thought whimsically. Bells should be ringing. Whistles should be blowing. Winged cherubs should be strumming soft harps.

Actually, bells *were* ringing—at least, the telephone was. Smith stroked his fingers across her lips, still parted, and murmured, "Do you need to answer that?"

She didn't give it a moment's thought. It couldn't possibly be anyone important enough to compete with what she and Smith were doing. "The machine will pick it up. Kiss me like that again."

He willingly obliged, sliding his hands into her hair, dislodging the combs there, taking her mouth in a way that already, after only one time, some part of her hidden deep inside would always recognize. But before he'd gone any further, before his tongue parted her teeth, before he claimed her sweetly, hungrily, thoroughly, the answering machine on the desk in the corner clicked on, and a long-forgotten greeting drifted between them.

"Hey, *jolie blonde*," Jamey said, the sounds of O'Shea's—a television, conversation, the clinking of glasses—muted in the background. "Just wanted to see if you're going to keep our date. Tonight, same time as usual, same place. If it's a problem, give me a call and we'll reschedule." With another series of clicks, the machine shut off again, and the room grew quiet.

It wasn't a bad message, she thought with regret as Smith put her away from him. Jamey could have come right out and said that Nick Carlucci wanted to meet her at the Serenity Street park at midnight. But no, he'd been careful. He had left a message that wouldn't arouse suspicion in anyone... except the man who had just stopped kissing her.

Slowly she lifted her gaze from Smith's shirt to his face. There was a little bit of tension in his blue eyes that hadn't been there a moment ago, taut lines at the corners of his mouth that had just appeared. He looked serious. So very serious.

"It's not a date," she said quietly. "It's just a..." She didn't know what to say. A what? A meeting? An appointment? They both smacked entirely too much of business, and Smith knew too well what most of her business these days consisted of: her source in Falcone's organization. But what other word could she possibly substitute? Conference? Engagement? Rendezvous?

It was just business—business that she didn't want anyone but Jamey to know where and when she was conducting it.

"I should have asked before I invited myself over this evening." His voice was as quiet as hers, his manner subdued. "The next time I get pushy, don't hesitate to tell me that you already have plans."

"I don't have other plans—at least, I didn't. I wouldn't even bother going except..." Except Nick wouldn't have had Jamey call if it wasn't important. Except she wanted to see if he had some new information for her. Except she wanted to ask him yet again if he would talk to Smith, if he would help her out of the mess they'd gotten her into.

Not that she expected an affirmative answer from him. Nick was an expert at making messes. When it came to cleaning them up, he was usually long gone.

"You don't owe me an explanation, Jolie." Smith's voice and his attitude put an emotional distance between them, one that he made physical as he rose from the sofa and started toward the kitchen. "If you have time, I'll help you do the dishes. If not—"

"Damn it, would you stop being so reasonable?" she snapped, rising onto her knees to watch him.

He stopped halfway through the dining room and for a moment simply stood there before turning to face her. The tension radiating from him was strong enough to make her stiffen there on the other side of the room. "I thought you liked the idea that the assistant U.S. Attorney was a reasonable man."

"I'm not talking to the assistant U.S. Attorney, and I damned sure wasn't kissing the assistant U.S. Attorney... was I?"

He drew a deep breath, then noisily blew it out. "No," he sighed. "It was just me." Coming back, he brushed his hand over her hair. "'Jolie Blonde.' You know that song?"

She nodded. It was impossible to live long in Louisiana without hearing the traditional Cajun tune about a pretty blonde—especially when your name was Jolie and your hair color was blond.

"You are a pretty woman."

She caught his hand as he started to withdraw. "Come and sit down. I'll take care of the dishes later."

Turning his hand so that he was holding hers, he pulled her to her feet. "Let's do them now, then I'll go on home and you can get ready for your..." He hesitated, then shrugged. "Non-date." Once she was on her feet, he let go and, in a few long strides, disappeared into the kitchen.

Jolie sighed regretfully. With his request—command?— for tonight's meeting on such short notice, Nick had once again proven a lesson she would never forget: his timing was incredible. Absolutely incredible. She would tell him so when she saw him tonight.

When she was sneaking around with him, hidden in Serenity's shadows.

When she should be safe at home. With Smith. Doing heaven only knows what—something sweet. Something special. Something reckless.

She gave a disgusted shake of her head.

Absolutely, god-awful incredible.

Monday afternoon found Smith in the middle of a meeting, staring out his office window, hearing the voices behind him but listening to nothing. The impromptu meeting had been going on for more than an hour, since shortly after the secretary, with a disapproving sniff, had delivered an envelope "from that reporter" to his desk. He had been waiting impatiently all morning, not for the delivery, not for the documents inside the envelope, but for a chance, however brief, to see Jolie. He had been disappointed—and still was—that she'd come so close, literally within feet of his desk, and had left without seeing him.

She had chosen to leave without seeing him.

Because of what had happened Saturday night.

Exactly what *had* happened? he wondered darkly. Who was this man she met often enough for him to tack an "as usual" onto his "same time, same place"? And if it wasn't a date, then exactly what *was* it, and why had she had such trouble finding a word for it? She was a reporter, for God's sake, with an enviable gift for language. Words were her specialty, her talent.

Yet she hadn't been able to find the words to describe the nature of her relationship with Saturday night's caller.

Because it was business? He had considered that possibility, had considered that maybe the mystery man was her source, that the casual reference to a date had been designed to mislead anyone who might hear the message or have a tap on the phone.

He had also considered the possibility that it wasn't business. That whatever was between her and the guy was very personal. After spending the better part of Sunday morning alone at the Café du Monde, he had given that possibility very serious consideration indeed.

It had been a weekend for breaking Wade traditions. First she had invited him to share the cruise she usually took alone... and then she had missed her Sunday morning ritual of beignets and café au lait at the Café du Monde.

And he couldn't help but wonder why.

"I've never seen you so distracted before."

Alexander Marshall's voice, composed of equal parts amusement and concern, penetrated his thoughts. Looking up, he realized that he and his boss were alone in the office. Shawna and the other FBI agent who had accompanied her were gone.

Smith was embarrassed by his obvious preoccupation. His thoughts occasionally wandered in meetings—when he was tired, when the material being covered was all too familiar, when he had other, more pressing business matters on his mind—but in the past few weeks, it was as if his mind had taken a vacation on him. How many times now had he been caught totally oblivious to his surroundings?

"I'm sorry, Alexander. I was thinking."

"About anything connected to this case?"

Smith's mouth formed a thin line. That was their problem: Jolie's connection to this case. If only she covered other kinds of news or he prosecuted other kinds of cases.

If only he knew where she'd gone Saturday night... and with whom... and if she had returned home alone... or if she hadn't gone home at all.

He couldn't remember ever in his life being jealous over a woman, but damned if he wasn't now, so jealous that he could taste it.

"You're wandering again." There was a faint censure in Alexander's voice. "Do you want to talk?"

Smith took a deep breath, then turned his gaze to his boss. He didn't want to go into this, didn't want to discuss his private life with anyone in the office. But since neither he nor Jolie had made any effort at secrecy and since hiding her away was something he would never even consider, their relationship was going to become public knowledge sooner or later. Under the circumstances, it would be to both his advantage and hers if he broke the news to his boss himself. It was the best way to avoid even the appearance of a conflict of interest. "I've been seeing a lot of Jolie Wade lately."

His boss sat motionless for a moment. "What do you mean by seeing? That you're friends outside the office? That you're involved in a personal relationship with her? That you're intimately involved with her?''

Smith didn't answer. He simply returned Alexander's level gaze and let him interpret that however he wanted.

"There are dozens of beautiful, rich young women out there who would be delighted to occupy your free time, gracious young women who are eminently suitable for an assistant in this office, women who were raised to be proper companions to men like you. And who do you choose?'' Alexander shook his head. "A feisty, five-foot-nothin', hell-raising, stubborn little blonde who doesn't give a good damn about being rich or gracious or suitable—and one who's involved in your current case, no less. You do know how to pick them.''

Smith remained silent.

"Well, hell. Can you honestly say this...involvement hasn't had any bearing on the way you've handled the case or the advice you've given Shawna?''

"Yes.'' He spoke without reservations, without doubts. "Jolie's cooperating with us as much as she can. I haven't done anything for her that I wouldn't do for any other reporter who was willing to work with us.''

"Can you honestly say that it won't affect the way you'll treat her in court?''

"Yes, sir.'' He could separate the demands of work from his personal life.

But he wasn't so sure Jolie could. Even Saturday evening, after those too-few and too-brief kisses that had tempted and tantalized and ultimately frustrated him, she'd had a few doubts. *I damned sure wasn't kissing the assistant U.S. Attorney... was I?* He had wondered then—and again now—if she had been aware of the soft plea in those last two words, if she had known that there was a shadow of hurt in her emerald green eyes. How would she react when he questioned her in court? How would she feel when he asked the judge to send her to jail, to lock her up with the criminals she wrote about? If she couldn't separate the prosecutor from the man in a clinch on her living room sofa, how could she ever manage it in a courtroom or a crowded jail cell?

"Isn't your life difficult enough, Smith? Don't you have enough to do without going out looking for trouble?" Alexander chuckled. "You're one of the smartest people in this office. I'd give up my retirement for another two or three just like you. But, damn, son, couldn't you have been satisfied with some sweet young demure thing who could actually help rather than hinder your career?"

Smith smiled faintly. Isn't life tough enough on its own? he had once asked Jolie. *Do you have to go and complicate everything?* And she had smiled one of those brilliant smiles that could outshine even the hot July sun and replied, "It keeps things interesting." Interesting. Hell, yes, Jolie was indeed that.

"Demure would bore me to death," he replied dryly. "Feisty, stubborn and hell raising are more to my tastes."

Rising from his seat, Alexander shoved his hands into his pockets. "If you want, when it comes time to put her on the witness stand, I can take over."

It was a tempting offer—to let Alexander be the bad guy, to let him ask her questions that they all knew her principles wouldn't let her answer, to let him tell the judge that they thought she should be locked up—but Smith shook his head. He had an obligation to do his job properly. He couldn't shirk his responsibilities in the courtroom because of his personal relationships outside.

And he couldn't shake the feeling that somehow Jolie would think less of him if he did.

"Well, keep it in mind." At the door, Alexander paused and turned back. "It would have come out sooner or later anyway, but . . . thanks for telling me. I appreciate the courtesy."

Alexander closed the door behind him, leaving Smith alone in the silence of his office. He tried for a moment to turn his attention to work, but when that failed, not surprisingly, he reached for the phone instead. It took only a moment to look up the number for the newspaper in the directory, only a moment longer to dial and a moment longer than that for the cheerful young woman who answered to tell him that Jolie was out.

Out? he wondered moodily after hanging up without leaving a message. Or not taking calls? Maybe avoiding him as she'd avoided him earlier this afternoon?

Repeated calls through the afternoon earned the same response. A call to her house got him the answering machine, where he left his only message, short and simple. "Jolie, it's Smith. Call me, will you?"

At six o'clock, he stuffed his briefcase full of files and was heading for the door when the phone rang. Wishing it would be Jolie, expecting it to be anyone but her, he returned to his desk and picked it up only to have his expectations met.

"Hey, Smith," Remy greeted him. "Do you have plans for dinner tonight?"

"No." Only hopes, he thought with a grim sigh.

"Why don't you meet us at Ralph and Kacoo's—Michael and Valery, Susannah and me?"

"I don't know. I have work—"

Remy interrupted. "Come on, the workday is over. We haven't seen much of you lately. Leave your briefcase in the office, take a break, come and have dinner. You can even bring Wade along if you want."

Smith gave it a long moment's thought. He liked the restaurant, he had to eat dinner, and he could certainly use the company. And Remy was right; they hadn't seen much of each other recently. It was only natural, he supposed, considering that Michael and Valery had been married only four months, Remy and Susannah less than that. They needed time to adjust to the changes marriage had brought to their lives, and he certainly didn't mind giving them that time and space. But he didn't want so much time and space between them that their friendship suffered. Married or not, Michael and Remy were still his best friends. They were still his family.

"All right," he finally agreed. "What time?"

"We're meeting there at six-thirty."

"I'll see you there. If I'm late, go ahead and get a table."

After saying goodbye, he glanced at his watch, then left the office. He had less than half an hour to go home, change, drive to the Quarter, find a parking space and walk to the restaurant. Less than half an hour to try once again—maybe twice again—to reach Jolie, to try yet again to put her and this jealousy that nagged at him out of his mind. Less than half an hour to straighten up and search for a better mood that might fool his friends.

No doubt he *would* be late.

Watching fish was supposed to be relaxing, to relieve stress and ease tension and generally make you a mellower person. Jolie had read that somewhere, but after spending some time gazing at the brightly colored fish in the large aquarium that separated the restaurant lobby from the bar, she couldn't honestly say she felt any mellower. In fact, she didn't feel much of anything at all except edgy. Tired. In need of a vacation.

She wished she could leave the fish to their lazy swim, go home and go to bed with the covers pulled over her head. But she had spent the better part of the past two days at home, using her answering machine to screen her calls, huddled on the sofa with the newest packet of information from Nick scattered all around her, and it hadn't made things any better.

Their meeting Saturday night hadn't been particularly productive. She had asked him to talk to Smith, and he had refused to even consider it. He wasn't interested, he was doing things his way, end of discussion. Typical Nick.

But, if his self-centered stubbornness was typical, his mood hadn't been. It had been different—darker, more reckless, more dangerous. When she had paused Sunday morning on her way out for beignets and coffee to thumb through the documents, she had found a reason for the impression of danger. She had sat down on the sofa, had gone through everything carefully—had listened to the tapes, had studied the photographs, had read the constructed-from-memory transcripts of phone calls and other conversations. She hadn't finished until late Sunday evening, and she had gone over it all again today.

Her thorough scrutiny of the evidence had left her with nothing but questions. Had Nick simply gotten careless with the documents he'd given her this time, or were his actions deliberately reckless? Was he really looking for justice, as he claimed? Revenge, as Smith suspected? Or penance, as she was beginning to believe? Was he really trying to bring an end to Jimmy Falcone's reign as the undisputed boss of organized crime in southern Louisiana? Or was he trying to bring an end to something else, such as his own ten years of criminal activity?

Such as his own life?

Behind her the door opened, letting the muggy evening air drift in, but she didn't bother looking over her shoulder. It was only six forty-five. Cassie was already fifteen minutes late for their dinner date. If she lived up to her reputation, she would be at least another fifteen minutes late.

Another fifteen minutes to brood over Nick. And Smith. And the decision facing her.

Back in college, when she was a young, idealistic journalism student, she had vowed she would be among the noblest of the noble. She would never betray a source, not even if it meant going to jail for months on end. Not even if it meant disappointing someone whose opinion had too quickly come to mean too much to her. Not for *any* reason.

But back in college, she had never imagined the situation she now found herself in. She had never dreamed that she might one day find herself about to have an affair with the attorney prosecuting the man she was writing about. She had never dreamed that she would be so disturbingly close to falling in love with a man whose goals, personally and professionally, were so at odds with her own. She had never dreamed that Nick Carlucci might come back into her life, as arrogant and selfish as ever, but with one major difference: his drive to succeed replaced by something more dangerous, more morbid, more threatening.

And it had been. While Nick might not be actively trying to destroy himself—he wasn't drinking himself into an early grave, wasn't playing Russian roulette with a loaded pistol or contemplating stepping in front of a speeding train—he *was* actively taking steps to make his own death not only possible, but damn near probable.

And he wanted to use her to do it.

"Do you think they know that, while they live a life of leisure here in this tank, back in the kitchen their distant cousins are being broiled, steamed and fried by the thousands so that we can enjoy them for dinner?"

Smith's voice startled her, then filled her with a rush of pleasure that chased away all thought of Nick. She looked from the fish in the aquarium to him, then guiltily back again. "Do you think they care?" she responded. "They're beautiful, pampered, fed daily and kept safe from predators. What's happening to the less fortunate redfish, catfish and crawfish doesn't matter to them at all." After a moment she glanced at him again. "What are you doing here?"

"I'm meeting Michael and Remy."

"Guys' night out?"

"No, their wives are with thcm. They've already been seated. I'm late."

"I thought you were never late."

"I had to make a couple of phone calls before I came." Phone calls to her? she wondered when he hesitated. Then he went on. "If you're alone, you're welcome to join us."

She would like that—spending time with Smith and his friends. Feeling for an evening that she was a part of his close-knit family. Putting aside work and worries and simply having a good time. It frightened her just how much she would like that. "Thanks, but I'm waiting for Cassie."

He moved to stand beside her, his attention focused, like hers, on the fish. "I called the paper a half-dozen times today."

"I was working at home."

"I called there, too."

She'd heard his message, brief and to the point. *Jolie, it's Smith. Call me, will you?* By the time she'd gathered up the papers on her lap and scattered around the sofa cushions, by the time she'd managed to step over a pile of cassette tapes and untangle herself from the extension cord running to the nearest outlet, the tape had stopped and he had already hung up. It was just as well. She hadn't really wanted to talk to anyone right then.

She wasn't sure she was ready now.

"I was working," she repeated, her gaze fixed on a large fish whose colors were so vivid that they were almost surreal.

Abruptly he turned to face her. Although she could see him peripherally, she continued to watch the fish. "Jolie, I don't like the way things are between us right now. I feel as if you're pushing me away, and I don't know why." He paused briefly, but when she showed no inclination to speak, he went on. "Does it have something to do with the man you met Saturday night? Are you involved with him?"

She settled for a version of the truth, the one that she thought he would probably prefer. "I'm not seeing anyone else, Smith." Continuing, she forced an uneasy little smile that the glass and water of the aquarium reflected back at her. "I haven't gone out with another man, or gone to bed with another man, or even kissed another man, in a very long time. In fact, until you came along, male companionship has been noticeably missing the better part of my life."

He didn't look reassured by her answer. If possible, his blue eyes had grown even more sober. "Then what's wrong?"

She wanted to confide in him, she realized with a slight jolt of surprise. Even if she had to confine herself to generalities, even if she had to be overly careful to say nothing that might lead him to Nick's identity, she wanted to share her suspicions with him. She wanted to show him the evidence Nick had given her this time, wanted to voice her fears, wanted to hear his opinion. She wanted his advice. She wanted the benefit of that reasonable nature of his.

Jolie Wade—who rarely confided in anyone, who often didn't care for even her editor's opinion and who never asked for advice—wanted to disclose everything to Smith and ask for his guidance. It was a miracle, she thought self-mockingly, how things could change.

But a restaurant lobby was hardly the place for unburdening herself, and this evening wasn't the time, not with his friends waiting for him and Cassie walking in the front door at that moment.

"Can we talk later?" she asked softly.

He glanced from her to Cassie, giving her sister a smile and a distracted greeting, then looked down at Jolie again. "You know where to find me." With a nod to them both, he walked away, disappearing into the rear dining room.

Cassie waited until they were seated underneath a fantastic display of Mardi Gras finery to comment. "Trouble in paradise?"

Jolie dredged up another smile. "Honey, there is *always* trouble in the adult world. Take my advice. Stay seventeen forever."

"Time moves on regardless of what we want. August fifteenth is going to be here in three more weeks no matter what."

"I remember the day you were born," Jolie murmured. "It was hot and humid, and a storm was forming on the horizon."

Cassie's laugh was as cool and quiet as that day had been sultry and loud. "You've just described the majority of my birthdays. The day I made my entry into the world wasn't remarkable."

"No, at least, not in that aspect." But it had seemed pretty damned remarkable to Jolie. What would Smith, dining in the next room with his friends, think if he knew that? Probably that he had a chance, after all, to change her mind about having kids of her own—kids of *their* own.

But if Smith, dining there in the next room with his perfectly suited, disgustingly happy newlywed friends, knew all there was to know about Jolie, there would be a change of minds, all right. *He* would change *his* mind about wanting her.

And right now, she very much wanted him to want her.

Even if it was wrong.

Even if it was only temporary.

Even if it led only to heartache.

"So what's the problem with Smith?"

Jolie's gaze drifted to the broad doors connecting the dining rooms. She couldn't see him or his friends, but she could envision them. The men's conversation would eventually come around to work; it always did. Remy or Michael would ask about the Falcone case, and Smith would tell them whatever he could. She wondered if he ever told them anything about her and, if he did, what he said and how he said it. She wondered if he called her Jolie, as Michael did, or Wade, as Remy did, or that damned reporter, as some of the others on their side of the law did. She wondered if he complained about her in that derisive way he spoke of people who interfered in his pursuit of justice.

She wondered if he had acknowledged his relationship with her to them.

Selecting a hush puppy from the bowl in the center of the table, she flippantly replied, "Smith doesn't have any problems. They're all mine."

"Have you gone out with him?"

"A time or two."

"Have you gone to bed with him?"

Jolie stopped in the act of spreading butter across the fried cornmeal to direct her startled gaze at her sister. "I don't believe that's any of your business."

"No one thinks twice about asking *me* if I'm sleeping with Trevor."

"*I* haven't asked you that. But..." Jolie grinned. "As long as you brought it up..."

Cassie's responding smile was serene and told her nothing. "Do you remember Mama's introduction to sex education? 'Sex is a wonderful experience when shared by...'"

"'A woman and her husband,'" Jolie finished. "She gave all of us that little speech. I can still remember how surprised I was when I discovered that it's pretty damn wonderful whether you're married or not. Then, of course, there's Daddy's guidelines for having sex." With a laugh, they spoke simultaneously. "'*Don't.*'"

"Naturally, that was just for the girls. He told the boys, 'Do it, but be careful.' Excellent advice from the father of thirteen." Cassie's expression grew serious. "How old were you the first time?"

Melancholy swept over Jolie, and she sighed heavily. "Not old enough."

"Did you love him?"

"As much as one foolish child can love another."

"Did you regret it?"

Did she have regrets? Without knowing or caring, Nick had changed her life in ways both good and bad. He had taught her lessons no teenage girl should ever have to learn. He had set her on the path that had brought her to where she was today. She didn't regret the loving—could never regret that—but the losing...

Oh, yes, she regretted what she had lost.

She had a heart full of regrets.

And she didn't want Smith—either loving him or losing him—to become another.

"Sometimes," she answered at last. "In some ways."

"Overall, we Wade women have good taste in men," Cassie remarked. "Seven marriages—eight counting Mama and Daddy—and not a divorce in the bunch. I think you and I have made good choices, too. In spite of his appearance and the family's prejudice against him, Trevor has some admirable qualities, and Smith...he's strong in ways that you aren't. He provides balance for you. He'll make a good husband for you."

Such a comment spoken by a seventeen-year-old girl who hardly knew the man in question shouldn't make Jolie's heart hurt, but it did. It took all her strength to hide it, to inject a careless note into her voice. "A husband?" she asked dryly. "Aren't you getting ahead of yourself there? We've only gone out a couple of times. Why, we haven't even—"

Cassie smiled that slow, serene smile again. "I didn't think so. But that's all right. Neither have Trevor and I. We're waiting." Then she shrugged, setting her long, dark hair ashimmer. "Of course, we're just a couple of kids. You and Smith, on the other hand...you're not getting any younger. What are you waiting for?"

"Similar ambitions would be nice," Jolie replied, thinking of Smith's desire for a family and her own hunger for success. "Similar backgrounds would be a plus. Jobs that didn't put us at cross-purposes would be wonderful."

"Is he still threatening to have you locked up if you don't come clean?" Although Cassie's expression was sober, there was an unmistakable hint of amusement underlying her voice.

"Not at the moment. But the trial starts next week. It's coming."

This time Cassie made no effort to hide her humor. "I'll come and visit you at the jail every week. I'll even bring you a piece of my birthday cake." Abruptly she became more serious than ever. "Daddy says the man you're protecting is scum. He talks as if he knows him."

Jolie raised her gaze to one of the costumes on the wall. Hung with its flowing cape, the dress was long, satiny, beaded, sequined and feathered in brilliant, vibrant colors. Paired with the matching headdress, it was flashy, flamboyant, outrageous—a perfect match for Carnival in the French Quarter.

Of all the people she didn't want to discuss Nick with—even more than the FBI, the U.S. Attorney's office and Falcone's people—Cassie headed the list. By the time she was born, he had been long gone from Serenity and mentioning his name in the Wade house had been strictly forbidden. It was a fair bet that most of the family had forgotten his existence.

Except Jolie.

And her parents.

They could never forget.

"*Does* Daddy know this guy?"

Jolie sighed heavily. "Sort of."

"Is he worth going to jail for?"

She didn't need to consider her answer. "No."

"Is he worth jeopardizing your relationship with Smith?"

"It's not really about him, Cassie. It's about my job and ethics and keeping promises. Journalists have to be free to report the news. They have to be able to provide some measure of protection to their confidential sources or those sources won't come forward.''

"Information that comes from sources who hide behind the shield of confidentiality isn't news, Jolie. It's rumor. Gossip.''

"Not when it's supported by documentation.''

With a careless shrug, Cassie brushed her off. Right now she wasn't really interested in a debate on ethics, Jolie knew. There were more important questions on her mind, and she asked one of them next. "How does Daddy know someone who worked for Jimmy Falcone?''

Jolie understood her curiosity. Patrick Wade was a hard-working, God-fearing man. For years he'd held two jobs to support his family, to give them the best he could. He didn't gamble, didn't run around, didn't drink more than an occasional beer or utter more than an occasional profanity. After nearly thirty-eight years of marriage, he still loved his wife more than anything in the world. He still showed respect to his elders and still had the same two best friends that he'd had in first grade. He provided guidance to his children, adored his grandchildren and attended church faithfully. How, indeed, had he come to know the kind of person who would make his career with Falcone? How had he become acquainted with someone so immoral, so dishonorable, so corrupt?

That was the problem with the mistakes Jolie had made in her lifetime. She didn't make the kind of typical little screwups that everyone else made. Her mistakes were big ones, ones that affected not only her but the people around her. Eighteen years after Nick had walked away from her, he was still affecting her life, and her mother's and her father's and, now, even Cassie's.

"He was from the old neighborhood,'' she replied at last. It was true, as far as it went. It just didn't go far enough. There had been plenty of disreputable people in the old neighborhood—poverty had a way of increasing their numbers—but her father had kept his distance from most of them, and he had urged his family to keep their distance, too.

But Jolie hadn't been able to stay away from Nick. Friendship had turned into a crush, a teenage romance into a two-year affair that had ended in heartache, depression, sorrow and major changes.

That was how her law-abiding father had come to know someone who worked for Jimmy Falcone.

That was also how her father had come to...

A small crowd of diners leaving the back room caught her attention and sent her thought trailing off, forgotten. She wanted to drop her gaze, wanted to pretend that she didn't see them, that she was too focused on Cassie to notice the Bennetts, the Sinclairs and Smith. But all she could do was look.

He was bringing up the rear, and he saw her almost immediately. He smiled, but there was something so serious about it, something almost melancholy. For a moment, she thought he was going to separate from the others and approach her—his steps slowed, and he looked as if there were something he wanted to say—but as the others went through the next doors into the main dining room, Michael turned back and spoke to him. With one last, faintly regretful look, Smith turned away and caught up with them, taking two steps out of sight.

Jolie felt more alone than she ever had in her life.

Cassie settled back in her chair, the fringe on her black dress swaying with the movement, and folded her hands together, resting them on the edge of the tabletop. "You never did give a really suitable answer to one of my earlier questions," she remarked softly.

Jolie sighed wearily. No more talk about Nick, their father or Jimmy Falcone, she silently vowed. She wasn't in the mood.

But none of them was on her sister's mind at the moment.

"Explain it to me, would you?" Cassie asked, her tone so reasonable, her gaze so knowing. "Exactly what *are* you and Smith waiting for?"

Chapter 8

Smith sat on the textured floor of the patio, his back against the glass door, his arms resting on his knees, and stared at the darkness across the river. He still wore the suit he'd worn to work that morning, though the jacket was tossed across the sofa inside, his tie dangled from a table and his cuff links had been dropped into one of Lily Andrews's ugliest and most useless contributions to his home, a free-form ashtray for a man who didn't smoke and didn't have any friends who smoked.

He had unfastened the top few buttons of his shirt, had rolled the sleeves to his elbows, but he was still uncomfortable. The fine fabric, soaking in moisture from the muggy air, clung to his skin. The temperature was typical for a summer evening—hot—but the humidity was higher than normal tonight, the air heavy and thick. Black clouds gathered overhead blocked the moon and the stars and seemed to absorb the light that filtered up from the city, allowing nothing to bounce back down. It was as if a black hole had opened up above downtown New Orleans, stealing its energy and recycling it into brilliant lightning that occasionally flashed in the night.

He should have skipped dinner tonight. If he had known that he was going to run into Jolie, if he had known what the major topic of conversation among his friends would be, he would have refused Remy's invitation and come on home. His mood had been bad enough before he'd gone to the restaurant. He hadn't needed five of the people he cared most about to make it worse.

Jolie and babies.

There had been a purpose behind the last-minute get-together: twin announcements, although neither couple had known about the other's beforehand. Valery and Susannah were pregnant, Valery about six weeks so, Susannah twice that long. Michael and Remy were going to be fathers.

It wasn't fair, Smith thought with a scowl. In less than a year, both of his best friends had fallen in love and gotten married; in less than another year, they would each have a son or daughter.

And *he* was still alone.

He was happy for his friends, truly, he was. Even though neither couple had been married long, he fully understood why they had wanted to start their families as soon as possible. Michael and Remy were his own age—thirty-seven. Michael had been through a divorce, and Remy had indulged in a number of insignificant relationships before meeting Susannah. They had both undergone major traumas in the past year or so. Michael had gotten shot, and Evan had died saving him. The resulting grief and guilt had sent Michael on a drinking binge that would have destroyed him, if he hadn't pulled out of it, as surely as a bullet to the head. Remy had survived his own shooting and a second attempt on his life, and both he and Michael had seen the women they loved threatened by Falcone.

After a tough sixteen months, they were both healthy, happy, alive and in love. They were facing futures brighter than any they had hoped for. Having children was only natural.

It was exactly what he would do if he was in their place.

But, thanks to Jolie, he wasn't in their place. He might never be.

The wind picked up a little, ruffling his hair, cooling the perspiration that dampened his skin. It was the only movement in a curiously still night. Everything seemed subdued, stifled. Sound was muted by the sheer weight of the air; scents were unable to penetrate the dense moisture-laden particles. If he was any judge of Louisiana weather—and, after sixteen years, he thought he knew his adopted home state's quirks fairly well—they were in for one hell of a storm tonight. The thunder would rumble, the lightning would crack, and the heavens would open up. Parts of the low-lying city would flood, the power would go out, and for a time, life in the Crescent City would be difficult and harsh.

Then the storm would pass and the floodwater would drain off. Closed streets would reopen, power would be restored, and the people would take stock, repair damage, deal with losses and go on with their lives. Louisianans were admirable that way—strong willed, self-sufficient, independent.

There was no denying that Jolie Wade was a Louisianan through and through.

In the darkened room behind him, the doorbell sounded, a harmonious chime, soft and subtle, that reached into every room. He considered not answering. He was tired, bad company. It was late. He wanted to sit out here in the heat, alone and gloomy, and commiserate with the weather.

But it *was* late. People rarely dropped in on him without calling ahead, particularly after eight o'clock or so. It could be important. It could be an emergency.

Or, he discovered when he crossed the room and opened the door, it could be Jolie.

Shifting uncomfortably, she looked past him into the apartment. The only light came from a small Art Deco lamp down the hall; the housekeeper turned it on when she left so he wouldn't come home to a dark, empty place.

As if a lighted, empty place was much better.

"Am I disturbing you?"

He smiled thinly as he leaned against the door. "Only for the past six months or so."

She looked puzzled, but he didn't offer an explanation. He didn't tell her that he could pin down almost to the minute when his awareness of her had changed from politely professional to purely personal. It had been in January, a sunny cold day, and she had walked into his office unannounced to take him to a meeting at the shabby motel where Michael and Valery had gone into hiding from Falcone's thugs. She had driven—as Cassie so eloquently described it—like a bat out of hell, weaving in and out of traffic, paying more attention to her rearview mirrors, watching for a tail, than to the road ahead. She had been bright and alert, excited by the story she was uncovering, and so sublimely self-confident, and he had found himself thinking as they sped along Interstate 10 that this woman was exactly what he needed in his life.

This brash, bold, aggressive woman who, frankly, scared the hell out of him.

There wasn't anything brash or bold or aggressive about her now, but she was still, now more than ever, exactly what he needed.

And she still scared him.

"I—I'm sorry. I would have called, but your number's unlisted."

"Hell, Jolie, you could have talked it out of anyone who knows me."

Her discomfort increased, showing in the shadows that darkened her eyes, and she took a backward step toward the elevator. "Maybe I should call you at the office tomorrow—"

"Please don't go." His plea was little more than a whisper, but it was enough to stop her retreat. The smile he managed to summon was shaky. "It's been a tough couple of days. I was just sitting out on the patio waiting for the storm to break and wash everything away."

Her own smile was crooked. "I used to do that when I was a kid."

"Did it work?"

She shrugged. "Everything looks brighter when it's wet and clean."

Releasing his grip on the door, he stepped back and waited for her to enter before closing it again. She walked to where the black tile of the hallway gave way to the high-gloss gray gleam of the living room and stopped. "Want a drink?" he offered. He didn't drink often and doubted that she did, either, but this night—this mood—seemed to call for something strong, with a bite.

"No, thanks. Could we go out on the patio again?"

He gestured for her to lead the way, and she did, stopping only briefly to lay her purse on the table where his tie had fallen. Outside, she walked to the rail, then turned into the wind that was picking up, kicking up dust and bits of stray leaves and blossoms from the potted geraniums. It moved her hair, too, lifting it from her neck, blowing it back and around, whipping her bangs first to one side, then the other.

He stayed near the door and watched her.

"You said it had been a tough couple of days," she said at last. "Problems at work?"

"No more than usual." He waited for her to glance his way before he went on. "I told Alexander that I've been seeing you."

It was difficult to read the emotion that accompanied the slight widening of her eyes. Was it surprise or dismay? Likely the latter. They hadn't discussed whether they would try for some semblance of privacy in their relationship, although, considering what they each did for a living, they probably should have. But he wasn't going to lie, wasn't going to sneak around, wasn't going to act as if his association with her were something to be ashamed of.

"Was that what made the day tough?"

"No. Alexander doesn't care...as long as I can still be ruthless with you in court."

She smiled faintly. "Any chance I'll be out of jail in time for Cassie's birthday the fifteenth of August?"

"I doubt it. You may not get out in time to sail to the Caribbean with me this winter."

Her smile grew a degree or two stronger. "No fair. I was looking forward to learning to swim."

"Says something about our preferences," he said dryly. "*I* was looking forward to making love to you under the sun."

His admission made her smile flicker, then fade, and she turned away again, standing this time so that the wind blew her hair around her face, hiding her expression from him. For a moment he watched her again, judging the stiffness of her spine, trying to read emotions he couldn't see. Finally he broke the silence between them. "Why did you come here tonight, Jolie?"

She faced him not because she wanted to, he knew, but because that was how she usually approached life: head-on. But it was hard for her this time, hard for her to look at him and answer his question. "I wanted to be with you."

It was a good answer, but not good enough. He wanted more. "You wanted to talk?"

"Yes. Later."

Later. A very good answer. "You wanted to watch the storm?"

She opened her mouth, moistened her lips, found nothing to say. On her second try, she smiled a sly, shy, lazy smile. "Hell, Smith, I wanted to *create* the storm."

Desire, comfortably familiar, curled in his stomach. He couldn't think of any way he'd rather spend a sultry, stormy summer night than making love, couldn't imagine any woman he would rather make love with than Jolie. Still, he didn't move away from the door, didn't approach her, didn't pull her close for a kiss. "I think you could do a damned good job of it." She possessed a brilliance, spark and heat that made lightning pale in comparison, could stir up a maelstrom of need and hunger, could take the very energy from the air and make it crackle, and she could bring relief, damp, soothing, heart-stopping relief.

Knotting his fingers behind him, he asked one more question. "Why tonight?"

Jolie had been asking herself the same question ever since she'd left the restaurant and had realized that she was headed for Smith's condo instead of her own little yellow house. None of the answers she had offered herself were particularly satisfying. Because they were adults. Because this was something they both wanted. Because there was no reason to deny their desires. Because, as Cassie had so sweetly pointed out, what were they waiting for?

The truth, plain and simple, was that she wanted him.

Plain and not so simple, she needed him. She needed his companionship. His embraces. His sweet kisses. She needed his strength. His understanding. His quiet, reliable, make-her-feel-safe presence.

She hadn't relied on any man since Nick. When she needed strength, she supplied it herself. If she needed to feel secure, she accomplished that for herself, too. She didn't lean on anyone, didn't ask support of anyone.

But tonight, in two brief instances at the restaurant, she had realized how much she had come to rely on Smith. When he had first spoken to her there at the aquarium, the pleasure that had rushed through her had been intense. It had been as if her gloomy day, for a few sweet seconds, had suddenly brightened, as if everything had been made right. Later, when he had left with nothing more than that long, disquieting look, a sudden, empty loneliness had settled over her, making her feel bluer than she'd ever been.

She had desperately wanted to be with him.

Had desperately *needed* to be with him.

At least for tonight.

Why tonight? he had asked. Why not tonight? she wanted to lightly reply, but she didn't think he would buy the response. He wasn't in the mood for teasing, for flippancy, for smug, pat answers.

"Because I need you tonight." She waited for his next question, for the question so obvious that she could read it in his eyes. *What about tomorrow?* Would she need him then, too?

But he didn't ask it. Maybe he was afraid of the answer. God knows, *she* was.

Lightning flashed around them, fingers of heat and brilliance arcing across the sky in long jagged trails, and a clap of thunder exploded, making the deck reverberate under their feet. The intensity sent shivers up her spine.

Or maybe those shivers came from Smith, who was moving a few steps toward her, extending his hand.

She hesitated a moment. It wasn't too late to turn back, to tell him that she'd been wrong to come here, to rush out the door and save herself.

Oh, but it was, a small voice whispered. It was far too late to save her heart.

Moving away from the railing, she placed her hand in his, holding on tightly as he led her inside. Behind them, the rain started, not gentle drops but a torrent falling with such force that even the closed glass doors couldn't block the sound. It softened as they reached the broad hallway, blending now with the quiet hum of the air-conditioning, then picked up in intensity again as they entered the bedroom.

He didn't reach for the light switch as they passed. The little bit of illumination that came from the lamp down the hall, coupled with the lightning outside the wall of windows, was more than adequate. It showed Jolie all she needed to see: the big bed that dominated the room.

And Smith.

He released her just inside the door, and she stayed for a moment where she was. She had never been nervous about making love—except for the very first time, when she hadn't expected pain but had gotten it, and the second time, when she had expected it but didn't get it—but she was nervous tonight. Not uncertain or having doubts—no, she was very sure that she wanted this—but *nervous*.

But she had never made love with a man so important, so sweet, so special.

She had never made love with a man like Smith.

He was waiting beside the bed, unrolling his sleeves, doing it slowly to give her time, she thought with the beginnings of a little smile. Not to entice her. Not to arouse her. Not to make her admire the way he moved, the way his long fingers folded the fabric down, smoothing it bit by bit, stroking over it. Not to make her jealous of a damned piece of cotton because he was touching it and not her.

As he finished with the second sleeve, she moved a few steps closer. He was looking at her now, watching her watch him. He began unbuttoning his shirt, his fingers finding the buttons by instinct, again taking his own sweet time at working each one free. It was such a simple act to be so erotic. To spread such heat through her. To fire such need.

When the last button was undone, before he could move to remove the shirt, she spoke. "Wait." Her voice was husky, the word thick and hoarse, but he understood. Standing motionless, saying nothing, he waited.

She was only a few feet away, but it seemed to take forever to close the distance between them. Reaching up, she slid her fingertips beneath the shirt, making only the smallest of contacts with his skin until her palms glided across his shoulders. She pushed the shirt away, following it with her caresses, sliding across his chest and down his arms, brushing feather light across his back. She touched him far more than was necessary to remove the shirt—and far less than was necessary to satisfy herself.

When at last she held the shirt in her hands, she wrapped its folds around her fingers. It was soft, damp from the humidity outside, warm from his body, and smelled of cologne—rich, sexy, designer named, but uniquely his own fragrance.

Smith gazed down at her, watching as she focused on his shirt, resisting the urge to draw her attention back to him, to pull the shirt from her hands and toss it to the floor, to add her own clothing to it in an untidy heap. He knew already that she was a sensory sort of person. She paid attention to details, to the way things felt and smelled, to the way they looked and sounded and tasted.

Moving with the leisurely grace he associated with runners, she laid the shirt aside and turned back to him, touching his arms, his shoulders, his throat, never breaking contact until her hands cupped his face. She had to stretch onto the tips of her toes to kiss him, and even then her lips brushed his throat, not his mouth. She was so forceful, so dynamic, that sometimes he forgot how short, how slender and delicate, she was. Tonight, facing the prospect of making love to her, of drawing her beneath him on the bed, of literally joining his body with hers, he found it too easy to remember. It made him feel big and clumsy.

And incredibly aroused.

She gave him a second kiss, and he bent his head to meet the third. Details. Yes, he could share her pleasure in them. Her skin was softer than he had imagined—as soft, he would wager, as a baby's. Her hair was like strands of cool satin, fine enough that the tangles from the wind fell right out. She tasted of something sweet and creamy, laced with the richness of chicory-blended coffee, and she smelled... Angling his head to deepen the kiss, he drew a full breath of wind and rain, of heat and need. Of hunger.

Jolie's hungry, Michael had told him one hot Saturday afternoon. Damn right she was—and tonight she was hungry for *him.* For the next few hours, maybe the entire night, her passion was for him. Not her career, not her ambition, not the damned Pulitzer prize she wanted so badly, but for *him.*

He wanted a lifetime of these nights.

But he would be satisfied—would pretend to be satisfied—with whatever he could get. With whatever she would give him.

While they kissed, she touched him. She stroked him, teased and tickled and tempted him. Her hands were small, her touch delicate, sometimes fleeting, sometimes tantalizingly slow. Her nails scraped across his stomach, just above his belt, making his muscles clench and ripple. When one hand slid lower, his breath caught in his chest. When she brushed her fingers in a lazy, lingering, tormenting caress across his arousal, a groan shook through him with a rumble that equaled the storm's fiercest, most intense thunder.

Ending the kiss, he raised his head and, by lamp light and lightning, for a moment he studied her upturned face. Her eyes were closed, her lips slightly parted, her expression one of desire, need... and the slightest hint of fear. There was nothing he could do about the fear, no assurances he could offer, no promises he could make, because he knew it wasn't him she was afraid of. It was herself—what she wanted, what she needed and, most of all, what she was feeling. She didn't want to be feeling things for him. After all, she was Jolie I-don't-need-a-man-in-my-life Wade, Career Woman.

And she was discovering—really discovering—that she *did* need him.

He wished he could be sympathetic... but he was too damned grateful. Too damned pleased. Too damned much in love.

After a long moment under his scrutiny, her eyes fluttered open, and she gave him a seductive smile. "In case you were wondering," she began in that husky voice that made his muscles twitch and his heart beat a little faster, "I wouldn't be offended if this first time was wicked, wild and quick."

He grinned as he began unbuttoning her blouse. "And miss out on touching you and seeing you and kissing you all over?"

"There's always the next time. And the next. And the next..." Her voice trailed off as he slid his hands inside the open shirt, filling them with her breasts, stroking them through the thin lace of her bra. Her nipples were hard, and his little caresses through the lace made them even harder—made *him* even harder.

Her suggestion, to make it wild and quick, was gaining appeal with each contact they shared, with each kiss, with each brush of her body against his. His muscles were taut, his body achingly stiff. Even her most casual touch sent sensation, edgy and hot, rippling through him... and there was nothing casual about the way she was touching him. Nothing casual about the way her hair brushed his arm or the way her breasts were pressed against his chest. Nothing casual at all about the way her fingers lightly stroked his arousal.

When she unfastened his belt, unzipped his trousers and wriggled her small fingers inside, he swore fiercely and caught her hand in his. He didn't push her away, though. For one torturous moment, he pressed her hand closer, molding her fingers more intimately to him; then, swearing again, he pulled free, stepped back and began removing the rest of his clothing. "You want wicked, wild and quick?" he asked, his voice little more than a growl.

She gave him a slow, languid smile as she slipped out of her own clothes. "This time," she murmured. "Next time we'll take it slow and easy."

Out of his clothes first, he helped her with the last of hers, then pulled her down to the bed with him. "What if we don't last next time, either?"

Wrapping her arms around his neck, she drew him close for a kiss, all heat and hunger. "Then we'll keep trying," she whispered, sliding her hands down his spine, silently guiding him between her thighs. "Until we get it right."

His own voice was as weak, as whispery. "Even if it takes all night?" Probing, he found his place, pushing against her, pushing into her, until they were intimately joined. His groan was low and strained and almost overpowered her own soft, satisfied little sigh.

It did overpower her softer, littler words. He wasn't sure what she actually said, but he knew what he thought he heard.

"Even if it takes all our lives."

Jolie lay on her side, her head resting on Smith's arm, the burgundy comforter tucked around them. They were lying close, his chest against her back, his arm over her ribs, his arousal softening now against her hip, and they were watching the storm. It had been more than an hour, and it hadn't abated.

They had made love twice, and her need hadn't abated, either.

She had been right when she'd thought that Smith's bed—and Smith's arms—would be a wonderful place to watch a storm. The openness of the glass walls served to bring nature's fury right up close and personal, but she had never felt so secure. She had never known such certainty that she was safe from harm.

That certainty should be setting off every self-defense mechanism she possessed, but she felt too sleepy, too warm and satisfied. Maybe tomorrow morning she would be alarmed, but not tonight.

Rain lashed the windows, the only way she knew for sure that the fierce winds still blew. If they were at her house, in her bed, they could hear the branches of old oaks and magnolias scraping against the siding. They could see the limbs swaying wildly, sending fantastic shadows dancing across the bedroom walls. They could hear pinecones torn free and dashed to the roof and could see the slender crape myrtles bending nearly to the ground under the onslaught. When they went outside the next morning, they would find broken flowers fallen in the mud, leaves blown everywhere, small branches torn from trees and scattered across the yard.

Lightning lit the room with a brilliance that made her instinctively shield her eyes. It was followed by a muted explosion, and the light from down the hall disappeared. The air-conditioning shut off, and the red-glowing numbers on the bedside clock went black.

"It's a good thing you came over tonight," Smith said, his voice a sleepy murmur in her ear. "You couldn't have gotten home before the storm broke, and this rain would have swept you and your little toy car away."

"And you law-and-order guys would have declared a day of celebration at finally getting that thorn out of your side," she teased. "But sooner or later, you would have missed me."

"Honey, I already miss you. Every day that you're not with me, every night that you're not lying beside me . . ."

She tried to ignore the lump forming in her throat. "Don't try to sweet-talk me, Smith. I've been too smart to fall for lines like that since I was seventeen."

"Was that when the man you were in love with left you?"

Jolie drew a deep breath. She had come here to talk about Nick—at least, that had been part of her reason—but she had wanted to discuss Nicholas Carlucci, lawyer, crook, Falcone attorney and federal Grand Jury indictee. Not Nicky Carlucci, teenage friend, sweetheart, lover and heartbreaker. "Yes," she admitted. "It was."

He was quiet a long time, quiet and still. She wished he would say something. When he didn't, she did. "You're probably thinking that, at seventeen, I was too young to know what love was."

He moved his hand, tucked underneath her between her ribs and the mattress, and began gently stroking her stomach. "I don't think you were ever young, Jolie. I think from the time you were a small child, you had grown-up needs, grown-up worries and grown-up understanding. If you say you were in love at seventeen, I believe you."

She didn't need his faith. *She* knew. No matter how young seventeen was, she *knew* what she had felt for Nick. She knew it had been real and special. But in accepting her word, in trusting her to know her own feelings, Smith had just moved her a step closer to something even more real, something even more special. How different, she wondered, was a teenage girl's love for a teenage boy from the love of a woman for a very special man?

How much more could it hurt when it ended?

"What went wrong?"

She shrugged and, in doing so, snuggled back a little closer to him. "You just said it—he left me. He fell in love with someone else, someone who made him happy in ways I didn't."

"Were you planning to get married?"

"I thought so. We had talked about it. But after he was gone, I realized that *I* was the one who had done the talking. He had simply listened, nodded and agreed, then changed the subject." Nick had never encouraged her dreams of marriage, but she'd had them anyway. After all, he loved her—he told her so every night they went out, every time they made love. Didn't that mean he wanted to marry her? Wasn't that what people in love did?

She had been such a fool. Nick hadn't loved her. He had loved being loved by her. He had loved having someone to count on and being important to someone. He had loved the effortlessness of their relationship, had loved the way she put out so easily, requiring no effort or real commitment on his part. They had been the only teenage couple among all their friends with a regular sex life, which had made him look important to the guys—and had made her look cheap.

"Were you willing to have children with *him?*"

Her chest growing tight, she injected a note of warning into her voice. "Smith..."

"Valery and Susannah are both pregnant. Michael and Remy are going to be fathers. I just found out this evening."

The tightness extended into her throat, making her sound hoarse instead of flippant. "Give them my sympathy."

Lifting his hand, he brought it down with a sting on her hip. "Don't be a smart ass, Jolie." After a brief silence, he spoke again. "Tell me one thing, would you?"

"That depends."

"The day we took the riverboat cruise, we talked about having kids, and you said, 'I can't even consider it.' Do you remember?"

She simply shrugged, although, of course, she did.

"Is this a conscious choice that you've made or...is there something physical?"

"It's a choice," she said flatly. She had to clamp her jaw shut to keep from going on, to stop herself from adding, But not *my* choice. None of the important choices had ever been hers.

"So...if it's a deliberate choice, then it can be changed."

Instinct warned her not to even consider the question within his statement, and she *always* trusted her instincts. But instead of turning away from the subject, instead of making clear to Smith once and for all that she couldn't be budged on the issue, instead of doing something seductive and bold to make him forget it, she found herself wondering about it.

Could she change her mind? After living her entire adult life utterly convinced that she shouldn't have children, that there wasn't any mothering left in her, could she suddenly decide that it was all right, after all? That there was room in her life not only for kids but for their father, too? That she was entitled to the sort of normal life that all her sisters were living? That she could make her career not her first priority, not her second but somewhere down there around number three or even lower?

Could she live with the guilt?

She was well acquainted with guilt. Nick had put her on a first-name basis with it the summer she was fifteen, and her parents and Father Francis had added to it over the next three years. Her parents were entitled—after all, they loved her no matter how badly she had disappointed them and were concerned for her—but the priest...he was a sanctimonious old man who'd had no intention of ever letting her forget her sins. Was it any wonder that she avoided church now as religiously as her parents attended?

Could she bear the guilt? It would mean new lies and new secrets. It would mean being haunted once more by old memories that had taken years of struggle to lay to rest. But she could live with it. She'd lived with guilt of some sort and of some degree for twenty years. This would simply be a different sort and a different degree.

All that aside, there was one very basic question she hadn't asked herself, one question she had never dared ask for fear the answer, no matter how deeply buried, would find its way out. Did she want a baby? Not would she have one or could she have one, but did she *want* one?

The answer was inside her, wrapped in layers of hurt and sorrow, anguish and guilt. It was a little word, a tiny word with the power to break her heart if she ever allowed it to escape. It was only three letters, a short little glide of three sounds, but she had never let herself say it. She had never let herself even think it.

Yes.

Until now.

Yes. She wanted a baby. She wanted to know what it was like to hold her own child in her arms. She wanted to nurture him, to protect him, to be there for him when he needed assurance or comfort or just a little love. She wanted to be able to claim that child at age five, age ten and age twenty, to be able to point him out and say this is my son. She wanted all the experiences—all the joys, all the tribulations, all the heartaches—of being a mother.

God help her.

God forgive her.

"I guess ignoring me is your way of saying you don't want to have this conversation." Smith pressed a kiss to her forehead. "All right. It's dropped."

For now. He didn't say it, but he might as well have. The thought hung between them.

"At the restaurant you asked if we could talk later. Is this a good time for whatever you wanted to discuss?"

Jolie held back a bleak sigh. After babies, Nick was the last thing she wanted to talk about tonight. She knew him too intimately. She didn't want him intruding any more than he already had on this new intimacy with Smith.

However, without Nick, his evidence and her articles, Smith wouldn't have gone to her house that sultry Friday evening a few weeks ago. He wouldn't have talked her into a relationship, and she wouldn't have come here tonight. She wouldn't be lying here in his arms tonight. She owed Nick something for that.

But tomorrow would be soon enough to think about repaying him.

Swallowing the lump in her throat, blinking back the moisture that thinking about a baby all her own had brought, she moved, twisting in Smith's arms until she was facing him. "I don't want to talk at all," she announced, her voice consciously provocative.

In the dim light she could see his responding smile, could hear it in his response. "What *do* you want to do?"

Laying one hand on his chest, she pushed until he was lying on his back and she was leaning over him, their bodies in close contact. "I want to see you." She pushed the covers back, exposing them both. The longer the power stayed out and the air-conditioning remained off, the warmer the room would get and the heavier with moisture the air would become. But that was all right. Even if the room temperature registered somewhere below frigid, what they were about to do would leave them sweaty and hot...and that was a damned sexy way to be.

"I want to touch you." She did so, gliding her fingertips over his chest, paying particular attention to his nipples, flat one second, pebbly hard the next. "And I want to kiss you." Rising to her knees, she bent over him, leaving a trail of kisses from his jaw down his throat, wicked, wet kisses that made him suck in his breath and caused the muscles in his belly to contract beneath her fingers. When her kisses moved lower, he groaned, and when they went even lower, became hotter, more intimate, he swore aloud. He was ready for her, she thought with a private smile. With so little coaxing, so little touching, so little playing, he was harder, hotter, needier, than ever before.

When he reached for her, ending her kisses, she let him, and when he lifted her over his hips, she settled into place, wrapping her fingers around him, guiding him inside her, sinking down until she had taken all he offered.

She sat still, her body adjusting to the intrusion of his. It was a powerful feeling, knowing that she had created such arousal in him, knowing that she could satisfy it and leave him weak...but no weaker than *he* left *her*. Such power that they shared. Such passion. Such need.

"What are we aiming for this time?" he asked teasingly, reaching up to stroke her breasts, stiffening as she finally moved against him. "Wicked and wild? Or slow and easy?"

Supporting her weight on her palms, she leaned forward and kissed him, sliding her tongue inside his mouth, tasting and testing him as she shifted back and forth, slow, lazy strokes, her hips rocking against his. Wicked and wild had its fine points—there was no denying that. Heated passion, pleasure so sweet and fast, a whirlwind of need feeding, devouring, consuming, then releasing them.

But slow and easy had its finer points, too—intensifying the arousal one achingly sweet degree at a time. Time to caress. Time to savor lazy, hot kisses. Time to absorb the myriad sensations—the feel of him, long, thick and hard, inside her. The intensity of the heat deep in her belly where she sheltered him. The tickle of his fingers where he stroked her. The sharp bite of his teeth on her nipple, shooting tiny jolts of erotic pain straight through to her core. The rough texture of his tongue and the strong sucking of his mouth as he eased the pain and made her throb for more.

Yes, wicked and wild was wonderful, but this time she wanted it...

Breaking off the thought, she claimed his mouth for a breath-stealing kiss before finally answering his question in a murmur of sound that passed from her mouth into his.

"Slow," she whispered. "And easy."

Tuesday morning was sunny and hot and promised to deliver even more of both as the day wore on. Smith stood on the patio, a cold soda making his hand damp, and gazed down at the city below. From eighteen stories up, it was impossible to see signs of damage from last night's storm, although according to the morning news, there had been flooding, trees uprooted and power lines blown down. From up here everything looked fine. Normal. Life as usual.

Power had been restored to the condo sometime in the night. He had awakened about four o'clock, according to his wristwatch, to find the hall lamp on again, the alarm clock flashing and Jolie snuggled practically underneath him as she sought relief from the air-conditioning. He had ignored the lamp, reset the clock and retrieved the comforter from the floor where it had fallen before going to sleep again. He had slept holding her close and had awakened the same way when the alarm went off at six.

Life as usual.

Not after last night.

Not without Jolie a permanent part of it.

How could he have fallen in love with a woman so totally unsuited to him? She wanted to leave New Orleans, and he intended to live the rest of his life here. She didn't want kids, didn't want marriage, and he wanted both so damned badly that it hurt. She wanted to take every risk her career offered, and he wanted to keep her safe. She was stubborn, difficult and so damned determined, and so was he.

All she wanted was her career, and all he wanted was her. A home with her. A future with her. A family with her.

Behind him the patio door slid open, and she stepped outside. She had been asleep when he'd gotten up to take a shower. By the time he'd finished, she was awake and awaiting her turn in the bathroom. They'd done little more than exchange a brief greeting before he turned the room over to her, got dressed and came out here. How would she feel? he wondered. Mornings after could be awkward, especially the first one. Would she be shy? Regretful?

Or would she be unaffected by what had passed between them last night?

He could deal with anything—reticence, embarrassment, anger, remorse. He could handle any emotion from her except no emotion at all.

She joined him at the railing, her face scrubbed clean of makeup, her hair wet and combed back from her forehead. Her clothes were rumpled, a little the worse for having spent the night on his bedroom floor.

Damn, she was beautiful.

"Good morning," he greeted her.

"Morning." Leaning over the rail, she gazed down at the street below. "From up here, you can't see any sign of the storm last night."

"What storm? I thought that was just you and me heating up the night and making the earth move."

She tilted her head back and gave him a long, level look; then abruptly sobriety gave way to a sweet, oh-so-smug and confident grin and an okay morning became good. Hell, it was better than good. It was damn near the best morning of his life.

"You're pretty damn good, you know it?" she remarked.

"You're not bad yourself, lady." He reached for her, and she came willingly into his arms. "You think you might be interested in doing it again?"

"I think I might." The teasing note faded from her voice to be replaced by regret. "We need to talk, Smith."

A chill chased away the warmth created by her body against his. Struggling to keep the accompanying tension out of his voice, he offered a soft warning. "If this is where you tell me that last night didn't mean anything, that it was only about sex, I don't want to hear it."

She didn't look up at him. Instead, her gaze stayed locked on his tie. "Last night was about a lot of things, the least of which was sex."

"I don't want to hear that it can't happen again, either."

"We both know it will."

He gently forced her head up so he could see her face. She let him, but her eyes were still downcast. "And I don't want to hear that you're sorry."

At that she finally met his gaze, and she smiled just a little. "No. I'm not sorry."

Satisfied, he slid his arms around her again. "Then I suppose it's business. Do you want to talk over breakfast? Since it *is* business, it'll be my treat." He tried to coax a brighter smile out of her. "It's not often the U.S. Attorney's office is willing to buy a reporter a meal."

She rewarded him with precisely the smile he'd wanted. "Are you kidding? Your people are just itching to provide me with not only three squares a day but also a jail cell to eat them in." She glanced around, then gestured toward the glass doors. "We can talk inside, all right? It won't take long. Then I need to go home and get ready for work."

Agreeing, he released her, then followed her into the living room. She chose a seat at one end of the sofa and sat for a moment studying the sculpture across from her before she finally spoke. "The man I met Saturday night? That was my source. He gave me some new information."

Smith sat down on a low table, a steel and granite piece strong enough to hold far more than one ugly ashtray, one discarded tie and one oversize handbag. It was solid and hard, the stone cold. "When will this stuff show up in the paper?"

"I'm not sure it will." She looked troubled, as if she would rather not be having this conversation—and definitely not with him. He understood that. No matter what had happened between them last night, no matter what happened in the future, this was always going to be a separate part of their lives. There was always going to be a time when he was, if not her enemy, well, not her friend, either. Their professional relationship would always have to contain a certain amount of distance. There would always be a certain adversarial flavor to it.

Which meant that whatever was troubling her was serious indeed if she would bring it to him for advice.

"Is there a problem with his evidence this time?"

"Yes, I think so."

"Do you think it's manufactured?"

She shook her head.

"Then what is it, Jolie?"

She started to speak, stopped, then with a heavy sigh, tried again. "I think he's trying to make it easy for Falcone to figure out who he is."

Her words hung between them, tentative and uncertain—not because she didn't believe them but because she didn't *want* to believe them. Because she didn't want to think what Smith was starting to think. After a still moment, though, she put the thought, however reluctant, however repugnant, into words.

"I think . . . I think he's trying to get himself killed."

Chapter 9

"What makes her think so?"

Two hours had passed since Smith's conversation with Jolie in his living room. She had left after giving him a hug that could only be described as clinging in all the best usages of the word. It had been as much a boost to his ego as the fact that she had confided in him about her source. He would bet Jolie Wade had *never* clung to any man—not ever.

It was a sure thing that she'd never confided in a prosecutor.

Now he was standing next to a bench that overlooked the Mississippi River. Jackson Square was behind him, Algiers Point across the wide expanse of water. Much closer in either direction were Remy, sitting on the bench, absently rubbing his thigh where the gunshot wound had healed, and Michael, at the edge of the boardwalk, his attention on the ferry making its way from Algiers to the landing at the foot of Canal Street. It was Michael who had spoken.

"Everything he's given her so far has been more or less common knowledge within Falcone's organization," Smith said. "It could have come from any of a number of people—his employees, his bodyguards, his women, his house staff or even his gardening staff. A lot of it wouldn't even have to come from someone inside. Some hotshot electronics whiz could have bugged his house and tapped his phones. A computer hacker could have gained access to his records. The photographs could have been taken from a distance with a very long telephoto lens."

"We've been studying everything, trying to narrow it down," Remy spoke up. "We've ruled out a few people who weren't around at the right times, but there's still a long list of possibles. The people closest to Falcone are loyal. They tend to stick with him until they die."

"So what's changed?" Michael asked, still watching the ferry.

Smith watched it, too, for a moment, then shifted his attention to the *Natchez*. "Jolie says the new stuff he gave her narrows the field of suspects—*significantly*. She says Falcone would have to be an idiot to not be able to figure out the guy's identity, just based on what information he's made available."

"Maybe the source is the idiot," Remy suggested. "Maybe he doesn't realize what he's given her."

Smith shook his head. "She says he's not. She says he's very bright, very logical and methodical. She says there's no doubt that he understands exactly what he's done."

"She doesn't happen to say who he is, does she?" Remy asked sourly.

"No."

"And she hasn't turned over the documents that would allow us to figure it out... or does she think we're not as smart as Falcone?"

Finally Michael turned from the river to face them. He was grinning. "You can't blame her for having doubts about the FBI," he said mildly. "After all, it *was* Jolie who discovered that your partner was on Falcone's payroll. That one sort of slipped by all you special agents."

Remy's scowl deepened, Smith noticed as he forced back his own smile, but their friend didn't say anything in his own or the bureau's defense. He couldn't, because Michael was absolutely right. The government's background check into Remy's former partner had turned up nothing out of line, while Jolie's had revealed a history of gambling, bad debts and a steady flow of cash from sources unknown. It had been exactly the information they had needed to stop the man and to make a move on Falcone.

"So what is Wade going to do?" Remy asked.

Leaning back, Smith braced himself against a square wooden planter that stood about three feet high. "I don't know. If she doesn't use the information, she's not keeping the agreement she made with her source—that he would provide the documentation and she would expose Falcone's wrongdoing. If she does use it, Jimmy will be able to figure out who's betraying him, and he'll have the guy killed. If she doesn't use it and gives it to us, *we'll* be able to figure out who it is, which, again, will be breaking the agreement she made with him to protect his identity."

"But if she doesn't turn it over," Michael went on, "she'll be breaking the agreement she made with you to cooperate in exchange for you keeping Shawna away from her. Hell, she's damned if she does and damned if she doesn't."

"An ethical dilemma," Remy said. "Who ever would have guessed that reporters even had ethics?" Before anyone could respond, though, he raised his hand to stall them. "I know, I know. Jolie's not your typical reporter. You've got a dilemma or two of your own, Smith. If she chooses to sit on this material and do nothing with it, you've got to tell Shawna."

"And when I do, Shawna's going to figure that all deals are off," Smith said ruefully. He had realized that—and its implications—pretty quickly. "She'll want to put Jolie under surveillance, get a line ID on her phone, start an investigation into her background and activities ... I know."

Michael shoved his hands into his hip pockets and rocked back on the heels of his run-down sneakers. "At least you'll be out of the decision-making process. That ought to save you a little grief."

"How do you figure that?" Smith asked.

"Well...under the circumstances...hell, you've already acknowledged to Marshall that you and Jolie are...that you're having an af—" With a shrug, he broke off and looked away.

Smith looked from him to Remy, who seemed to find the river as interesting as the tree that held Michael's gaze. "A relationship," he said quietly. "I have a relationship with her. So...I told Alexander. He told Shawna. Shawna told you—" he looked at Remy before shifting his gaze back to Michael "—and he told you."

Neither man spoke.

Now it was his turn to walk over and stare out across the river. It wasn't fair. Michael and Remy had both been allowed to fall in love privately, without anyone looking on, without censure, while for him, it had to be front-page news. Then he thought of Jolie, whose stories were almost always on the front page, and he smiled thinly. Maybe that was a bit of exaggeration...although a front-page announcement couldn't be a whole lot worse than the scrutiny they were getting from the FBI and his own office. As for the scrutiny they would face if Jolie stopped cooperating...

Every move she made would be watched. If she went to his house, if he went to hers, if they met innocently in the middle of Jackson Square, the government would be watching and making notes. There would be no more nights like last night. There would be no phone calls, no more kisses, no shared dinners, no steamy lovemaking.

If the bureau placed her under surveillance and initiated a background investigation, she would have no privacy for a relationship.

Until Falcone's trial was over, she would have no privacy at all.

They would have no privacy at all.

And that, he acknowledged grimly, meant no relationship at all.

With the television tuned, volume down, to a twenty-four-hour news channel and a guitar solo blasting from the stereo, Jolie sat curled on the sofa Tuesday evening, comparing transcripts she'd made from some of Nick's tapes against her own notes from an earlier interview. The interview had been conducted back in late February when Falcone's house of cards had come tumbling down around his ears. It had been Jolie's first meeting with Susannah Duncan—now Sinclair. Susannah had recounted for Jolie the details of her numerous phone conversations with Nick Carlucci regarding Falcone, who had used Susannah's younger brother to blackmail her, and his plans for getting rid of Remy once and for all.

Much of the interview had gone into Jolie's article; the rest was documented in these notes and preserved on a cassette tape neatly filed away at work. Although Jolie hadn't listened to the tape in months, with the help of her notes, all the pieces of the conversations remained clear in her mind. She knew what threats Nick had delivered for Falcone, knew what questions he had asked and what answers Susannah had given.

Now she knew something else, too.

In passing Susannah's information on to Falcone—information that the old man had intended to use to track Remy's movements, to learn his habits, to make it easier to kill him—Nick had lied.

He had lied to his boss.

He had taken all the information Susannah had given him and twisted it and turned it into something believable but bearing little resemblance to its original form and then had given it to Falcone. Granted, Jimmy had made his move against Remy anyway, but Nick hadn't helped. Susannah hadn't helped. The fact that Jimmy's hired killers had almost succeeded had been purely the luck of the draw.

The other woman had felt so badly over what she'd done, Jolie remembered, that she had been willing to die to give Remy a chance to live. At least this news ought to ease her lingering guilt a bit. Thanks to Nick, she'd done no harm.

They had briefly touched on his dealings with Susannah in one of their conversations, Jolie recalled. *You made a big mistake when you tried to use Susannah Duncan to get to*

Remy Sinclair, she had taunted him. *You didn't count on her falling in love with him, did you?*

And his response had been flat, empty of emotion. *I didn't count on her doing anything. I didn't count on her at all.*

What was his game? What did he want from Jimmy Falcone? Justice, he had claimed—but justice for what? What had Jimmy done that had driven Nick to such elaborate lengths to punish him? Which of his innumerable crimes had affected Nick personally?

The loud knock at the door behind her startled her from her musings. Rising quickly to her feet, she stuffed the papers into a file folder and hastily slid them underneath the sofa before approaching the door, barefoot and wary.

It was Smith waiting there. She had invited him over, but she hadn't expected him until seven, and it was only... A quick glance at her watch made her sigh exasperatedly. It was seven o'clock straight up.

Opening the door, she stepped back and waited for him to come inside. Once the door was closed again, it seemed the most natural thing in the world for her to step into his arms for a long, leisurely kiss.

This wouldn't be so bad, she thought as he pulled her closer, kissed her harder, more greedily. To come home from work every day to this—to Smith, to a kiss and a family and so much more. Maybe she could do that. Maybe she could be happy working the rest of her life for the *Times-Picayune.* Maybe she could give up the crime scenes and the criminals and the trials—or at least give up some of the risks associated with them. Maybe...

Maybe.

Smith ended the kiss, raised his head and gazed down at her. There were stress lines at the corners of his eyes and around his mouth, as if he'd had yet another tough day. It couldn't have been any worse than her own day.

Raising his hand, he brushed her hair back from her face, then let his fingertips glide along her jaw to her throat. "Hell, Jolie, what are we going to do?" he asked, his voice soft, his smile tired.

"I don't know." She wasn't sure if he was referring to their professional problems or the more personal, more intimate, situation between them, but her answer remained the same. "We could rent that sailboat we talked about and run away for a while."

"Maybe by the time we got back, this entire case would have gone away."

"I don't know. I don't think Shawna's going to let it go away without the pleasure of seeing me behind bars for at least one night."

"She doesn't have much tolerance for you," he agreed.

She chuckled. "Remy tolerates me. Shawna hates me. So..." Leaning back against the cradle of his arms, she smiled up at him. "How was your day?"

"Not good. How was yours? You reach a decision yet about your guy?"

"He's *not* my guy, and no, I didn't. I will, though. I'm convinced that if I give it enough thought, I'll come up with a thoroughly brilliant solution that will make everyone happy."

She expected him to laugh or at least smile at her smug confidence, but he looked even more melancholy than she'd been feeling lately. "I certainly hope you do," he murmured. He brushed a kiss across her temple, then finally released her. "Do you want to go out somewhere or order in?"

What she wanted was to forget about dinner and simply take him upstairs to her bedroom, but she didn't suggest it. Somehow it seemed too forward.

Then she rolled her eyes heavenward. What were the first words that most people used to describe her? Bold. Brazen. Aggressive. Pushy. Brash. Who would ever believe that Jolie Wade found herself in a situation where she didn't want to seem forward?

"Order in?" she echoed, feigning surprise, thickening her Southern accent. "Honey, when I invite someone over for dinner, I spare no effort or expense. I intend to make our dinner myself in my own kitchen."

He did smile just a little at that. "You can cook?"

"I'm the oldest of thirteen children. You bet I can cook."
After a moment, she relented. "However, that doesn't mean
I ever do. I stopped at the deli on the way home and picked
up sandwich stuff. When we're ready to eat, I'll make our
sandwiches and dish up the potato salad and baked beans
with my own hands."

"By all means, use a spoon," he said dryly. Then, after
giving her a long look, he softly asked, "Are you hungry?"

She swallowed hard. "Not particularly. Are you?"

"Not at all."

"I guess we'll have to amuse ourselves for a while."

He nodded agreeably. "Maybe work up an appetite."

She tugged the collar of her shirt, then fingered the top
button. It seemed to be growing much warmer in the room,
even though the air conditioner was running and the ceiling
fan turned overhead. Chances were good, of course, that it
was just the way Smith was looking at her that made her so
warm. As if he'd been without a woman far too long. As if
he couldn't imagine any other woman he'd rather be with.

Hell, he was looking at her in exactly the same way she
was looking at him.

Wickedly.

Wantonly.

Returning to the door, she twisted the lock, then headed
for the stairs. When she passed Smith on the way, she caught
his hand and pulled him along—up the stairs, down the hall,
into her bedroom at the back of the house. Evening light
filtered through heavily leafed trees to dimly illuminate the
room and its furnishings. Knowing they would likely wind
up here, she had taken a little time after work to straighten
up, but he probably couldn't tell. She had too much stuff
and too few places to put it.

But he wasn't looking at the room or the things that cluttered it.

He was looking at *her*.

Using his hold on her hand, he pulled her closer until only
their clothing separated them, and he kissed her. It was a
sweet kiss, tentative, promising passion, pleasure and
delight...all in good time. It was the sort of kiss given by

people who were intimately familiar with each other, people who had shared a past, people who were guaranteed a future. It was a serious, beyond-an-affair, more-than-just-lovers sort of kiss.

It threatened to break her heart.

Or put it back together again.

When it ended, he slid his fingers through her hair, gently tugging out the glittery band that held it off her neck, letting it fall to cover his hands and to swing lightly across her shoulders. "I like your hair," he murmured.

Of its own will, her mouth curved into a smile. "I like yours, too. Of course, I like damned near everything about you."

"You're not too crazy about my job, huh?"

"No more than you are about mine."

"I'll turn in my resignation tomorrow."

As he began a series of slow, lazy caresses across her scalp and down her neck to her shoulders, she sighed softly and let her eyes flutter shut. "Right. And miss out on the biggest case of your career?"

"Big criminal cases come along often enough. There will be one bigger, more important and more complex than this one."

"Ah, so you wouldn't give up prosecuting the bad guys. You would just change the office you do it from."

"That wouldn't help much, would it?" He added kisses to his caresses, little ones, light, teasing, soothing. "I could always go into private practice. Instead of prosecuting the bad guys, I could start defending them."

"No, you couldn't." She spoke with certainty. He was too honest, too by-the-book, to use his brilliant career and his sterling reputation to help people like Falcone walk away scot-free from their crimes. "You could only defend the innocent, and so few people are innocent anymore."

"Then that would give me more time with you."

"And what would we do with this extra time?"

He kissed her again, stealing her breath, making her knees go weak, sending heat searing through her. She clung to him for support, pulling at his clothes and her own as they made

their way blindly to the bed, as they sank down together,
powerless, powerful, hot and ready. He shifted over her as
if he'd been there a thousand times or more. She opened to
him as if she had welcomed him often, as if she would welcome him always. He filled her, pushing slowly, sinking
deeply until she sheathed him, heated, moist, tight, and then
he gave her a long, lazy kiss before answering her question.

"I'm sure we'd think of something."

The sun had set and night had truly fallen before either
Smith or Jolie stirred from the bed. He was the one to move,
to untangle his arms and legs from hers, to slide back the
quilt she had pulled over them, sit up and turn on the bedside lamp.

The lamp's light was softened by its frosted glass globe,
but it was enough to banish the darkness from all but the
distant corners of the room. It was enough to show him the
details of the room where Jolie slept. Where she dreamed.

It was as cluttered as his bedroom was spare, as old-
fashioned as his was modern. The walls were papered in a
floral print of cream, pale green and paler rose, and the
furniture consisted of mismatched pieces—a brass bed, a
cherry armoire, a wicker settee and an oak dressing table,
complete with marble top, framed mirror and a low, petit-
point-topped stool. The settee and a rattan trunk in the
corner held quilts, both relatively new in comparison to the
one that covered the bed, and there was lace everywhere—
the curtains at the windows, the pillows on the settee, the
doilies that protected the top of the dressing table and the
nightstands.

Soft colors, old lace and quilts, antique furniture. He
smiled. Jolie, tough and independent though she was, had
a romantic streak.

He wondered how he could make it pay off for both of
them.

Rising from the bed, he picked up the rumpled pile that
was their clothing and sorted through it until he'd located all
but his shirt. He took his time dressing, in no rush because

he felt lazy and perfectly relaxed and because Jolie, lying in bed, seemed to enjoy watching him.

"Do you want to have dinner now?" she asked, her voice thick, her smile satisfied.

He zipped his trousers, then fastened his belt. "That's a tough choice."

"In what way?"

"Do I stay here and watch you lie there naked, or do I become quite possibly the only man in Orleans Parish to enjoy a dinner prepared by Jolie Wade's very own hands? Fixing dinner for a man...you know, that's such a womanly, wifely sort of thing to do."

She threw a pillow at him, then drew the quilt back over her, tucking it underneath her arms as she sat up.

"Covering up does no good, sweetheart. I'm intimately familiar with what you're hiding. I remember every little wonder and every little flaw."

"What flaws?" she asked indignantly, lifting the quilt and giving herself a quick once-over.

He returned to the bed and bent to kiss her full on the mouth. "You don't have any flaws—not a single one. You're gorgeous. Beautiful. Thoroughly desirable."

"And you're a very smart man." She took the pillow he was holding and tucked it behind her back.

Leaving her there, he turned his attention once more to the room. Cobalt blue bottles shared the broad windowsill with small pots of ivy. Crystal atomizers in deep amethyst, citrine yellow and faceted rose were lined up on the dressing table, and strings of cheap plastic beads in garish colors—throws, or souvenirs thrown from Mardi Gras floats during past Carnivals—hung from the top corner of the mirror.

Stopping in front of the dressing table, he picked up the only atomizer that held perfume and sniffed the sprayer. Jolie's fragrance filled his senses before he returned it to the marble top and moved on to the next area of interest: a wall filled with framed photos. In the center was a backyard shot, informally posed, of the entire Wade clan, with Jolie sitting on the ground in front, a nephew on each knee and a niece hanging around her neck. In a haphazard pattern around that one were individual and family pictures, snapshots and portraits commemorating births and birthdays, graduations, weddings and anniversaries.

"Let me make a wild guess and say that Cassie is your favorite sister," he said, noticing that a disproportionate number of the photos were of the youngest Wade.

"She was born just before I started college over in Mississippi," Jolie replied, an odd tone to her voice. "She's the only one of the kids that I didn't help raise."

He took down one of Cassie's pictures from the wall for a closer look. In it her gaze was direct and level—no shyness, flinching away or mugging for her. She simply looked straight into the camera and, in exchange, let it look straight into her. "She's a beautiful child. She must leave a trail of broken hearts wherever she goes."

"Starting when she was born." The strange quality in Jolie's voice grew stronger, prompting Smith to glance over his shoulder, but she wasn't looking at him. Instead, her gaze was focused on her hands, folded tightly together in her lap.

He turned back to the wall, intending to replace the frame on its hook, then go back to the bed, but the cardboard in the frame had slipped a few inches. "This back is a little loose," he remarked, turning the frame over to slide it into place. As he did so, a small piece of paper slid out from between the layers and fluttered to the floor. He bent to pick it up. "If you add an extra sheet of cardboard, it will hold it more securely...."

His voice trailed off, the thought forgotten while he studied the fallen item. It wasn't paper but another photograph, three and a half by five inches, the colors faded. It was a snapshot of Jolie, very young, short and reed thin but somehow stronger looking than today. Standing in front of a shabby house with a cluttered porch and barren yard, she was with a young man—a boy, really—who stood behind her, his arms possessively around her, and they were laughing for the camera.

Smith smiled as he looked at her captured-on-film image. Even in this flat, lifeless medium, she had presence. She looked so damn alive that he almost expected to hear her laughter. "No wonder Cassie's breaking hearts," he said softly. "She learned from her—"

A choked sound from the bed interrupted him. He turned and saw that Jolie had risen to her knees. Her face had gone pale, and she was clutching the quilt with one hand. The other hand was extended to him in an unspoken plea.

He followed her gaze to the snapshot. She obviously wanted it, obviously didn't want *him* handling it. But why? It was just a picture of her and an old boyfriend. It wasn't as if he were going to get jealous of a relationship that had ended years before he'd even met her. He might envy the young man with the dark hair and dark eyes for being a part of her life at a time when *he* hadn't been, but...

Suddenly he became still, focusing on the boy. The young man with the dark hair and dark eyes... the *familiar* young man with the dark hair and piercing, intelligent, empty dark eyes. Only they weren't empty in the snapshot; there was emotion there—passion, happiness. *Now* they were empty. *Now* they were soulless.

The muscles in his jaw growing tight, he stared harder at the boy, willing the familiarity to fade and the features to shift and change into the face of a stranger. But the longer he looked, the harder he looked, the more offensively familiar the boy became.

The more distraught Jolie became.

The colder Smith became.

Forcing air into her constricted lungs, Jolie maneuvered free of the covers, slid to her feet and wrapped the quilt tightly around her. She took the few steps necessary to bring her close to Smith and took hold of the photograph. For a moment he tightened his own grip as he continued to stare, although now he couldn't see anything, because she had placed her fingers dead center over her and Nick's faces.

But he didn't need to see.

He had already recognized them.

He had already recognized Nick.

After a time, she pulled, and he let the slick paper slide from between his fingertips. She didn't look at it but simply opened the nightstand drawer, dropped it inside, then closed the drawer again.

A glance at Smith showed that he hadn't moved. He was standing utterly still, a stunned—and more than slightly repulsed—look on his face. Would he think less of her because of her poor taste in boyfriends twenty years ago? Under ordinary circumstances, she had no doubt that the answer would be no. He was too incredibly reasonable and logical for that.

But these weren't ordinary circumstances.

Nick wasn't merely a sorry excuse for a teenage boyfriend.

And Smith was probably feeling none too reasonable.

She traded the quilt for her robe, belted it tightly, then went to the window to gaze out. After more heavy silence than she could stand, he finally spoke. "You were in love with Nicholas Carlucci." His voice was strained from the effort he made to keep it level and flat, but accusation slipped in anyway.

"I was *seventeen*. I was a child."

"With *Nicholas Carlucci*." He shook his head in dismay. "For God's sake, Jolie, the man is *scum*."

"He was a boy who had the same dreams I had. He understood me better than anyone else ever had. He wanted what I wanted." She smiled faintly, remembering all the years she and Nick had been friends and the short time, less than three years, that they'd been more than friends. As a rule she preferred not to remember anything good from that time, but she *did* have some good memories. They'd just been forgotten under the weight of all the bad.

"He was the one who left you—the one who fell in love with someone else."

She nodded, watching her reflection shift and shimmer in the window glass.

"Is he the reason you swore off men? The reason you decided to devote your entire life to your career? The reason you decided you don't need a man in your life?"

"He's part of it. Not all, but part."

Behind her, Smith combed his fingers through his hair. "For God's sake, Jolie, you were a kid. Kids date, fall in love and break up all the time. It's a normal part of growing up. You don't let it affect your entire life. You don't let something a teenage punk did eighteen years ago determine how you live now."

"I said he was part of it," she repeated, turning to face him, wrapping the loose ends of her belt tightly around her fingers. "Just part."

He started to speak, then broke off. Coming to stand directly in front of her, only inches away, he forced out the question. "Do you still care for him?"

"I quit saying nightly prayers asking God to punish him about fifteen years ago." Then she blew her breath out in a heavy sigh. "For a long time I hated him as much as I had loved him. For the better part of the last eighteen years, I've despised him. He had such potential, such incredible promise for a kid who grew up the way he did. Just getting into college was such an accomplishment, and earning his law degree... and he threw it all away on Falcone. He sold out. He became exactly what he had been hoping to escape."

"Do you still care for him?" Smith repeated, the edges of his words a little sharper.

"I feel sorry for him." Though, heaven knows, Nick would hate that. He had endured years of pity and charity and had hated every moment of it. He'd had a wealth of pride but nothing else; having to accept all the things—food, clothing, a place to live—that others gave him had cost his pride deeply.

Smith came even closer, and his voice dropped to little more than a murmur. "Do you still care for him?"

She drew a deep breath. "In ways."

He withdrew fractionally. His eyes narrowed, and his mouth thinned.

"I don't love him. I never could. But he was too important a part of my life for me to feel nothing."

For a moment he stared at her, disappointment darkening his eyes. Then, abruptly, he turned away and began searching for his shirt. It had been kicked underneath the bed; one cuff stuck out, bright white against the multihued hooked rug there. "I have to tell Shawna," he remarked, sounding all business except for the tightness in his voice.

She couldn't control the dismay that colored her own voice. "That Nick Carlucci and I were teenage lovers?"

He shot her an annoyed look. "Come on, Jolie. Don't deny that he's the source you've been protecting all this time."

Surprised, she leaned back against the window jamb. Her source. She had forgotten about that. Somehow the conversation—for her, at least—had been totally personal. Business hadn't entered into it, hadn't crept even partway into her thoughts. She had forgotten about the articles, about Nick's role as her source, about her promise to protect his identity from the government.

But Smith hadn't forgotten.

How ironic. Here *she* was the one who was supposed to be so thoroughly professional, the one whose career was supposed to be the focus of her entire life, and yet, in the past few minutes, she hadn't given one thought to work. But Smith—you-can-have-it-all—career-marriage-children-Smith—had been dealing with the information on both a personal and professional level from the start. He had immediately understood the implications of her history with Nick.

She couldn't help wishing the situation was reversed—that *she* had shown a little more awareness professionally... and that Smith had shown a little more concern personally.

"You can't tell her, Smith."

He finished buttoning his shirt before looking at her. "Give me one good reason why I shouldn't."

She had no reasons to offer, nothing rational, nothing reasonable. Nothing but the most personal reason of all. "Because I'm asking you not to."

For a moment, just a moment, he looked sad enough to break her heart. Then his gaze hardened, his jaw tightened, and his demeanor turned chilly. "I'm sorry, Jolie," he said stiffly. "But that's not good enough."

He turned away, making little noise as he left the room. Feeling more than a little sore inside, she went after him. "Smith, please... I gave Nick my word that I would protect his identity."

"But *I* didn't."

She stopped at the top of the stairs, gripping the banister tightly with both hands. "I'll deny it," she said, her voice steady in spite of the quaking inside. That brought him to a stop near the bottom of the stairs, made him slowly turn back to look up at her. "We both will. We've been careful. We've covered our tracks. There's no way—" as long as the government didn't connect either of them to Jamey O'Shea "—to tie us together. You won't be able to prove anything."

"You had an affair. You were in love with him." His smile was icy. "I think that ties you together."

"An affair that ended *eighteen years* ago. Not even Shawna will be impressed by that. I'll swear that I haven't seen him or spoken to him since he dumped me."

His smile faded and was replaced by myriad emotions— regret, sorrow and, hurting most of all, disappointment. She had lived half her life with disappointment—her mother's, her father's, her own. It had helped shape her, had helped make her into the woman she was today. The woman who wasn't quite good enough. The one whose mistakes were infrequent but major. The one who couldn't help but let down the people she loved. The one who didn't quite deserve the people she loved.

Now one of those people was looking at her with such disappointment.

"You would lie to the FBI to protect Nick Carlucci." He spoke flatly, not needing an answer, but she offered one anyway.

"As easily as you would betray the trust he placed in me."

He stood there a moment longer, infinitely weary. Then he took the last few steps down, crossed to the desk in the corner and picked up the phone there. His gaze never wavering from her, he dialed Shawna Warren's number. In a few cold, clipped sentences, he gave her the information she'd spent the past couple of weeks trying so hard to find out.

Jolie sank down on the top step. Her decision all those years ago to deny herself personal relationships had been a good one, it seemed. For the first time since Nick, she had gotten involved with a man, and for the second time, including Nick, she had somehow screwed up. She had failed again...only this time the failure extended into business. She had violated her professional ethics by making it possible for Smith to learn the identity of her informant. She had broken her promise to Nick. She had betrayed his trust.

Downstairs in the center of the room, Smith was uncomfortably watching her. "They're going to bring him in tonight for questioning."

She didn't respond.

"I need to be there."

She still said nothing.

"I'm sorry, Jolie, but...you have your ethics, and I have mine. If I hid Carlucci's identity from the FBI, I'd lose my job. I'd be no better than he is."

She knew what he was saying was true. She understood. She didn't even blame him for what he had done.

She blamed herself.

"It's better this way, Jolie. We need him to testify against Falcone next week. Until then we can keep him safe. We can protect him from Falcone *and* from himself. And it gets you off the hook, too. If we have Carlucci, we won't have to subpoena you." He tried a smile, but it wouldn't form. "I won't have to ask the judge to lock you up."

She was ashamed to admit even to herself that she found some small measure of comfort in that. But she still said nothing.

"Jolie, please..."

"You'd better go." She spoke at last but refused to look at him. "You don't want to keep them waiting."

He stood still for a time, then finally turned toward the door. There he stopped and looked back at her. "I'm sorry, Jolie."

After the door closed with a click behind him, she sighed. It sounded lost and unsteady in the quiet house. Then, her shoulders rounded, her movements lethargic, she got to her feet and headed for the bedroom. She went to the phone on the night table, and as she dialed the number she'd memorized a few weeks ago, she voiced her own regretful apology.

"I'm sorry, too, Smith. I'm so damned sorry."

When Smith arrived at work Wednesday morning, he was summoned to a meeting in the conference room. Though it was still early, Alexander Marshall and the others—Shawna Warren and a number of other agents who were working with her on Jimmy Falcone and the many associated cases—all looked as if they'd been up and working for hours, which they probably had.

They hadn't picked up Nick Carlucci last night. When the agents assigned that task had arrived at his house, a small guest residence on the grounds of Falcone's estate, they had found him gone. They had waited the rest of the night—their replacements still had his place under surveillance—but he hadn't returned.

Smith hoped Carlucci's sudden disappearance was mere coincidence. He hoped the lawyer had spent the night with a woman or made a long-scheduled visit to family or had some other mundane, ordinary excuse for being gone last night of all nights.

He hoped Falcone hadn't figured out the identity of his betrayer and eliminated him.

He hoped Jolie hadn't been foolish enough to warn Carlucci of his impending incarceration.

Dear God, he hoped she wasn't involved.

Alexander greeted him with a weary nod and gestured for him to join them around the conference table. Acknowledgment from the others varied, ranging from uneasiness to outright hostility from Shawna. So much for his hopes, he

thought, suspecting what she was about to say before she
even opened her mouth, but still praying he was wrong.

He wasn't.

"We know why we missed Carlucci last night," she announced. "What time did you leave Wade's house last
night?"

"Right after I called you."

"About 9:15?"

He shrugged. He hadn't looked at his watch, hadn't had
any interest at all in keeping track of time last evening.

"I got off the phone at 9:10 exactly," she said. "I figure
you took a few minutes to say good-night, then you were
probably out the door by 9:15."

Smith shrugged again. "That sounds reasonable. Why?"

"You know we have a line ID on Carlucci's phone."

He nodded. They'd had it for months; *he* had been the
one to go before the federal magistrate and ask for the warrant that allowed them to install it. It had come in handy in
connecting Susannah Sinclair to Carlucci, and her cooperation, along with her brother's, had led to a string of indictments against Carlucci, his boss and a number of his
partners in crime.

"He got a call last night at 9:17. It lasted three minutes
and twenty-one seconds." Shawna paused to give import to
her next words. Smith knew all too well what they would be.
"The call came from Jolie Wade's house."

"She warned him, Smith," Alexander said quietly. "The
minute you walked out the door, she was on the phone to
him."

He couldn't say he was surprised. He *could* say he had
used bad judgment in leaving her. There hadn't been any
reason for him to leave right away. He had known it would
take time for Shawna to contact the two agents she would
send, had known it would take more time for them to drive
to the compound where Falcone and Carlucci lived, get
Carlucci and drive back downtown. At the very least, he had
been looking at about an hour's wait—had everything gone
according to plan.

But he hadn't wanted to wait out that hour at Jolie's. Not feeling the way he had felt. Not with her looking the way she had looked. He had needed to get away, to consider what he had learned, to put everything into perspective. He had needed to examine the state of their relationship and whether there was anything left to salvage.

He had wanted to be alone.

And that made it *his* fault, not Jolie's, that Carlucci wasn't in protective custody. *His* fault that they'd lost their best witness against Falcone.

"Didn't it occur to you that she might do just that?" Alexander asked.

Smith looked at him. "No, sir, it didn't." What *had* occurred to him after he had left was that he and Jolie might have made love for the last time. That this could be a test their relationship might not survive. That, in fact, their affair might have already ended, even though there was so much they hadn't done yet, so much he hadn't said yet.

Such as *I love you.*

He had never considered the possibility that while he was feeling miserable over her, *she* was warning her old friend. Her old boyfriend. Her old lover.

But he should have. It was so typical of her. Her behavior—to anyone thinking clearly—would have been predictable.

"For all we know, Carlucci could be out of the country by now," Shawna said glumly. "Since we don't have him, I propose we make the best of what we do have—Jolie. We can make a number of charges against her. Then, maybe the next time something like this comes up, she and her fellow journalists will think twice before they interfere."

At the head of the table, Alexander stood up. "That will be all for now, Smith."

For a moment he ignored his dismissal. He had never been excluded from such a meeting before, not in all the years he had worked in this office. But it was his own fault. He had chosen to get involved with Jolie, even knowing that the job—his or hers—might come between them.

Now it had.

They were going to discuss the action they would take against Jolie—surveillance, investigation or outright arrest were a few of the options—and he was being excluded from the conversation. He wanted to stay, wanted to argue on her behalf, wanted to make them see things from her point of view, that she'd had an obligation to Carlucci.

But he could never make them fully understand her motivation, because he didn't fully understand it himself. Even knowing what had once been between her and Nick Carlucci, he still couldn't understand why she would put herself at risk to protect him.

He didn't understand at all how she could place her loyalty to Nick above her feelings for *him*.

Rising from the chair, he turned stiffly to Alexander. "I'm sorry. I should have expected..."

"You're a lawyer, not a cop. At least you got us a name. Now it's the FBI's responsibility to find him and bring him in."

His boss's words were intended to make him feel better. They didn't.

He left the room—left them to plan their strategy against Jolie—and went to his own office, settling into his chair, turning as he so often did to gaze out at the city.

You're not too crazy about my job, he had acknowledged to Jolie last night. *I'll turn in my resignation tomorrow.* At the time, he had been teasing, and she had known it. He had never considered exactly how long he would stay with the U.S. Attorney's office... but he had never considered leaving it, either. He had never thought about what he would do when—or if—he left government service. He had a job he liked, a job that challenged him, one that he'd proven he excelled at. The salary was decent, the location perfect, the people he worked with likable. He was satisfied with everything about this job, so why waste time even thinking about looking for something new?

Because of Jolie.

Because, as far as she was concerned, this job was a liability.

Because, as far as his job was concerned, *she* was a liability.

What would he do if he left the U.S. Attorney's office? Going to work for the Orleans Parish District Attorney was one possibility…but that wouldn't resolve the problems. He doubted that Jolie was held in any higher regard by the D.A.'s office and local-level law enforcement, Michael and a few others excepted, than she was at the federal level. Private practice was always an option, but he really couldn't see himself handling divorces and civil suits, and she had been right last night about criminal law. He couldn't defend people he knew were guilty. He just couldn't.

That didn't leave much. Corporate law, which would bore him in no time. Teaching, something that held zero interest for him. Maybe politics. There were lots of Kendrickses in politics, although he had never imagined he might be one of them. Beyond that, he was fresh out of ideas.

Since both his career *and* Jolie's were a problem, it would be easier if *she* would switch. She wouldn't even have to quit her job. She could simply give up the crime reporting and do something else. The *Times-Picayune* was filled every issue with non-crime-related stories; someone was writing those stories, and there was no reason why that someone couldn't be Jolie.

But they didn't give Pulitzer prizes for writing about street repairs or garden parties or new industry coming to town. She would never give up her shot at being the best, and, in her opinion, the best wrote the hard-hitting stories. Neither street repairs nor garden parties nor new industry come to town packed a hard enough punch to qualify.

But if he was willing to give up *his* job, if he was willing to change the entire focus of his career, then *she* had to be willing to give him something in return.

A baby sounded just about perfect.

What he was suggesting was a compromise, a concept that was probably damn near alien to Jolie. She gave in on occasion, but always unwillingly and only when she felt she had no choice. Did he want her that way—unwilling and without choice?

His scowl slowly gave way to a smile, one that was thin, humorless and filled with regret. Did he want Jolie that way?

Damned right he did.

He wanted her any way he could get her.

Chapter 10

Jolie sat on a bar stool at O'Shea's, her feet dangling inches above the floor. If she pointed her toes straight down, she could rest them on the crossbar—just barely. She didn't try, though; she simply let them dangle.

She had never been one to hang out in bars, had never had the money or the time or the inclination, but she could understand the appeal such places held for people who were down. The worn, torn shabbiness of O'Shea's was a perfect match for the way she felt in spirit.

It was Wednesday morning, a few minutes after ten, and she felt as if she carried the weight of the world on her shoulders. She hadn't slept well last night—had blamed her restlessness on the heat, although the air conditioner had kept the temperature at a chilly sixty-eight degrees, or on mysterious hot-and-muggy-weather ions or on full-moon craziness. Truth was, she had been restless because she was alone. Because her pillows and the old quilt that covered her bed had smelled of Smith. Because he had looked at her with such disappointment. Because he had left her with that quiet apology and that sorrowful expression in his eyes.

Because she was afraid he might not come back.

She had already heard that the FBI's plan to pick up Nick last night had been a bust, and she knew that they must know—that Smith must know—she was the one who tipped him off. She hadn't meant to send him into hiding. She had simply wanted him to know that she hadn't intentionally betrayed him. She had wanted him to be prepared so that when the agents arrived, he wouldn't do something foolish or reckless. She hadn't intended for him to go on the run and possibly place himself in danger.

She had wanted, she admitted gloomily, to salve her conscience. She had wanted to be able to say to herself, "All right, I made a mistake. I shouldn't have allowed Smith to discover Nick's identity, but since I did, I've done what I can to make it up to Nick."

But what she had done was wrong. It was liable to drive her and Smith even farther apart. It was sure to increase the disappointment she'd stirred in him. It could even cost Nick his life.

God help her.

With a sigh, she glanced at her watch. Less than ten minutes had passed since Jamey had arrived at the bar from somewhere down the street and unlocked the doors. Time sure flew, she thought sourly, when you were utterly miserable.

After dozing fitfully toward dawn, she had gone for her morning run, only to give up after less than a mile and return home. There she had showered and dressed for work, then gathered all the material Nick had given her at their last meeting. It was still in her car, tucked under the seat in its green accordion folder. She would do something with it today—would give it to Shawna or maybe take it by Smith's office. She wasn't above trying to buy her way back into his good graces.

In fact, that was why she was here. After a few fruitless hours at the paper, she had mumbled some excuse, wandered out and wound up here. She needed Jamey's help.

She had been waiting outside, along with a painfully shabby old gentleman, when Jamey had opened the doors five minutes before ten. He had greeted her with no more than a nod before turning his attention to the old man, fixing him a cup of coffee and sliding a couple of beignets onto a napkin to accompany the whiskey he was also serving. The two men were talking now—or, at least, Jamey was. His was the only voice she could hear, his questions unimportant, his remarks casual. *How are you feeling today? I didn't see you around yesterday. What do you think of this heat? Is there anything I can get for you?*

She wondered if there was anyone else to ask the old man about his health, anyone else to notice when he didn't come around. Probably not. At least he had Jamey.

Finally Jamey returned to the bar, offering her a cold soda, fixing himself a glass of iced water. She had never seen him drink, not even beer, not even when they were kids. Granted, his father *was* an alcoholic; that was the best reason of all, she supposed, not to drink.

But, if that *was* his reason, he had certainly picked a strange profession for himself.

"You're a good man, Jamey O'Shea," she remarked, popping the tab on her soda can.

He followed her glance to the old man, then shrugged. "Uh-huh. I know you well. When Jolie Wade comes around with compliments, she's wanting something. What is it you want today, half-pint?"

Her flippant answer came automatically, without an ounce of lightheartedness. "To be five foot ten and beautiful."

"You don't ask for much, do you?"

"Only six inches and a new face." And a chance to relive the past twenty-or-so hours. But as long as she was wishing, she wouldn't turn down a chance to relive the last twenty years.

"There's nothing wrong with the face you've got." He went to turn on a fan at the end of the bar, then returned. "Nothing wrong with being short, either. Plenty of men like women who are little and delicate." With a sidelong look and something close to a smile, he added, "I hear Assistant U.S. Attorney Smith Kendricks is one of them."

The mention of Smith's name added a new shade of blue to the moroseness she was already feeling. She had wanted to call him—in the middle of the night, around dawn, this morning—to apologize for warning Nick, but she had been afraid to, afraid that he wouldn't understand why she'd done it, that even if he did understand, he wouldn't forgive her.

She wasn't exactly sure she understood herself.

And if anything happened to Nick, she knew she would never forgive herself.

"Right now Smith Kendricks prefers any kind of woman over the kind that I am," she said bleakly. "He found out about Nick."

"That he's behind your articles about Falcone?"

She nodded. "And that he and I were..." She let it trail off with a shrug. She didn't have to be more specific. Jamey probably knew more about her and Nick twenty years ago than anyone else... but even he didn't know everything.

"And it makes a difference to him?"

"I don't know," she replied honestly. "Maybe it does."

His expression made it clear what he thought of that. Of course, Jamey had a strong streak of forgiveness in him; he'd had to develop it in order to deal with his mother and father. He'd had plenty of practice at forgiving people their shortcomings.

She doubted that Smith had ever known anyone with failings like hers.

And he didn't yet know her biggest secret of all.

That was something he might never understand. She would know how Smith would react—if Jamey could help her, if Nick would—tonight.

With a sigh, she got down to the point of her visit. "Have you seen or talked to Nick since last night?"

He looked at her head-on, his blue gaze steady. He could be about to tell her God's honest truth or to spin the most outrageous tale, and his expression would never change. There would be nothing in his eyes to declare that this was the truth, nothing to hint that it was a lie. "If you're going to ask where he is, save yourself the trouble. I don't know.

I imagine someplace where the FBI and Falcone can't find him." He used a metal scoop to pour ice into his glass, then refilled it from the tap. "If you're going to ask if I know how to get hold of him, I think I could manage. I can't guarantee, though, that he'll want to talk to you or meet with you or anything like that."

Her mood sank a notch lower. "He must be pretty angry."

"Not angry. Just looking out for himself. You know, you're probably pretty hot right now. Having any contact with you could get him caught."

"I imagine they're running a background check on me, and they've probably tapped my phone, but I'm not being followed—not yet, at least. I never would have come here if I was."

Jamey shrugged. "It doesn't matter to me. I can't tell the feds anything that two dozen other people on this street can't. I don't have anything to hide from them. My business is legit, my background is clean." Leaning on the bar, he grinned. "I'm a responsible, law-abiding, upstanding citizen. Who ever would have believed it?"

Jolie smiled faintly in response. There had been more than a few uncharitable souls on Serenity twenty years ago who were convinced that none of them would amount to much of anything—not Jamey, Nick or her.

They had been more right than wrong.

Mimicking his position, she took a deep breath. "If you can get in touch with him, ask him to meet me as usual tonight. Tell him I'm sorry I screwed up, and tell him that, if he'll come, I'm bringing Smith Kendricks with me."

It wasn't a great plan—she would be the first to admit it. Smith might not agree without notifying the FBI first or insisting that they be present. She might get him there, only to find that Jamey was unable to reach Nick or that Nick had chosen not to trust her again. Even if Nick did show up, even if Smith did go without notifying Shawna Warren, there was still plenty of room for things to go wrong. Nick could refuse to listen to Smith. Smith could refuse to listen to *her*. Smith could feel that what little she was offering—a face-to-face meeting with Nick, no more, no less—wasn't enough to make up for what she'd done last night.

In fact, the plan was downright lousy. But it was the best apology she could offer.

"Do you want me to let you know what Nicky's answer is?" Jamey asked.

"No. I'll be there either way. If he doesn't show, then I'll know."

"That park's not a safe place at night."

"Hopefully, Smith will be with me."

He made a face at that. "Big deal. Like prosecutors don't get mugged in this city?"

She forced a halfhearted grin. "I run fast and scream loud. If I get into trouble, you'll hear me all the way down here."

"You need to get into a new line of work, one where running fast and screaming loud aren't considered vital skills."

She slid slowly to the floor, her gaze steady, her voice quieter. "I've been thinking about that." All too often lately she had found herself thinking that maybe being a reporter wasn't all there was to life. Maybe she could be a few other things, too.

Like a wife.

Or maybe...

Even thinking about it hurt, but maybe, just maybe, she could even be a mother.

If it wasn't too late.

If she hadn't ruined everything.

Balancing her purse on the bar stool, she rummaged inside for some money. When she offered a buck for the drink, he shook his head. "My treat."

Digging inside again, she came up with a five and laid them both on the counter. "Buy your friend some lunch," she suggested as she turned away. She was halfway to the door before he spoke.

"Hey, *jolie blonde*."

When she looked back, he looked as serious as ever.

"You're not so bad yourself." Then he grinned. "If things don't work out with Kendricks, come on back here. I'll fall in love with you myself."

She thought of that heart-sore possibility—that things might not work out with Smith—but managed a faint smile anyway. "Watch out, O'Shea," she warned over her shoulder as she walked away. "I just might take you up on that."

The last person Smith had expected to see when his door-bell rang late that evening was Jolie, but there she stood, looking lovely and nervous and as if the past twenty-four hours had been as difficult for her as they had been for him. He wanted to draw her into his arms, wanted to kiss her, wanted to pretend that they didn't have more problems than any couple should ever have.

But, unsure that she would come to him willingly, unsure that he could let her go if she did, he didn't reach out. He didn't touch her at all, even though he ached to. He simply looked at her.

She hesitated, obviously uneasy, then gestured inside. "Can I come in?"

She had been nervous the last time she'd come to his house on a sticky, hot evening. They had made love that night—only two nights ago, he realized with a jolt of surprise. He felt as if he'd known her forever, as if they'd been lovers forever.

He felt as if he had loved her forever.

He stepped back, far back so they wouldn't accidentally touch, and waited for her to enter. After she did, after the soft shuffle of her footsteps on the tile floor had faded, he closed the door and moved to follow her. She was waiting for him in the living room, not seated comfortably but standing, as she had once before, in front of the sculpture. She wasn't looking at it, though. Even from this side view, he could tell that her gaze, and her thoughts, were far from this ugly mass of glass, stone and steel.

Finally, when the silence in the room grew heavier, thicker, taking on a form of its own, she faced him. "I'm sorry I warned Nick."

The apology should have been enough. He shouldn't need an explanation, but he did.

"Why did you? You were worried about him. You were concerned that he was setting himself up so Falcone could kill him. If we had been able to pick him up last night, he would be in protective custody. Falcone *couldn't* get to him. He would be safe. But, thanks to you, he's still out there somewhere. He's still within Falcone's reach." Hearing the accusatory note in his voice, he broke off, drew a deep breath and asked once again, more quietly this time, "Why did you do it, Jolie?"

"I made a promise to Nick that I would protect his identity, and I broke it. It wasn't intentional, but the results were the same. I betrayed his trust. I screwed up." She shrugged, setting her hair ashimmer. "I had an obligation to tell him what I had done. I asked him not to leave his house, not to go into hiding, but that was his choice. Don't you see, Smith? Whatever he did had to be *his* choice. I had no right to reveal his identity to you, and I had no right to decide that he should be taken into protective custody or forced to co-operate with you against his will. He had to make that decision for himself. I had to let him do it."

He wrapped his fingers around one of the sculpture's protruding glass rods. It was smooth, cold, lifeless. In this condo he was surrounded by cold, lifeless forms. As soon as the Falcone trial was over, he decided, he was going to hire some movers to get rid of every piece that could be moved except Michael's painting, and he was going to start over, choosing his own furniture, his own art. Better yet, instead of movers, he might just call a Realtor and start looking for an entirely new place to call home. Someplace cozy. Someplace warm and inviting. Someplace that suited him.

Someplace like Jolie's place.

But he could move into the coziest, most inviting house on the market—hell, he could duplicate Jolie's little yellow house right down to the cobalt blue bottles on the windowsill and the framed bits of lace on the walls—but without her, it would still be cold. Empty. Unwelcoming.

The way his life would be without her.

Compromise, he reminded himself. That was what they had to learn to do.

In that spirit, he could see the logic that had led her to warn Carlucci. The rational part of him could even understand it. Carlucci had made it clear from the beginning that he didn't want to deal with the government. He had known that, at any time in the past few months, he could walk into Smith's office with his evidence and cut a deal to hang Falcone and save himself, and he had chosen not to. He had turned down Smith's request through Jolie for a meeting. Whatever his reasons, he had wanted to handle things *his* way, and being taken into protective custody by the FBI wasn't part of his plan.

But Smith still thought Jolie had been wrong to call him.

"What if he gets killed, Jolie?" he asked quietly. "What if Falcone figures out who his leak is and kills him?" He paused, but she wasn't eager to reply. "Carlucci lives in one of the houses at Falcone's compound. It's maybe a hundred yards from one house to the other. Do you think Jimmy hasn't noticed that he's gone? That he took off in a hurry last night and hasn't come back? Do you think that doesn't make Jimmy wonder? Maybe he asks a few questions, maybe he figures out a few answers...and maybe Nick Carlucci turns up a floater in Lake Pontchartrain. What then, Jolie?"

For a moment she looked so weary, so defeated. He had never imagined that the brash, bold, aggressive woman he knew so well could look so utterly lost. And there was nothing he could do to help her.

"I made a mistake," she said, her voice low and empty of life. "I shouldn't have warned Nick. I should have let your people surprise him. I just wanted him to know...."

"Know what? That his cover was blown? That we were coming? Or that you didn't give him up voluntarily?" He knew that last was her answer. Her promise, her integrity and her reputation meant too much to her. She had wanted Carlucci to know, above all else, that she hadn't broken her word, that Smith's uncovering of his identity had been a fluke and nothing more. "Why, Jolie? Why do you care what Nick Carlucci knows? Why do you care what he thinks? He's a corrupt lawyer, for God's sake—a criminal. He's as dirty as the man he works for. He's—''

Fixing her gaze on him, she quietly interrupted. "He's the father of my daughter.''

Smith walked to the French doors and faced out but saw nothing of the night-dark sky or the lights that pierced it. All he saw was Jolie's face reflected in the glass, burned into his mind. Jolie's sweet, lovely, immeasurably sad face.

He's the father of my daughter.

Jolie had had a child.

Jolie—who had used up all the mothering instincts inside her, who had no room in her life for kids, who would spend time with him, go out with him and even go to bed with him but would not consider the possibility of ever having children with him—had already had a sweet little baby girl.

With Nick Carlucci.

He hadn't been prepared for that one. Of all the surprises she could have thrown at him, that was the biggest one of all.

"I've known Nick all my life," she said from behind him, her voice tautly controlled but barely audible. "We were neighbors, friends. As we grew up, we became more than friends."

In the glass, he saw her move a few feet closer. She seemed smaller than usual, and with her arms folded across her chest, she looked chilled. Frightened. In pain.

"When I was seventeen," she went on, "Nick went away to college. At first, he came home on weekends to see me, but it wasn't long before that stopped. I thought it was because he couldn't get a ride or because of the demands of his classes or the jobs he was working to pay his expenses. I finally got to see him at Thanksgiving—we spent the entire weekend together—but then he didn't come home again until Christmas. He came to tell me that he'd been seeing someone else, that he was in love with her and he wanted to marry her. A few weeks later I found out that I was pregnant.''

"And you didn't tell him." He sounded as empty and blank as she did.

"No. He had already made it clear that he didn't want me."

"But he had an obligation—if not to you, then to his—" Smith didn't finish. He couldn't.

"For two and a half years, he had told me that he loved me. He told me every time we—"

Every time they had made love, Smith silently finished, hating the idea, the images, the mere suggestion that what she did with *him,* she had done with Nick Carlucci first.

"But he lied," she went on. "He didn't love me. He used me until he found someone better, and then he dumped me."

She moved again until she stood beside him but at the opposite side of the glass door. If he turned his head just a little to his left, he could look directly at her, but he chose instead to remain focused on her reflection. Somehow it was easier that way.

"It wasn't long before I had to tell my parents that I was pregnant. Unwed mothers weren't a rarity where we lived, but Mama and Daddy had expected better of me. As far as my goals and ambitions, we didn't agree on much, but we did agree on one thing. They wanted a better life for me as much as I wanted it for myself. But there's no future for a pregnant seventeen-year-old girl who's not even out of high school and has been abandoned by her baby's father. All they could see ahead for me was welfare and shame and a tough life for the baby. People in the neighborhood, in the church and in the family still cared about small matters like legitimacy back then." Her voice dropped to a whisper. "They were so disappointed in me."

And that, Smith suspected, had probably hurt her far more than Carlucci ever could.

He waited for her to go on, but when seconds passed into minutes and she still said nothing, he finally spoke. "I suppose abortion was out of the question."

Her laughter was choked. "My parents had twelve children. Abortion was a profanity that was never mentioned in our home. Besides, except for my lapses with Nick, I was a good Catholic girl. Abortion was never an option."

"So you put the baby up for adoption."

"Yes." Another whisper.

"And you've regretted it ever since."

Jolie remembered the day the decision had been made. It had been winter—late January—but the day had been beautiful, sunny and warm. It had been a Sunday, her father's only regular day off from both jobs. They had gone to St. Jude's—her parents didn't make major decisions without advice from their priest—where the four of them had talked in Father Francis's office. It was a small, close space with dark paneling, heavy velvet drapes closed over the single window and a grimly uninspiring painting of Jesus on the wall. The depressing office was the perfect place for the man Jolie had regarded even then as small, closed minded and grim.

The priest, who had helped raise Nick after his mother's abandonment, who had felt a cleric's responsibility toward the boy but had never yielded to one moment's affection for him, had argued against her parents' plan. He hadn't been concerned with what was best for the baby, definitely not with what might be best for Jolie. She had believed then and still believed now that he had wanted only to see her punished. She had sinned, and he had wanted her to pay for it. He'd shown no compassion, no benevolence, no mercy.

For a man of God, he'd had a great deal of narrow-minded, mean-spirited malice in him.

On a matter of less importance, she supposed, her parents would have given in to him. As far as she knew, that was the only time they had stood against him. With or without his blessing, they had decided to raise her daughter as their own.

And they had done an outstanding job. There was nothing for her to regret.

Although she did.

"Not for her sake, but for mine, yes. I knew it was best for her. I knew the only kind of life I could offer her—living on welfare on Serenity Street, trapped in a despair I would never escape—was no life at all, but still I wanted to try." She sighed softly. "I wanted so very badly to try."

"Does Cassie know she's adopted?"

She looked at him for a long time, for so long that after a while he broke contact and looked away. She wasn't surprised that he'd figured it out, that he knew that the daughter she'd given up, the daughter she'd kept secret in her heart all these years, was Cassie. Still, she asked, "How did you know?"

With a shrug, he met her gaze again. "You said she was born just before you started college, that she was the only one of the kids you didn't help raise. You said she started breaking hearts the day she was born." He hesitated. "She started with yours, didn't she?"

Knotting her fingers together, she thought briefly of the box of papers she had stored in her parents' garage when she had first feared that the FBI might come knocking at her door with a search warrant. The photograph she had slipped inside the box—a Polaroid, blurry, with bad color—was the only tangible reminder, besides Cassie herself, that she had of that stormy August day. Her mother's younger sister had taken the snapshot of Jolie, wearing a drab green hospital gown, her hair sticking to her head, her face etched with fatigue, and of Cassie, six and a half pounds of peaceful, red and wrinkled baby. Even then Cassie had had entirely too much class to make a fuss.

"No," she answered at last. "And she never will. That was part of my agreement with Mama and Daddy."

"What about her birth certificate?"

"It shows that a baby girl was born in Louisville, Mississippi to Patrick and Rosemary Wade." At his questioning look, she went on. "Cassie was born in a little country clinic, delivered by the doctor who had tended Mama's family for forty years. When he supplied the information for the birth certificate to the state, as a favor to the family, he was willing to replace certain names with others."

"So you pretended not to be pregnant for nine months when you were, and your mother pretended to be pregnant when she wasn't. And because she had been pregnant so much of the last eighteen years anyway, people probably didn't even notice. It was more or less a chronic condition for her."

Jolie almost smiled at that last part. "She often wore maternity clothes even when she wasn't pregnant. Money was always so tight that she couldn't see any sense in not wearing perfectly good clothing just because it was too big. And when I started wearing clothes that were big, my friends assumed I was wearing hand-me-downs that didn't fit or was going through a sloppy phase or something. Then, as soon as school was out, I went to stay in Louisville with my aunt."

After her last words faded away, another of those heavy silences descended over the room. She waited for Smith to say something else, to ask another question, to probe a little deeper, but for a time he simply stood there, gazing out the door. Was he absorbing what he had learned? Judging what she had done?

Condemning her for it?

Finally he faced her again, focusing all of his attention on her. "Is that why you don't want children now? Because you couldn't keep the one you had? Because you failed your daughter and you aren't willing to try again?"

Moving away from the door, she sank down onto the nearest seat, an armless leather chair that was cool through the thin cotton of her pants. She was too tired to stand another minute, too tired to finish the discussion she had started. How did she ever expect to last through a midnight meeting between Smith and Nick?

"I should have been able to make it work," she explained wearily, repeating arguments that had echoed in her mind for eighteen years. "I should have found some way. I was a smart kid, a straight-*A* student. I was resourceful as hell. But I took the easy way out. I put her up for adoption. Do you understand what that really means, Smith? I *gave* her to someone else to raise. What kind of mother gives her own baby away?''

He sat down on the table in front of her and leaned forward, resting his arms on his knees. "One who loves her. One who wants what's best for the baby regardless of how very badly she wants to keep her. Letting her be adopted was the mature thing to do, Jolie. It was the responsible thing."

"But it wasn't the motherly thing." She blinked back the moisture that was filling her eyes. "A mother—a *good* mother—would do anything in the world to hold on to her child. A good mother would fight like hell to keep her. A good mother wouldn't make the choices I made."

"You're wrong," he said very quietly. "*Only* a good mother would make the choices you made."

She wished she could believe him. It would be such a relief if she could allow herself to be convinced...but she'd been living with the guilt and the disappointment for so long.

"You could have kept the baby, Jolie. You could have given up your dreams and your future, and somewhere along the way, you would have given up hope. You could have raised her on welfare and in poverty, and you could have watched her make the same mistakes and the same bad choices that so many poor teenage girls make, and, unless you were both very lucky, you could have watched *her* give up her dreams and her future. You could have watched her lose hope. But because you gave her up, because you were willing to make that sacrifice, instead of making mistakes and bad choices, she's got a bright future ahead of her. Instead of being trapped someplace like Serenity Street, she'll be starting college soon. Whatever she decides to do after that, you know she'll be a hell of a success, in part because she's got your example to follow—and that's an example you couldn't have set if you hadn't given her up."

They were nice arguments, enticing arguments that someday she might invest her time, her heart and her soul into believing.

But this wasn't the day.

Tonight she knew that she'd made some big mistakes that she wasn't finished paying for. One was Cassie.

Another was Nick.

She prayed that the way she'd handled her relationship with Smith wasn't a third one.

"The bottom line, Jolie," he said quietly, "is that no matter how hard the decision was, it was *right*. Cassie's had a good life. She has parents who love her, a family who dotes on her, a big sister who adores her. She's a bright, well-adjusted, remarkably mature girl with all sorts of opportunities ahead of her. She would be the last person in the world to begrudge you whatever makes you happy. She would be appalled if she knew that she was the reason you won't get married. She would be devastated to find out that *she's* the reason you won't have children."

Knowing that he was right, that Cassie more than anyone would want her to have a normal life, but unable to deal with the knowledge—with the longing—she surged to her feet and paced the length of the room. "Good closing argument, counselor, but I still have a reasonable doubt. Anyway, I didn't come here tonight to talk about Cassie and me and babies." Although she managed a careless, flippant tone, those last words pierced all the way through her. "I came to invite you to a meeting."

"Jolie—" Breaking off he watched her, his gaze troubled. Then he stood up, slid his hands into his pockets and detached himself from the situation, professionalism overtaking and blotting out his personal feelings. "A meeting with Carlucci?"

"I hope so."

"You know how to get in touch with him?"

"No. But I know someone who can." With a grin that she knew bore only a vague resemblance to her usual cocky one, she hastened to add, "Don't bother asking who. I can't tell you. So... are you interested?"

"Of course I am."

"I'll warn you—I don't know if Nick will show, and if he does, I don't know if he'll talk to you."

"So why are you inviting me?"

Her grin fading, she turned serious again. She had a number of reasons for the actions she was taking tonight. She wanted one more chance to persuade Nick to cooperate. She wanted to try to protect the father her daughter would never know. She wanted to make things right with Smith, wanted to apologize in a manner more concrete than the trifling words—*I'm sorry I warned Nick*—she had offered when she arrived. She wanted to erase the disappointment she'd seen in him and prove herself worthy once again of his respect.

She chose the simplest of the reasons and delivered it in the most casual of manners. "Consider it an apology. So... are you coming or not?"

Smith had assumed that he was at least slightly familiar with all of the French Quarter, but he had never seen Serenity Street. It was a depressing sight in the dark night, all gloom and shadows. He would like to believe that it looked better under the midday sun, but he knew better. Harsh daylight would show the shabbiness, would glint off the broken windows and spotlight the shuttered storefronts, the broken sidewalks and the utter lack of hope.

It was hard to imagine Jolie living in this place. He had always appreciated her ambition; now he knew where it came from. What a place to face every day. The fact that she had nurtured any dreams at all said something about her spirit. The fact that she had achieved a number of them said plenty about her drive.

No wonder she had wanted out. No wonder she had wanted better than this for her baby.

Her *baby*. Her daughter. Cassie.

It still hadn't quite sunk in. Logically he could process the information. After all, her situation wasn't that unusual. For a number of generations, boys had been getting their girlfriends pregnant, then ducking out of their lives. They shared the fun, but none of the responsibilities. None of the sacrifices. None of the heartaches.

But emotionally... he was having a little trouble accepting that the woman he wanted to be the mother of his chil-

dren was already the mother—albeit secretly—of a child of
her own. He was having even more trouble accepting that
the father of this nearly grown child was a man he despised, a man who had conspired to kill one of Smith's best
friends, a man who stood against everything Smith stood
for.

With a shudder, he realized what that meant: if he and
Jolie managed to work things out, if he ever persuaded her
to marry him, he would be stepfather—again, albeit secretly—to Nick Carlucci's daughter.

Wouldn't *that* be a hoot? he thought without humor.

At his side, Jolie sighed softly. "I guess we'd better head
back."

Since they had arrived early at the meeting place—a
scruffy, ragged little park that no child should have to play
in—she had suggested a walk down Serenity. From one end
to the other, she had pointed out important places from her
childhood. Her tone had been even, empty of emotion, as
if she were merely pointing out historical sites to a disinterested tourist.

But the history in these sites was less than thirty years old.

And he was far from disinterested.

They had walked the length of the street; now they went
back to the park. The only businesses open this late were
bars, each one barely distinguishable from the other. They
were all small, all dimly lit and stinking of smoke. They were
all depressing little places—not boisterous like the Quarter
bars that catered to tourists or the clubs that provided lo-
cals with a place to socialize as well as drink, but quiet,
bleak places where the patrons cared more for the oblivion
liquor could provide than the drink itself.

As they crossed the street onto the final block where Serenity dead-ended—such an appropriate word, Smith
thought—a gang of young men across the street caught his
attention. "That's certainly a fine-looking bunch of boys,
isn't it?"

Jolie smiled at the dryness of his tone. "Don't worry. If
Nick's doing business as usual, they're being paid for

standing on the corner and looking out for anything suspicious or unusual.''

"Does the fact that they're here mean that he's also here?''

"No. But if he *is* here, they won't be looking to get into any trouble until he's gone.''

They crossed the street just before it ended at a brick wall and entered the park through the rusty gate. Either Michael or Remy would be more comfortable out here in a place like this in the middle of the night, he reflected ruefully. But then, Michael and Remy both carried guns most places they went. They were trained and prepared to deal with hostile criminals. Tonight he would trade his own ability to deal with hostile witnesses and, on occasion, jurors for theirs in a flash.

Just inside the gate, Jolie signaled him to stop with her hand on his arm. The stone beneath his feet rocked as he abruptly obeyed. She moved a few feet past him, peering hard into the shadows, listening, even it seemed, sniffing. Satisfied with whatever she'd discovered, she pushed her hands into her pockets and spoke into the darkness. "Nick, it's Jolie. I've brought Smith Kendricks with me. He wants to talk to you.''

Smith strained to identify whatever it was that she saw or heard or smelled. There were shadows that swayed in the light summer breeze, and a street or two over, a car's engine revved and its tires squealed across the pavement. From a nearby open window, music drifted out—heavy metal, discordant, harsh, hardly the soothing sort of music to accompany sleep.

There were also plenty of smells to identify. The sickly sweet stench of garbage rotting in the July heat. The lush, wet, muddy smell of the Mississippi, only a few blocks east. Closer by was the earthy, rainy scent of vegetation and, underlying it, too delicate to compete, an occasional whiff of roses, climbing spindly and sparse, along the iron fence.

And tobacco. It was light, little more than a hint, as if coming from a distance, barely brushing his senses before vanishing.

234 *A Man Like Smith*

Nick Carlucci was a smoker.

He was here.

Smith considered what he knew about Carlucci, excluding Jolie's bombshells tonight and last night. He was a good attorney, probably one of the best in southern Louisiana. He knew the law inside and out, could quote chapter and verse, could cite case law from memory that sent other, supposedly better-educated attorneys scrambling for their books. The first time Smith had ever faced him in court, he had regretted deeply that Carlucci wasn't on the government's side. They could have used his skills, his knowledge, his instincts.

Before Carlucci had gone to work for Falcone ten years ago, he had been in practice for himself. He had represented small-time crooks and had done it with flair. He'd built himself a reputation for being brilliant, for winning and for not giving a damn how guilty his clients were, and he had soon attracted Falcone's attention. It wasn't long at all before he was working exclusively for Jimmy... and, judging from the evidence he had so far turned over to Jolie, at the same time secretly working against him. Smith wondered why. Why did a man work hard for ten years at keeping his boss out of jail, then turn around and risk his life to undo all that he'd done?

"Come on, Nick," Jolie coaxed. "It's late, and we've all got better places to be and better things to do."

One long moment passed without a response, followed by another; then the shadows moved, shifted, and Nick Carlucci stepped into the light. He was dressed in dark clothes to better blend into the shadows. He wasn't smoking now, but Smith could still smell the slightly sweet flavor of the tobacco.

"All right, Jolie, I'm here," he said quietly. "What do you want?"

"I'm sorry about last night."

"Uh-huh." He sounded skeptical. "You get involved with people like him, things like that happen."

"Why did you run off, Nick? Why didn't you stay and deal with them?"

"Dealing with the feds isn't in my best interests at this time. Apparently, neither is dealing with *you*." He moved a few steps closer. "I haven't seen your name in the paper lately."

"Turning over the tapes and transcripts you gave me last time isn't in your best interests," Jolie replied. "That stuff about Remy Sinclair... Jimmy would have made you, Nick. He would have known it was you, and his boys would have killed you."

Smith wondered what she was talking about, but he resisted the urge to ask. When this meeting was over, there would be plenty of time to question Jolie—or, hopefully, Nick himself—about it.

"They would have had to find me first." Finally Carlucci turned his attention to Smith. "What is it you want from me, Kendricks?"

"Your cooperation would be nice, for starters."

His smile was thin and mocking. "Followed by all the evidence I've gathered and my smiling face on your witness stand next week?"

"That's about it."

"And what would you be willing to offer in return?"

Smith gave his question a moment's consideration. Even though the idealist in him despised plea bargains, the realist knew it was the way the game was played. You give me this, and I'll give you that. You scratch my back, and I'll scratch yours.

But damned if he wanted to be scratching Nick Carlucci's back.

The bulk of the charges in these cases were against Falcone himself and his boys, as Jolie referred to them; those pending against Carlucci were mostly conspiracy charges of one sort or another. The most serious as far as Smith was concerned involved the other man's role in blackmailing Susannah Duncan Sinclair and the attempted murder of both Susannah and Remy. They were family, and Carlucci had threatened them. He wanted him to pay for that.

But he could deal. He could let Carlucci walk as long as he hung his boss out to dry first.

"We could be persuaded to either drop or reduce the charges against you," he said evenly, "in exchange for your full cooperation in Jimmy's trial next week."

"And what else would you offer?"

"Protection."

"The federal witness relocation program?"

A new name, a new place, a new life. Nicholas Carlucci would cease to exist, and the man who had used that name for nearly forty years would one day resurface someplace far from New Orleans with a whole new identity. It was the ultimate in fresh starts and second chances. Smith wondered if Carlucci would make the most of it or if, like so many others who had tried, he would find that going straight was too much work.

"If it's considered necessary," he replied.

Nick seemed to be considering his offer; then he shook his head. "No, thanks. I'm not interested."

Disappointed, Smith took a step forward. "Then what was the purpose behind all this? Tapping Falcone's phone, eavesdropping on his conversations, photographing his meetings, documenting ten years' worth of illegal activity? Why pass all this evidence on to Jolie? Why expend all that time and effort and put your life on the line, only to stop short of where you could do the old man some real damage?"

"I intend to do the old man the kind of damage he can't recover from," Nick retorted. "But I'll do it on my own terms, not yours and not the FBI's."

"And what does that mean?"

Nick took a moment to shake a cigarette from the pack in his shirt pocket and light it, then blow a fat puffy cloud of smoke into the air before he replied, "It means I intend to see Jimmy in court ... and in jail ... and if there's any justice at all in this world, I intend to see him in hell."

His words were a promise, given without hesitation, without emotion, and leaving absolutely no doubt in Smith's mind that he meant exactly what he'd said. Whatever was driving Carlucci went beyond justice, beyond revenge. It was something stronger, something more powerful, that cut all the way through to his soul. Jimmy Falcone had once had a formidable ally in Nick Carlucci.

Now he had an even more formidable enemy.

Standing a little off center about halfway between the two men, Jolie felt a little shiver dance down her spine. She'd had dealings with a number of angry people before, with bitter, hopeless, frustrated, even murderous people, but she had never dealt with anyone as cold and empty as Nick.

"Why, Nicky?" she asked, not meaning to ask the question out loud, not intending to use the nickname he disliked, the name that connected them to a more innocent time. "What did Jimmy do to make you do this?"

For a time she thought he wasn't going to answer. That was so typical of him, of his arrogance. But then he proved her wrong. He responded in a flat monotone. "He killed someone."

It wasn't much of an answer. Falcone had killed, or been responsible for the killing of, a substantial number of people over the course of his career in organized crime. In the past thirteen years, she had covered many of those murders for the newspaper. Most of his victims had been business associates who had crossed him in one way or another; some had been competitors who had tried unsuccessfully to muscle in on his business; a few had been apparently innocent bystanders who had simply been in the wrong place at the wrong time.

But she couldn't recall a single one who might hold some significance for Nick.

She couldn't imagine anyone whose death he would consider worth avenging.

"Who was it?" she asked boldly.

He looked at her with the first real emotion he'd shown this evening. It was sorrow—the sort of pure, deep, heart-wrenching sorrow that stayed with a person forever. It was similar to the sorrow she had felt on giving up Cassie, only a hundred times stronger, a thousand times more powerful. "Who he killed doesn't matter," he replied, his voice softer, his tone gentler, than she would have believed possible.

"Why I'm doing this doesn't matter, either. All that counts is that I am."

It was a woman. Jolie knew it as surely as she knew her own name. Jimmy Falcone had killed a woman that Nick had cared about, had loved. Nothing else, other than the loss of a child, could explain that kind of sorrow. She wondered who, wondered how and when and why, but she didn't ask. She couldn't.

Smith came to stand beside her. "So you're saying that you'll testify against Falcone next week. You'll show up in court and swear to the authenticity of the evidence you provided Jolie. You'll answer our questions truthfully."

"I'll get you a conviction," Nick replied, quietly confident. "You won't need anything besides me and my evidence."

"But you won't go into protective custody."

He shook his head.

"Why not?" Jolie asked. "You know by now Jimmy's wondering about you. You know he must have some doubts about your trustworthiness."

"So let him wonder. Let him doubt. I'll take care of myself."

"But the FBI can protect you," she argued.

"Uh-huh. Remember last winter when Sinclair got shot? Remember *who* shot him? One of his fellow agents. One of Jimmy's people. Maybe everyone working for the FBI now is clean...but maybe not. I'll take my chances on my own."

"But—" The sound of traffic—at least two cars, possibly more—on Serenity Street made her break off, her argument forgotten. As she turned toward the street, she saw Smith, also distracted, also turning.

The cars—four of them altogether—were definitely bureau cars. Even without the antennas on the trunk and the blue lights on the dash, they would still look like cop cars to Jolie: plain, no-frills sedans, one gray, one burgundy, two white. The first one stopped at an angle, blocking her 'Vette in front; the second hemmed it in from behind.

She muttered a curse when Shawna Warren climbed out of the lead car. The temptation to interfere was strong—to create a diversion, to do something, *anything,* that would give Nick time to make it through the trees and the bushes to the gate in the back wall.

But she had interfered once already and made it possible for him to escape the FBI. She had no doubt that if she did it again, she would be spending the rest of the night in jail.

Maybe, in spite of Nick's wishes, this really was best for him.

"Hell, Jolie," he murmured as the agents approached them. "Is this your idea or his?"

She faced him again. "I didn't tell anyone about this meeting but Smith, and he hasn't left my sight since I told him."

"Didn't it occur to you after you called my house last night that they would have you under surveillance?"

"Of course it occurred to me." She made an effort to control the scorn in her voice. "But I wasn't followed, I swear. I was very careful. We drove around for nearly an hour before coming here. I would have noticed if someone was tailing us."

He swore softly. "Have you never heard of an electronic tracking device? They put it on your car, and they don't have to get close enough to be noticed."

"He's right," Shawna said as she joined them. "We've been keeping tabs on you from a distance all day. We followed you to work, to O'Shea's and over to Smith's. We figured chances were pretty good that eventually you would lead us to Carlucci, and you did."

Jolie looked from Nick, who seemed resigned, to Smith, who looked regretful. Had he known? she wondered. All those miles they had driven around the city while she made absolutely certain that they weren't being followed, had he known that the FBI was tracking them electronically?

As she watched him, he stepped forward. "Look, Shawna, I made a deal with Carlucci—"

The agent interrupted him. "And *I* made a deal with Marshall. You stay out of our way on this, and he'll overlook the poor judgment you've displayed in your dealings with this witness and this reporter. He'll still let you prosecute this case."

She put such derision into *reporter*. No doubt, Jolie thought, to Shawna's way of thinking, journalists ranked right down there with the other dregs of society—the prostitutes, the con men, the thieves and the murderers. She supposed it was only fair, though, because right now the FBI in general and this agent in particular, were at the bottom of her own list. Damn the woman, and damn Alexander Marshall.

And while she was at it, she might as well damn herself, she acknowledged grimly. After all, *she* was the poor judgment Smith was being accused of. It was his relationship with her, his faith in her, his *dealings* with her, that had left him open to criticism from a woman who wasn't half as smart or a tenth as talented as he was. If he got pulled from this case because of her...

She knew how important it was to him, knew all his personal reasons for wanting Falcone, as well as his professional ones.

She couldn't bear knowing that his association with her could damage his career.

"I haven't done anything wrong with either this witness or this reporter," Smith said coldly. "If it weren't for Jolie, we wouldn't have Carlucci or any of his evidence—which is better by far than anything you've been able to put together. If you don't trust my judgment, Shawna, I don't give a damn. If Marshall doesn't trust it, fine; I'll give him my resignation. But until then, this is still my case, and Carlucci is still my wit—"

The first shot sounded like a pop gun or a car backfiring, but instinct told Smith it was far more lethal. In the chaos that followed, he reacted automatically, grabbing Jolie around the waist, diving for cover, taking her to the ground with him. As a dozen more shots rang out around them, she wriggled closer, as if she just might crawl underneath him, and between the shouts and the shots, he could just barely make out her soft, frantic whispers. "Oh, God...oh, God...oh, God..."

Holding her tighter, he murmured a silent prayer of his own.

Oh, God, indeed.

Smith sat on the damp ground, his back against the stone wall that supported the iron fence across the front of the park. It was coming up on two in the morning, and he wanted to go home. Correction: he wanted to go home with Jolie, but he couldn't even get her attention. About half a second after the shooting had stopped, she'd undergone a remarkable transformation from frightened woman to on-the-spot reporter, and she had been as busy as the agents ever since.

The gunmen, presumably in the employ of Jimmy Falcone, had escaped unseen. Apparently—after his brief exchange with Shawna Warren earlier, Smith found some petty satisfaction in this—rather than try to follow Jolie herself, the men had instead followed the FBI agents who were following her, and neither Shawna nor any of her team had had a clue.

Nick Carlucci had also escaped. While everyone else had been seeking cover, he had made his way into the shadows and through a gate at the back of the park. By the time the shots had ended, he had been driving away. Since it had been Smith's intention to let the man walk away, he found some satisfaction in Carlucci's clean getaway, too.

With a weary sigh, he tilted his head back until it rested against the iron bars. It was funny how getting shot at could put things into proper perspective. This morning he hadn't wanted to even think about quitting his job. He had reached the decision that he could do it for Jolie, though . . . *if* she would have a baby for him.

In the past few hours, that decision had become so much simpler. He didn't need a job where he was distrusted, where his judgment was called into question, where his ability to do his job was second-guessed and doubted solely on the basis of the woman he was seeing. He didn't need to work with people like Shawna Warren, who saw only the problems Jolie had caused and not the tremendous amount of help she had given them. He didn't need to work with people who saw his relationship with Jolie as proof of his lack of good judgment.

And he didn't need a baby.

No matter how much he might want one.

All he really needed was Jolie.

Always.

"Is it all right if I join you?"

He lifted his head enough to see her face in the street-lamp light. The adrenaline was wearing off now, and she was wearing down. She looked tired, worried—about Nick, he thought without jealousy—and troubled—about *them,* he would wager. For once they were in perfect agreement. He was tired, too, and worried about Carlucci's safety.

And he was *very* troubled about them.

"Pull up a seat," he replied.

She sat down on the grass in front of him, her knees drawn to her chest, her hands clasped around her ankles. For a time, she sat in silence, her chin braced on her knees, resting. Relaxing. Seeking courage. Finally she spoke. "Do you think he'll show up in court?"

"If he's alive." It wasn't the answer he wanted to give, wasn't the answer she wanted to hear. It would be so much easier, so much more hopeful, to be able to say simply yes. *Yes, he'll show up. Yes, he'll help us. Yes, he'll survive this.*

Yes, your daughter will still have a father when this is all over—a father she'll never know, a father who will never know her.

But he couldn't offer false promises, and she couldn't accept them.

She spoke again, her voice lower this time. "Do you think he'll be all right?"

"Carlucci's been taking care of himself since he was...what? Six years old? I think he'll manage." Watching her closely, he asked, "Do you ever plan to tell him about Cassie?"

"No. I don't know how he would react—whether he wouldn't care, in which case I would hate him more than ever, or whether he would have some macho need to claim her as his own, which I couldn't allow him to do. I promised Mama and Daddy that Cassie would never know the truth. It's best for her."

Smith had to agree with her. Cassie was a bright and well-adjusted girl, but the truth could change that. It would certainly shake up her entire happy life to learn that her loving parents were, in fact, her grandparents, that the older sister who doted on her was her mother, that her father was a mob lawyer who might go to prison if his former boss didn't execute him first, who might change his identity and begin life anew, who might never want to know that he had a daughter.

After a brief silence, he asked another tough question. "Does it bother you that he loved another woman so much?"

She looked up abruptly, her expression faintly startled. "You saw that, too."

He nodded. It hadn't been a difficult guess to make. All he'd had to do was look at Carlucci's face when Jolie had asked which of Falcone's victims had been important to him and consider what it would take to bring out that sort of sorrow in *him*. The answer had been easy: losing Jolie. There were other people he loved, other people he would grieve for, but none so much as Jolie. None that could drive him to do what Nick Carlucci was doing but Jolie.

"No, it doesn't bother me." She smiled a little crookedly. "It makes me jealous, but it doesn't bother me."

"Why jealous? Because he loved her in a way he didn't love you?"

"No. Because I assume that if he loved her that much, she must have loved him a lot, too. I wonder what it's like to be loved like that."

Smith thought about the words she had chosen. Not *to love like that,* but *to be loved like that.* Did that mean she already knew what it was like to love someone that much?

Could it mean that she loved *him* like that?

He thought she loved him. Hell, he *knew* she loved him. He just wasn't sure she was willing to do anything about it. After all, she was the one who had insisted there was no place in her life for a man, no place for marriage. She was the one who looked into the future and saw only her career . . . while he had no future to look into without her.

"Sometimes there are problems," he said in response to her last comment. "Sometimes you disagree. Sometimes it seems you see everything from opposite viewpoints. Sometimes you fight . . . but you always make up. You never lose sight of what's important. You never stop caring. You never stop needing each other."

She studied him for a long time, her expression serious and a little, just a little, afraid. Twice she started to speak; twice she stopped. Then, drawing a deep breath, she asked in an unsteady voice, "And how would you know? You told me that you'd never been in love."

His own voice was none too strong. "That was before I fell in love with you." He tried to smile to ease the tension that was wrapping around him from the inside out, but he couldn't. This was too serious. Too important. Too damned vital to the rest of his life. "I do love you, Jolie. I love damned near everything about you."

She managed the smile that he couldn't. "You're not too crazy about my job, are you?"

They had had this conversation before, just last night, only the roles had been reversed. Now he gave the same answer she had given then in response to his question. "No more than you are about mine."

"I'll turn in my resignation tomorrow."

Her offer took him by surprise. Granted, she could be teasing—*he* had been when he'd made the same offer last night—although, as it turned out, he'd been more serious than he'd realized. But she didn't look as if she found anything about their conversation less than serious. Less than the-rest-of-their-lives important.

But she couldn't mean it. She couldn't actually be considering giving up her job for him. She *loved* her job. It meant everything to her.

At least, it used to.

She waited, her hands clasped tightly together, for some response from him. After a moment more, he gave it, his voice gently chiding. "You can't quit your job, Jolie."

"Actually..." She smiled edgily, showing him how nervous she was. She should be nervous, he acknowledged. This was a major, major decision for her. "I wasn't thinking about quitting. I was thinking about writing something else. How do you think I'd do on the society pages?"

Reaching out, he unknotted her fingers, then took both of her hands in his. "I think you would do fine no matter what you're writing about. I also think the society pages would bore you to tears in about six hours."

"Better to be bored than shot at," she replied. "Better than getting *you* shot at. Besides, maybe I could learn something from all those Southern belles."

"Like what?"

Her smile turned shy. "Like how to fit into your world."

Using his hold on her hands, he pulled until she had no choice but to move into his arms. "You fit into my world just fine," he murmured as he held her. "Hell, Jolie, you *are* my world."

She settled more comfortably in his lap, resting her head on his shoulder. "Of course, if I gave up my life of crime, I'd have a lot more free time. There'd be no more clandestine middle-of-the-night meetings."

"No more sneaking down alleyways or watching your back."

"No more worrying about the FBI snooping around in my belongings or in my past."

"Whatever would you do for excitement?" he gently teased.

She kissed him, slow, lazy and full of passion, then gave him a smile that matched and said in a thick, sultry voice, "I'm sure we'd think of something."

Feeling himself respond to her promise—not just physically, but emotionally, mentally, spiritually—he bent for another hungry kiss. "I'm sure we will," he agreed with a soft, satisfied laugh.

Just before his mouth touched hers, just before he satisfied the hunger she had created, she spoke again. She made one more promise.

One sweet, for-ever-and-ever promise.

"I love you, Smith."

Epilogue

Jolie sat cross-legged in bed, papers spread around her, a pair of recently acquired reading glasses perched on her nose. She was supposed to be working—yes, she had told Smith, she *was* bringing work along on the trip—but she hadn't accomplished much. First, there had been getting her sea legs to deal with; she had spent two entire days getting disgustingly sick. Then had come long hours learning to help Smith with the sailing and even longer hours staring out at the water. The ocean—beautiful, reasonably calm, incredibly soothing—fascinated her in a way that Smith, who'd grown up with the ocean lapping at the edge of his backyard, didn't quite share. Swimming lessons had filled a few afternoons; while she would never be as comfortable in the water as Smith was, at least she could stay afloat and get from point *A* to point *B*.

And, of course, they had spent hours—long, hot, sweet hours—making love.

Work had been the farthest thing from her mind.

Glancing at the clock, she leaned back against the pillows and sighed contentedly. It was ten minutes until midnight, New Year's Eve. If they were home in New Orleans, they would be in the midst of a giant party in Jackson Square, counting down to midnight, one of her personal traditions for as long as she could remember. But out here in the Caribbean, anchored off a sandy little uninhabited island whose name they didn't know, was a tremendously satisfying alternative.

It had been a hell of a year. Nick had stayed alive and had stunned Jimmy Falcone, his lawyers and the jury with his testimony. By the time he had finished his first day on the witness stand, a conviction on all charges had been virtually inevitable. It had taken a while—the trial had dragged on for weeks—but in the end, Smith had won. Nick had won. The people of New Orleans and Louisiana had won. Falcone had gotten slapped with a sentence so stiff that he would never see freedom again. He would likely die in prison.

She hoped that offered some bit of solace to Nick.

Before he had testified for the government, Nick had pulled out another surprise, this time stunning both her and Smith. He had pleaded guilty to the charges against him. He had refused Smith's attempts to make a deal, had refused to even discuss the possibility. Making a deal, he had insisted, could taint his testimony. If he got a reduced sentence or a free walk in exchange for his testimony, Jimmy's attorneys would twist that to their advantage. They would make it look as if the government had bought his cooperation. They would accuse him of saying whatever the government wanted in order to save his own skin. He hadn't wanted even the slightest doubt created in even one juror.

Now he was in prison, too, sentenced to five years in a federal penitentiary in Alabama. Jolie couldn't help but think that he'd gotten exactly what he wanted: revenge against Falcone and punishment for his own crimes.

With Falcone's conviction had come a number of job offers for Smith. He *had* been brilliant in court, she thought, immensely proud. Of course, he had turned them all down; the U.S. Attorney's office was where he belonged. Still, he'd told her, it was nice to know there were places that wanted him in case he ever changed his mind.

It *was* nice to know. She had gotten an offer herself from a regional magazine, a slick, thick publication that covered everything from politics and current events to restaurants and debutantes, from fashion to the arts to tourism. They had wanted to make use of her own particular expertise: the first article they had in mind from her would be an in-depth piece on Falcone's organization.

She had accepted their offer. It was that piece that was scattered around her now.

It was the first piece she'd written that would bear her new byline, Jolie Wade Kendricks. Once she was established, once everyone who had known and read her in the past had grown accustomed to the new name, she would drop Wade and use Kendricks exclusively.

She was just an old-fashioned girl at heart, she supposed.

"What are you smiling about?"

Removing her glasses, she looked up at Smith, standing in the doorway wearing a pair of gym shorts and nothing else, and her smile grew wider. "I've got a jillion things to smile about."

"Such as?" He crossed the room, stripped off his shorts, then waited while she gathered her papers, before joining her, naked, on the bed.

"I learned how to swim."

"Hmm."

"They've got the typical winter damp and fog back home, and *I'm* on a boat in the Caribbean." She laid everything, including her glasses, on the bedside table and slid down to lie beside him. "I've got a new job that I'm really going to like—one that will hopefully keep me out of trouble with you people."

"That's certainly something for *me* to smile about," he said dryly. "What else?" Balancing on one arm, he toyed with the top button of her gown. Made of batiste, falling to midcalf and buttoning up the front, the gown wasn't sexy enough to take on a honeymoon, her sisters had informed her.

But then, they had never been favored with the experience of Smith removing it.

"I had a beautiful wedding."

"*We* had a beautiful wedding," he corrected her. Finally he pushed the tiny white button through the hole and slid his hand an inch lower to the next one.

She acknowledged his correction with a nod. "Your parents liked me."

"They adored you." In fact, that had been his mother's first comment after meeting Jolie: *Oh, Smith, she's adorable.* Her next comment had dampened his satisfaction just a little. *You two will have beautiful children. Your father and I can hardly wait.*

He opened the second button and the third, then took a moment to explore what he had uncovered. Her skin was soft, a warm gold, browned by days under the tropical sun. Dipping his fingers lower beneath the gown, he brushed across her breast. Her nipple was already swelling, already growing hard in anticipation. "What else makes you smile, Jolie?" he murmured as he pushed the fabric back so he could bathe her breast with open kisses.

Her breath caught in her chest, and her voice sounded hoarse and strained. "You do," she whispered.

Moving to lie between her legs, he supported himself on his elbows and teased her with sweet kisses and feathery caresses before opening another button and yet another. The gown was open to her hips, heat was emanating from the oh-so-sweet place inside her, and he was hard and aching to fill her when she spoke.

"You know what else would bring me smiles?" She stroked him—his hair, his face, his jaw—before continuing. "After the wedding, Cassie was helping me change out of my gown, and you know what she told me? That she hopes we make her an aunt soon. She said..."

As he watched her, she swallowed hard, blinked back the dampness that filled her eyes and smiled ruefully. She was embarrassed by the tears, he thought, loving her so much that it hurt.

In control again, she went on. "She said that any child would be lucky to have us for parents. Do you know how much that means to me?"

Her daughter, who could never know that she *was* her daughter, thought she would make a good mother. He knew.

"I've thought about it a lot since then and...I think she's right. I think we can be good parents, Smith. I think we can be damned good parents. It doesn't have to be right away—I mean, we just got married—but..." she said, finishing in a whisper. "Having a baby, having *your* baby, would really make me smile, Smith."

Now it was *his* throat that was tight, *his* eyes that were suspiciously damp. He moved up the bed to kiss her, long and hard, and at the same time, he sought his place inside her, pushing until she was full, until she sheltered him completely. Breaking off the kiss, he closed his eyes for a moment, savoring the feel of her, so soft and heated, feeling his love for her, feeling *her* love for *him*.

Then, need growing stronger, he gazed down at her before he started moving inside her. "Then by all means, *jolie blonde*," he murmured, his lips brushing hers. "Let me make you smile."

* * * * *

Get Ready to be Swept Away by
Silhouette's Spring Collection

Abduction
& Seduction

These passion-filled stories explore both the dangerous
desires of men and the seductive powers of women.
Written by three of our most celebrated authors, they are
sure to capture your hearts.

Diana Palmer
Brings us a spin-off of her Long, Tall Texans series

Joan Johnston
Crafts a beguiling Western romance

Rebecca Brandewyne
New York Times bestselling author
makes a smashing contemporary debut

Available in March at your favorite retail outlet.

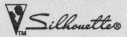

MILLION DOLLAR SWEEPSTAKES (III)

No purchase necessary. To enter, follow the directions published. Method of entry may vary. For eligibility, entries must be received no later than March 31, 1996. No liability is assumed for printing errors, lost, late or misdirected entries. Odds of winning are determined by the number of eligible entries distributed and received. Prizewinners will be determined no later than June 30, 1996.

SWP-S395

THE MACKADE BROTHERS

the exciting new series by
New York Times bestselling author

Nora Roberts

The MacKade Brothers—looking for trouble,
and always finding it. Now they're on a collision
course with love. And it all begins with

**THE RETURN OF RAFE MACKADE
(Intimate Moments #631, April 1995)**

The whole town was buzzing. Rafe MacKade
was back in Antietam, and that meant only one
thing—there was bound to be trouble....

Be on the lookout for the next book in the
series, **THE PRIDE OF JARED MACKADE—
Silhouette Special Edition's 1000th Book!**
It's an extraspecial event not to be missed,
coming your way in December 1995!

THE MACKADE BROTHERS—these sexy, trouble-
loving men will be heading out to you in alter-
nate books from Silhouette Intimate Moments
and Silhouette Special Edition.
Watch out for them!

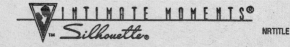

INTIMATE MOMENTS®
Silhouette®

NRTITLE

Silhouette celebrates motherhood in May with...

Debbie Macomber
Jill Marie Landis
Gina Ferris Wilkins

in

Three Mothers & a Cradle

Join three award-winning authors in this
beautiful collection you'll treasure forever.
The same antique, hand-crafted cradle
connects these three heartwarming romances,
which celebrate the joys and excitement of
motherhood. Makes the perfect gift for yourself
or a loved one!

A special celebration of love,

Only from

Silhouette®
™

—where passion lives.